ALSO BY M. T. ANDERSON

Feed

*The Astonishing Life of Octavian Nothing, Traitor to the Nation,
Vol. 1: The Pox Party*

*The Astonishing Life of Octavian Nothing, Traitor to the Nation,
Vol. 2: The Kingdom on the Waves*

*Symphony for the City of the Dead: Dmitri Shostakovich
and the Siege of Leningrad*

The Assassination of Brangwain Spurge

NICKED

NICKᴇD

M. T. Anderson

PANTHEON BOOKS · NEW YORK

Published in the United States by Pantheon Books,
a division of Penguin Random House LLC, New York, and distributed
in Canada by Penguin Random House Canada Limited, Toronto.

Pantheon Books and colophon
are registered trademarks of Penguin Random House LLC.

Library of Congress Cataloging-in-Publication Data
Name: Anderson, M. T., author.
Title: Nicked / M.T. Anderson.
Description: First edition. New York : Pantheon Books, 2024.
Identifiers: LCCN 2023038579 (print). LCCN 2023038580 (ebook).
ISBN 9780593701607 (hardcover). ISBN 9780593701614 (ebook).
Subjects: LCSH: Nicholas, Saint, Bishop of Myra—Fiction. LCGFT: Novels.
Classification: LCC PS3551.N37449 N53 2024 (print) | LCC PS3551.N37449 (ebook) |
DDC 813/.54--dc23/eng/20230922
LC record available at https://lccn.loc.gov/2023038579
LC ebook record available at https://lccn.loc.gov/2023038580

www.pantheonbooks.com

Jacket images (details): (skull) Michelangelo Caravaggio. Mondadori Portfolio /
Electa / Antonio Quattrone / Bridgeman Images; (hand) Giovanni Giampietrino.
The Metropolitan Museum of Art, New York
Jacket design by Zak Tebbal

Printed in the United States of America
First Edition
2 4 6 8 9 7 5 3 1

For Erin

The following story is based on real events.

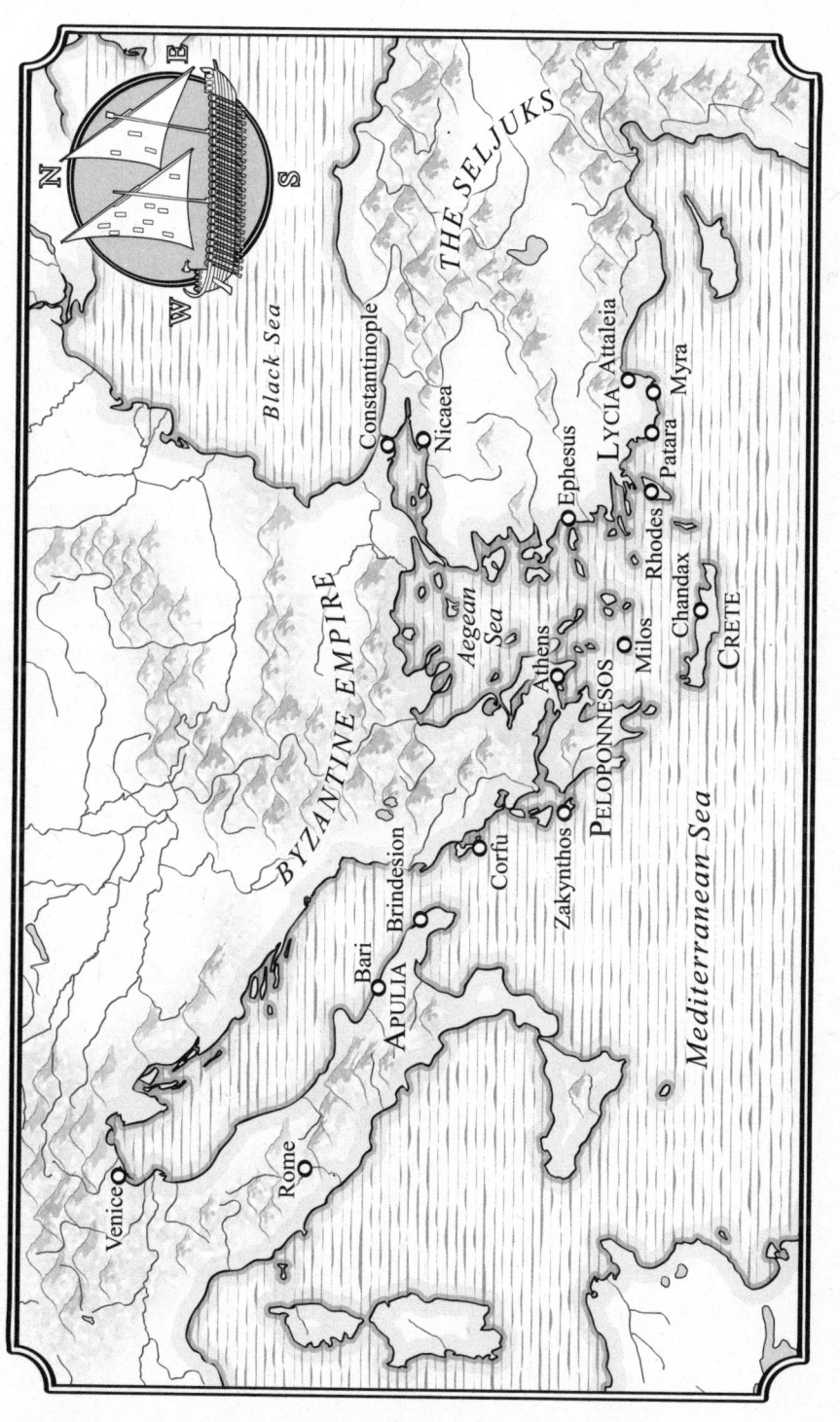

We keep his memory alive
In legends that our children and
Our children's children treasure still.

—ERIC CROZIER AND BENJAMIN BRITTEN,
Saint Nicolas

Foundationally marvelously aboundingly
illimitably with it as a circumstance.
Fundamentally and saints and fundamentally
and saints and fundamentally and saints.

—GERTRUDE STEIN AND VIRGIL THOMSON,
Four Saints in Three Acts

I

T HE MONK HEARD THAT A SHIP HAD ARRIVED CARRYING ONE OF THE DOG-HEADED PEOPLE WHOM TRAVELERS speak of when they tell tall tales of the one-eyed and the winged, and he went out to the docks to see if it was true. This is how he first laid eyes on the relic thief; this is how the voyage to steal the corpse of Saint Nicholas began.

In an age of sickness; in a time of rage; in an epoch when tyrants take their seats beneath the white domes of capitals—I call upon Saint Nicholas, gift giver, light bringer, wonder worker, who saved the living from drowning and pasted together the dead from their pickling jars, who even after death gave of himself in medicinal ooze; I ask Saint Nicholas to tell us a tale to pass a winter night, so that when we rise in the morning, we may feel resolute in the new dawn.

I will tell the story of the heist of St. Nicholas's body from its tomb. I will tell it as it was told to me by musicians and drunkards and guidebooks and lovers.

Though I am an unbeliever, I pray for faith.

There was a pox in Bari, and half the town had fevers. The countryside shunned the city and its narrow streets for fear of sickness. The monks of Saint Benedict's stayed locked within their walls, singing troped Kyries to ask God for clemency.

"Christ—who removed the blemishes from the sick man and banished demons in the hogs—have mercy upon us." Farmers who passed outside their sanctuary heard the echo of their chants and looked up to the sky to see if any of it was helping.

Word came down from the Archbishop of Bari that the monks should keep vigil each night for a week, praying to St. Nicholas for healing and guidance. They knelt in the cold chapel without sleep. Eventually, one, Nicephorus, fell asleep and was visited with a sacred dream.

When he woke, he said he wanted to go out and minister to the sick in the city, taking them food and water, despite all dangers. Nicephorus had an irritatingly pure and generous heart.

"In the dream, the saint told me we cannot wait," said Nicephorus. "We must leave our nest."

"You are sure?" said the Abbot. "The Blessed Nicholas?"

Nicephorus was uneasy. "He was dead. It has been six centuries. All the people in the dream were made of clay. But Saint Nicholas chanted and I heard. I will take it as a personal calling."

He went out with a basket of barley cakes and a ewer and visited the sick and drew water for them.

One said to him, "Put me in a wheelbarrow."

"You're not ready for the graveyard," said Nicephorus. "You're hale."

"I want to go over to the docks."

Nicephorus did not understand. He looked to the man's wife, who was leaning against the wellhead. She shrugged. "I'm already better," she said. "If he wants to die in a wheelbarrow, that's the kind of thing his father did."

"There's a dog-headed man on a ship. They're talking about it next door. I want to see it before I'm dead."

"You are not likely to die soon," said Nicephorus.

"I am not likely to see another dog-headed man who can

trim a lateen sail," the man said, and so he stood up roughly and shambled to the wheelbarrow and sat down in it.

Nicephorus rolled him through the tall, muddy streets and passageways toward the port.

The man said, to make conversation, "So you've had a sacred dream from the Blessed Nicholas."

"I cannot say that. We had sung hymns and sequences to St. Nicholas for a week. He was in my thoughts when I fell asleep. I do not know he sent the dream himself from his cloud."

"How did he seem?"

"Dead. Seven centuries."

"Did he seem discontented?"

"With us? He did."

"With death. He knows what it's like, now. Did he have advice? The weighing of souls?"

Nicephorus smiled. "What do you expect?"

"He might recommend we take ballast up with us. To tip the balances in our favor. He is a friend to sailors and knows the value of weight in the hold."

Nicephorus rolled the wheelbarrow around a rut. "There is no cargo on that final journey."

They bumped and rolled through a tunnel, out an old triumphal arch, and toward the blue Adriatic.

As they approached the wharves and warehouses outside the city walls, the piazzas of Bari were no longer empty. There were the crowds of sailors, the merchants, the grandees in their capes, the familiar heckling and haggling. Turbaned Byzantine workmen, Norman soldiers, accountants from the Caliphate in Egypt. Bari sat at the heel of Italy, the crossroads of the Mediterranean, a port at the center of the world: a city once Roman, once Arabian, twice Byzantine, and now Norman. Nicephorus had never been far from Bari, but he was used to foreign crowds: Jewish merchants who traveled back and forth from Córdoba to Samarkand; Christian pilgrims striking out for distant shrines with their trains of slaves; Muslim sailors stopping for a few days on their way to Venice; and those wanderers who spoke of no allegiance to nation and homeland, just to litanies of goods (Widhari cloth, Palermo silk, Basran sugar, borax from Lake Van). They teemed upon the Barese quays and thoroughfares.

Amid the grain ships and the fishing boats with their sails furled and the great warships, the dromons, at dock with their ranks of oars up like the flippers of Leviathan, there was a table set outside a taverna with a crowd gathered around it, pushing for a glimpse of the dog-headed man. Comedians shouted things like "Over here, boy—there's a good boy!" and "Bowwow!" which seemed blunt and unwelcoming. Nicephorus winced.

The man in the barrow yelled out, "Let me scratch you between your ears!"

"Maybe quieter," said the monk.

"Sure," said the man in the barrow. "He might be startled by loud noises."

The dog-man was seated at the table next to some sort of Tartar. Both were dressed in old brocade *qaba*s, scalded with sea salt and smudged with labor. The Tartar ate with his hands, like all decent men did. The dog-man had brought with him a weird metal claw on a stalk which held the meat down with three tines as he cut with a knife.

"All very entertaining, gentlemen, ladies," said the dog-man, waving irritably at the crowd agog.

"A dog-man and a Tartar in one day," said the man in the wheelbarrow. "Sometimes life serves me shit on a trencher, but today Fortune hands me a fucking dumpling."

"I will leave you briefly," said the monk. "I need to call

upon the Sisters of Saint Scholastica. If you need something, stagger."

Nicephorus went to see the sisters in their convent by the seawalls. They had suffered only one death within their whited chapel. Several more were fevered.

"Could you intercede with your new friend?" said the Abbess.

"In the wheelbarrow?"

The Abbess squinted. "The Blessed Nicholas. Abbot Helias told me you'd had a dream. The Archbishop is thrilled."

"I do not know the dream was inspired," said Nicephorus unhappily.

"Ask the saint what we can do to lift this sickness."

"I simply received a dream."

"Ask him on our behalf."

Nicephorus insisted: "I have no reliable avenue of communication with the undead Bishop of Myra."

The Abbess drew her fingers across the sacred linens on the altar. She did not meet his eyes. "He looks so severe in his icons."

"Not severe," said Nicephorus. "Just balding."

He asked whether the Abbess needed any little thing sent over from the monastery of St. Benedict. His abbot, he said, would be happy to comply.

When he got back to the taverna, the crowd had thinned around the Tartar and the cynocephale. The two adventurers were chatting with some port girls who Nicephorus knew from his dealings in the town: Gallenice and Aquilina. Nicephorus's sick charge was listening to the chitchat with wide-eyed curiosity. Some Samaritan had rolled the man's wheelbarrow closer to the table.

"You mistake me," said the dog-headed person. "I am no bitch."

"You look like a very good boy to me," said Aquilina huskily.

The man in the barrow said, "It talks really well."

"As do you, my malingering lazar," said the cynocephale.

"Do you get friendly with mankind ladies?" asked Aquilina.

"Not generally," the dog-man said, swallowing goat, his tail in a slow wag. "I find my sentimental evenings are often foiled by the oviform tang."

The Tartar and Gallenice were admiring each other.

"And you're . . . ?" said Gallenice.

"A relic hunter," said the Tartar.

"Any samples?" she teased. "Sell me your wares."

"I sold a church the very finger John the Baptist pointed with when he said, 'Behold the Lamb of God.'"

"Anything that might protect a girl from disease?" She leaned close to him.

Nicephorus found himself interested in the man's relaxed repose upon the bench, the sprawl of his legs beneath the table; and he wondered why he was so offended at the smile the man gave Gallenice, why he was irritated at the contract being drawn up in the air between saint hunter and provincial waitress.

"I retrieved a phial of the seed of Adam, First Man, from the mountains of the East."

"Did you now?"

"It was from a shrine in a walled garden near the gates of dawn."

"And you found it?"

"Imagine this, ladies," said the Tartar pirate. "Within our living seed float countless homunculi, waiting for life, each of which contains the next generation. And within those homunculi are curled, even smaller, the homunculi of our children's children. We were within our parents' seed. They were within our grandparents'. So, within Adam's seed, if you could examine it closely enough, you would find all human generations, the whole history of man, manikins of all of us nested within each other, like the ziggurats of Mataram—a series of steps, ever broadening, crammed with faces and carved figures striving and loving." At "loving," he gave her a kind smile, which made the monk step to the side of the wheelbarrow and announce to his friend, "We should return you to your wife."

"In Adam's seed, however," the Tartar continued, "there is one difference: Suspended within that blessed solution, we are all laid out, one generation to the next—but without sin. When this seed fell, that first bite from the Tree of Knowledge had not yet been taken. We had not yet been corrupted. Adam's seed is prelapsarian. During our conception, deep in our parents' viscera, we receive sin like the pox. We are born screaming with it. But within the seed of the first man, our images are perfect and unblemished. What floats in Adam's semen is God's hope for what we all should have been—a perfected history, not what we became outside the gates of Eden."

The monk couldn't stand any more flirtation. He lifted the handles of the wheelbarrow with an aggressively chummy "Heigh-ho, here we go!"; and despite the complaints of the sick man, he began to rattle him over the cobbles, back through the gate in the city walls.

The relic thief watched him go. "Benedictine?" he asked Gallenice, with a nod of his head.

"Yeah. Nice guy, though."

"Good," said the Tartar, as if calculating a strategy. And then he resumed his pitch: "You can imagine," he said, "the price we got for that phial. It contained the whole history of humanity, unmixed with sin."

Gallenice leaned close to hear the sum. The Tartar whispered it with lips that almost touched her ear.

This is how Brother Nicephorus met the saint hunter Tyun and the dog-head Reprobus for the first time, and how their disastrous heist began.

The infirmary. A cross painted above every bed.

"The disfiguration," said the Abbot, wincing. "We should all have incorruptible bodies."

Brother Nicephorus was distributing the morning meal. The monks on the pallets were not just fevered: some were showing pox.

"There is a solution," said the Abbot.

"Barley water?"

"You have been called."

"We do not know that." Nicephorus dipped his head.

"I think St. Nicholas spoke to you. He is dissatisfied."

Nicephorus turned away and considered the sick.

The Abbot pressed. "Nicholas is dissatisfied with his resting place. That is what I take from your dream. He is not in his chosen home."

"He is celestial. He sails among the stars."

"His body. In Lycia. If we had his relics here, there would be no pox among us."

Nicephorus looked up and down the ranks of pallets on the floor, his fellow brothers of St. Benedict, slumbering heavily or stirring uncomfortably with sickness.

The Abbot said, "You have perhaps heard: The Blessed Nicholas's body weeps an ichor. Every morning, in his sarcophagus, there is an ooze. It is medicinal. Those who drink the oil that cascades off his corpse are healed."

"It is a sure medicine?"

"It is better than theriac and masterwort for fevers. Nicephorus, the Duke and Archbishop Urso are arranging an expedition to liberate the corpse. Your dream shows us the saint no longer wants to be trapped, entombed, in Lycia. He wants to be here, in Bari."

"I do not remember him saying anything of that sort in my dream. It would be prideful to imagine he recommended any such task. It was a dream of clay people, long dead."

The Abbot was not pleased. "It would be *prideful,* Brother, for you to deny your abbot's interpretation of a dream sent straight from Heaven."

"What if my dream was simply a dream? The Archbishop asked that we hold vigils for St. Nicholas for a full week. My thoughts were on the Blessed Nicholas day and night. Maybe this was just a phantasm. Maybe the saint does not want to be removed from his Lycian tomb at all."

"Nicephorus, this is God's will: You will set out with a team of experts in the liberation of saints. You will sail to Lycia, to the city of Myra, where Nicholas was bishop and where he has lain in a coffin these seven hundred years. We need you because the dream was yours."

Nicephorus held up a hand. "The dream—"

"We need Nicholas to smile upon our efforts. We need you. You will return with his bones, his flesh, his oil." The Abbot indicated the sick men around him. "Will you let them fester? No. The dream was yours. You must answer the call of the undead Bishop of Myra."

Nicephorus laid down his wooden tray. Outside the window, a towering oleander rocked in the salt-scented breeze, and a swift darted at it, unsure whether it was shelter or foe.

"Why do you hesitate?" the Abbot asked. "Are you saying you are a fraud? That you had no dream? That you do not wish to exert yourself for the good of all Bari?"

"I will go," Nicephorus agreed uncomfortably.

"God go with you. You leave the day after tomorrow."

· · ·

Nicephorus could not have imagined the negotiation that
had gone on one day earlier in the chambers and colonnades
of the city baths. The Abbot of St. Benedict's was the first to
arrive at the meeting. He was shown into a dank room where
a marble bench, installed in the days when emperors still lit
fiestas with burning Christians, was greening. The Bari baths
had been built when Rome was capital of the world. They had
remained a luxurious retreat for the city's elite after Rome
fell and Justinian the Great ruled Byzantium and all the Adriatic coast. Now the marble was chipped and the gods were
defaced. Brick nogging held up sagging walls between the
pilasters.

The Abbot sat on the pagan bench and prepared himself
through prayer and self-affirmation. The powerful let him
wait. Distantly, something dripped.

"And thus I find you squeezing your own knees," said the
Archbishop, entering the antechamber surrounded by deacons. "Are they here yet?"

"They will call us," said the Abbot.

"Too many deacons," said the Archbishop, weaving his
head and miter to see around them. "Fewer deacons." Several
bowed and left. "All of you," said the Archbishop.

For a time the Archbishop and the Abbot waited side by
side.

"You are sure of the man's vision?" said the Archbishop.

"I am sure enough."

"Be certain."

"I am certain."

"May you be crowned in myrtle. Is it dank? Of course, they
know we are here. These games. Who enters first, who enters
last. Who sits, who stands." The Archbishop tugged at the
fringes of his cope. "On the Last Day, we know who shall enter
first and who last. Who shall sit and who shall stand."

The Abbot nodded, and wondered how long it would take to become an archbishop.

Three boys entered in period togas, designed to recall the glory that was Rome but already faintly smeared with algal green from the hand pumps. "We are sent to inform you they are ready in the cold bath," said the three boys, all of them, heads down so they did not meet any eyes. The youngest one added, "And will you bless me, Father? A sour stomach."

Archbishop and abbot followed the attendants while the Archbishop crossed himself and spoke the names of the Father, Son, and Holy Ghost and tapped the youngest on the back of the head. They passed through colonnades and by pools. Light sluiced back and forth across the ceilings. The water smelled of fish.

The Norman lords who had taken the city a decade earlier and the merchants of Bari who'd made their peace with them were gathered, frowning around a frigid impluvium. Their Duke stood in the midst of them, waist-deep in the pool, dressed in a floating garment of white linen. The rest were dressed in splendor. Their mantles were fastened with brooches inlaid with animals of predation: eagles, hawks, wolves, gryphons.

"I called out like a lamb in a ravine," said the Duke, "and you, great shepherd, have come."

"When the dearest of God's servants bleats," said the Archbishop, "I cannot refuse."

The Duke grimaced. "I of course do not bleat." He shook his head. It was shorn barbarically: the scalp shaved bald except long bangs. Wet, they clung to his face.

At the Archbishop's side, the Abbot, silent, tonsured like Christ's crown of thorns, considered how some haircuts bespeak brutality.

"This is your abbot?" said the Duke.

"It is," said the Archbishop. "Dom Helias of Saint Benedict's."

"Last week, Archbishop," said the Duke, "I asked you, as a favor, if you would beg the holiest men of Bari to pray to Saint Nicholas at the darkest vigils of the night and see if he delivered any messages."

"You did. I spread the word among the faithful. One of the brethren of St. Benedict's was visited."

"By?" said the Duke, and he slipped down into the pool, only the dome of his head floating above the water, his eyes blinking white like a fish's.

The Abbot spoke. "Blessed Nicholas himself, patron of merchants, friend of sailors, gift giver and repository of all virtues."

The head rose above the waters. "And he came to speak to a monk of your order." He sank again and watched.

"Not for any quality of our own," the Abbot said hastily, "for we are the least of the Lord's servants, but so the will of the dead might be made known."

The Duke blew bubbles. Around him, the great nobles and merchants of the city watched the Abbot. They were large men, accustomed to the violent death of others.

The Duke's head emerged. His bangs clutched the rocky scalp in black tendrils. "And how did your monk find the saint?"

"How . . . ?"

"How was the Blessed Nicholas? In health? In comfort?"

"Tell him," said the Archbishop.

The Abbot delivered his line: "He seemed—dissatisfied."

"With?"

"His neighborhood."

"And his request?"

The Abbot ventured: "That we rescue him from where he lies entombed at Myra?" The Abbot waited to see if he had answered correctly.

The Duke nodded and, with that, thrust himself backward out of the impluvium, splashing, rising up unseen steps. He stood for a moment, arms wide, water coursing off his linen smock. "So. Amen. A credible religious of our city has been visited by the Blessed Nicholas, who demands to be removed from Myra, in far Lycia, and to be housed here in Bari?"

"That was the message we received in the vision," said the Abbot, now more certain.

"I have been hoping to hear such a message," said the Duke. "Because last week, a gentleman wrote me a letter—a treasure hunter, a saint finder—and announced that Venice was about to hire him to go to Myra and kidnap the corpse of Nicholas."

"Venice already has Saint Mark," a Norman complained. "In a box."

"Those bastards," said a merchant.

"This gentleman offered to go on our behalf instead if we doubled Venice's offer. And if, of course, there was a holy vision, attested by an archbishop, to back up his expedition and demonstrate St. Nicholas's will. This saint hunter is no thief."

"Wise," said the Archbishop.

The Duke made a motion with his hand, and three shadows stepped out of the room to call the treasure hunter, the saint seeker. The Duke sat with his arms on his knees, like nothing more than a normal man, and the dark scrub of his pudendum could be seen through his wet shift.

It is a sign of his power that he can be naked before us, who are dressed in splendor, the Abbot reflected peevishly. *Only the invulnerable can afford such vulnerability.* The Duke's nakedness was itself a vivid threat to all around him.

The three boys in their costume togas returned with the treasure hunter. The Abbot was surprised to see the man looked utterly un-Christian. To the Normans and Apulians gathered there, his features spoke vaguely of the steppe, of the lonely, confusing distances that drew merchants east to God knows what scenes of barbarity. And yet there was an impudence in his eye that challenged them all to question his religion. (Demonic, the Abbot assumed: probably Apollyon. Maybe Baal. Children burned in a brazen bull. And yet these hearty Normans looked back at the Tartar in silent compact, a chilly politeness that suggested they would not question who his people were or his gods, so long as the deal was sweet enough.)

The Archbishop was appalled. "This is the man?"

"Tell them," said the Duke.

The Tartar surveyed all the men in the room, the powerful of Bari, and then he began. "I am Tyun, saint seeker, relic hunter. I have traveled from Kashgar to Zanj and served many princes of the earth and friends of Christ above."

"You claim you can get us Nicholas."

"This is the moment."

"You are sure?"

Tyun began his pitch. "The Seljuks have swept out of the steppe and across the face of the civilized world. The Arabs and Persians have fallen before them. They have taken Khurasan and Khwarazm. And now they have pushed deep into Byzantium."

A Norman said, "Alas, Byzantium."

"Alas, Byzantium," agreed the Duke, smiling.

"Alas, Byzantium," said another Norman, with a high titter.

Tyun smiled. "Myra, where the Blessed Nicholas lies, is in a state of chaos. The Byzantines, the Seljuk Turks: no one knows who rules that city now, or the whole state of Lycia. The coast there is in utter confusion. It would not be difficult to slip in, grab the corpse, and liberate the saint. Venice has asked me if I will go to fetch the bones for them. This is the moment. In a few days, I set off for Lycia, and I will bring the relics back to Italy." He clasped his hands behind his back. "If Bari does not want St. Nicholas, Venice does."

"The Venetians are bastards," a merchant clarified.

"You have asked us for twice what Venice offered you," said the Duke. "It is an appalling sum."

"So you might ask why you would want the corpse of Saint Nicholas," said Tyun.

The Normans waited for an answer.

"Saint Anastasia!" Tyun announced in a loud voice. "Saint Anastasia was born without hands. The daughter of an innkeeper. She did what work she could with her sleeves pinned shut. One night a husband and young wife came to the inn, seeking shelter, after a decree had gone out from Caesar Augustus, that all the world should be taxed. The wife was pregnant. There was no room in the inn. I presume you've heard this story. They slept in the stable."

His audience gawped.

"In the night, Anastasia, daughter of the innkeeper, woke. There was singing and the tolling of celestial bells. There was light coming from the stable. She rushed down to investigate, worried about fire. Instead, she found a glowing child laid in a manger, no crib for His bed. She knelt before him. She wished to bathe him as a midwife would do. But she had no hands. The Blessed Mother picked up the child and laid Him cradled in Anastasia's arms. Anastasia wished with all her heart she could care for the babe as the Virgin slept.

"And lo, an angel came out of heaven and delivered her a pair of hands, white as lilies. With these hands she tended the Christ Child through that long winter's night, as ox and ass stood by."

Tyun looked down upon the sitting Duke and his rapt company.

"I recovered Saint Anastasia's hands." There was an appreciative murmur from the Normans. "They were of ivory, inset with jewels and rare teak. I found them in a treasure house in the Maghreb. I penetrated the fortress, slipped the hands out of the vault without detection, and delivered them to the Church of Saint George in Fraxinetum. Within three months, Fraxinetum was drawing five hundred pilgrims a day. Ships arriving from all over the world. Caravans coming over the Alps, paying imposts. The city has repaired its walls and built a shrine. This is the power of a holy relic."

Nods of reluctant approval all around.

"Consider what a saint can do for a city. Venice wants to hire me to fetch Nicholas. But Venice—Venice already has Saint Mark. An Evangelist. One of a set of four."

Uneasy looks among the Normans.

"And they don't just have Saint Mark. Also Saint Athanasius, Saint Zacharias, and the foot of Catherine of Siena." The treasure hunter was now prowling between the men, restless with the energy of expertise. "Everyone has a relic. Rome's burial grounds have been picked clean. The tombs off the Via Labicana, the Via Appia—they're barren now, gentlemen. Not a bone left. All the Roman saints are spoken for. Don't even ask. The monastery at Fulda has Sebastian and Cecilia sewn up. One pierced by arrows, the other burned to death and then beheaded while playing the hydraulic organ. Sure, Fulda only has a few shreds of Cecilia, but they also have Urban, Felicity, Felicissimus, and Emmerentina. They have Boniface, Cornelius, Callistus—who was buried right next to Cecilia—and Columbana." He spoke these names directly into the faces of the astonished merchants, smacking his hands together with each martyr. "Agapitus, Georgius, Eugenia, Maximus, Vincentius, and Emerita. I got them Columbana."

"Fulda is a most prosperous abbey," said the Archbishop, in a fever of longing.

"Constantinople," continued the saint hunter, "seat of great Byzantium, has the True Cross, of course—and also the two more disappointing crosses the thieves hung on. They have the body of the Prophet Daniel, the robe and girdle of the Virgin Mary, the hair of John the Forerunner, and the rod of Moses.

"Gentlemen, if you wish Bari to remain a great port city, you need a saint. And you need a saint with draw. I can get that for you. Nicholas is no ordinary saint. You have all heard of his holy liquor. The oil that drips off his corpse. Imagine how many will come to your city to taste it. How does it taste, men of Bari? It tastes of lilies. It tastes of myrrh. It tastes of redemption. *It tastes of gold.*"

The saint hunter's spiel was done, and so he waited. The Norman Duke rose and pulled off his soaked linen shift. He handed it to the attendants. He stood before the most powerful men in the city naked. Two more attendants brought forth his shirt and, as he raised his hands, they slipped it over his head.

Dressing him like a child, the Abbot thought with disgust. *Again, an affront to all of us.* The undershirt was embroidered richly with flowers and hunters on horseback. And yet all that splendor, that needlework, would go unseen. *A reminder that beneath excellence lies excellence. Beneath power lies power.* The boys brought out a dalmatic of silk which was even more dazzling and lowered it over his head. His eyes re-emerged through the neck, locked on the treasure hunter. He held up his arms so the attendants could look to the pleats and belt him with gold.

"Why don't we just go ourselves and snag the saint?" asked the Duke. "Why pay you at all?"

The saint hunter shrugged. "My crew, my team, are just as happy working for the Venetians as for you. We have worked for kings and for caliphs. We know the business. All the tricks and traps. There are so many swindles, Your Lordship. Saints swapped or stolen. Small-time operators wander around in the Alps, digging up random bodies and passing them off as martyrs. The head of Saint John the Baptist lies garnished on a platter in Constantinople, and it's also being served up by monks in Gaul and in Swabia. Three heads at least on John. Many saint merchants deliver their promised corpses, sure, but they skim off a finger or rib to sell elsewhere. An unscrupulous priest of Soissons stole a pint and a half of Saint Marcellinus."

"How do we know you won't use us like that?" a canny merchant demanded. "How do we know you won't bring us some hick's corpse you just picked up in Illyria? We are paying for the true and only body."

"You will send an escort with us and a notary—someone incorruptible—who will watch the removal."

"Your Lordship," a merchant protested, "do you trust this man?" He pointed at the saint hunter. "He has a smirk. His manner is commercial and piratical. Is he even . . ." the merchant wondered, ". . . Christian?"

When the Normans looked to the Tartar, the leer was gone. His eyes were wide with piety. "These rough features may speak of the eastern steppe," he declared, touching his chest, "but Christ is engraved within my heart—a Christ as white as oyster shells and blond as wheat." He closed his eyes in reverence. "God has shown His favor by bringing thousands of pilgrims and their riches to all my clients."

It did not matter that no one believed him, or that he did not expect them to.

The Duke asked, "You require a military escort?"

"A warship to protect against the Venetians. They will not be happy I've accepted another offer. They were already prepared to set out for Myra."

"We will supply a warship," said the Duke, "and an agent of our own who will oversee the operation and authenticate the bones." He turned to the two men of God. "We also need a representative of the Church to notarize the corpse. Someone uncorruptible."

"Indeed," said the Archbishop. "It requires someone who may travel in—" he glared at the lazy smile of the saint hunter— "dubious company, and yet remain inviolate. He must sleep side by side with men of commerce and yet never be tempted by pelf."

"Your Lordship," said the Abbot to the Duke, bowing low. "If I may call my humble monastery to mind, the dreamer himself would be an excellent candidate. The one whose dream was visited by St. Nicholas. He is intelligent, with a quick eye and a store of learning. But he is unable—infuriatingly unable—to tell a lie.

"He would be ideal," the Abbot concluded. "He is, in short, a kind of . . . holy fool?"

"Do you know how I greet the morning?" said Brother Nicephorus. "I look up to the sky, whether it's bleached or blue, and I say, '*Haec dies*—this is the day!' And I think about how every dawn is like the first dawn when the earth was created, and the six six-winged angels stood around the new canvas of Creation, stretching it taut between them, and the new day rang with their chant as they sang the world into being, and as the sun comes up I greet it like they did, singing.

"Of course," he considered, "I always wonder how light came a few days before the sun, technically, because light was Monday and the sun was Thursday. You know, there was light before there was anything to draw it on, which I wonder about. How can you have light without surfaces? What does it shine on? Wouldn't it look just the same as darkness? These are the mysteries of Creation. Up north, I hear, they think it all came out of the body of a dead giant, which makes a lot less sense."

There was a silence after he spoke.

The servant said, "My hands are like this so you can mount."
It wasn't yet dawn.

"Sorry! Sorry, brother." The monk stepped in the servant's
cupped hands and pulled himself up onto the horse. "Excited
to meet my traveling companions. You know where we're
going?"

The servant did not answer.

They rode slowly along the causeway at the top of the city
wall. Below them, the dull morning waves broke against the
battlements. The sun was rising over the Adriatic. The monk
looked to the east and thought about how, the next day, he
would be sailing toward that rising sun and seeing impossible
sights.

Fifteen minutes later, they arrived at the old palace where
the Byzantine governor of Apulia had lived until ousted by
the Norman invaders. In the courtyard, the household was
unloading wood and drawing water, preparing for the day. The
tiles were smeared with mud, and someone was sloshing water
from a bucket onto nautical mosaics.

The servant led Nicephorus into the great house. Nicephorus deftly swiveled sideways to avoid a boy with kindling and
he whispered, "Who am I meeting?"

"The Factor," said the servant. This told Nicephorus
nothing.

They entered a grand triclinium, where the Byzantine governor had once dined with admirals and later had cried at his
loss.

The Factor sat by a small fire that had been built against
the morning's chill. He was a heavily chiseled Norman, his
hair cut blunt, his nose a wedge, his skin rough and red. He
was perhaps forty. He looked like business, presumption, and
impatience.

This kind of man made Nicephorus nervous. Next to them,

he felt young, like a gangly novice, though he was over thirty. He never knew what to do with his hands, which he tended to use during conversation to illustrate things like songbirds and the first rising of the sun at Creation.

"Brother Nicephorus?" said the Factor. "You had the dream?"

"I did," said Nicephorus.

"Hope it was right," said the Factor. "They're sending me to oversee it all."

He said his name was Rollo de Bailleul. He did not make it sound like Nicephorus would ever need to use it.

He explained the expedition would consist of two ships: the *Epiphany*, the saint hunter's ship, and a larger vessel, a bireme dromon manned by Bari sailors and marines, the *Dagobert*, which would act as an escort. The Venetians were also probably racing to Myra to claim the saint for their own. It was not impossible that the expedition would see "action at sea." This phrase alone seemed to make the Factor grimly pleased.

He explained that he had been engaged to watch out for the interests of the Norman overlords of Bari in the Nicholas matter. His specialty was military logistics. He would be in charge of the expedition as a whole. The saint hunter and his team of trained martyrologists would oversee the theft—the liberation—of Nicholas itself. But Bari was paying the saint hunter too well to trust him. The Factor also wanted Brother Nicephorus to stay alert. There were, apparently, many swindles in the saint business. They both would have to notarize the corpse when it was exhumed.

"Have you met the saint hunter?" the Factor asked. "He wants to hear the details of your dream."

"I have not," said Nicephorus.

The Factor called for the saint hunter to be brought.

While they waited, Nicephorus found the silence awkward.

The first light was coming in through the arched windows of the triclinium. "I like the dawn," he began. "Do you know how I greet the morning each day?"

The face did not respond: blocky, granitic.

Nicephorus would have just shut up, but he did not want to leave a question dangling. So he said uncomfortably, "I sing Lauds."

The face remained fixed.

They sat there, the monk who had never left the hot, flat plains of Apulia, and the invader from the muddy and obscure western fringes of the earth, those chilly Gaulish marches inhabited only by barbarians, bears, boars, and the pettier dragons. Out in the Frankish provinces, the princes were nothing but tribal chieftains. The kings were badly drawn Byzantine emperors scribbled in haste between battles. The Norman warrior sat motionless, speechless, needing nothing, offering nothing.

Then, "The saint hunter," he said.

Nicephorus turned to see the handsome Tartar from the taverna. Standing next to him was a pallid giant, shaved bald as a yam and dressed in lamellar armor: Rus, from the looks of him, and so tall his legs buckled inward at the knee.

"I am called Tyun," said the saint hunter. "This is my bodyguard, Shchek. You are the monk Nicephorus?"

Nicephorus blurted out to the Factor, "This man looks blatantly piratical."

The saint hunter regarded him evenly. "I shave every three days."

"He was telling stories of impossibilities down on the docks to seduce women."

"This is the dreamer?" Tyun asked the Factor.

"Apparently. Abbot Helias vouched for his probity and honesty."

"Then," said the saint hunter, with a half shrug, "I suppose we're seeing proof of it."

He walked forward and took a seat on one of the dining benches. The Rus giant, Shchek, stood behind him, tasseled spear held in military readiness.

"Dreamer," said Tyun, "no slander. I am a professional. I have touched the hand of Doubting Thomas in Mabar, which clasps into a fist at any untruth. I have located the caves of desert fathers and Shiite mystics to search for their sacred bones. I have gone diving for treasure in the Sea of Sodom among the ruins of the city Heaven blasted for sin. On the shore you can still see Lot's wife where she was transformed into a pillar of salt. Her features are almost unrecognizable, and there are holes through which the wind moans. The locals use her as a sheep lick." He leaned far forward and reached his arm out toward Nicephorus, almost touching the monk's face with a finger. Nicephorus reared back. The Tartar asked gently, with a sweet, dangerous smile, "What about you, dreamer? Have you ever swum in the Sea of Sodom?"

They stared at each other, the Benedictine monk and Tyun the saint hunter.

Something between a blush and a chill spread through the monk's chest. The finger quivered near the cleft of his chin.

Then Tyun sat back. "If we are going to unite your city with the Blessed Nicholas, I need to hear about your dream. What clues does it offer to the circumstances of the body?"

Nicephorus said uneasily, "The saint did not speak . . . directly of the theft of his body."

"Liberation," Tyun corrected.

The monk pointedly addressed Rollo de Bailleul rather than the saint hunter. He admitted, "It was a vague dream. The saint traveled through the air, through snow and a storm. He was gift giver and light bringer. He spoke to spirits, to men, to birds, and to beasts. He came and chanted and spoke to me . . ."

"What did he say?" asked Tyun.

"That we should walk forth boldly. That this was how we should do good. He marched out through a gate of ice and pointed at the wider world. I took it to mean we could no longer hide from the sickness behind our monastery walls, but should visit our friends throughout the city and give them aid."

"Walk forth boldly!" exclaimed Tyun. "There is your mandate!"

"I do not know if the dream was inspired," Nicephorus admitted to Rollo de Bailleul.

"You can express no doubt," the Factor said. "Thousands depend on this vision."

"It took place in a land of snow and ice. Lycia is hot. It has never seen snow."

"There are mountains in Lycia," said Tyun. "It probably snows on the peaks."

The monk raised his hand. "I cannot say absolutely—"

"There is no doubt," said Tyun. "Listen, dreamer: You will sail with me on the *Epiphany*. We will talk more about this dream." To the Factor: "The body of the thaumaturge saint is held in the city of Myra, in the basilica where Nicholas was bishop—peace be upon him. The church is about two miles from the port." The saint hunter reached into his sleeve and pulled out a letter, neatly folded. He untangled its quadrants. "I have written testimony from two pilgrims who visited the basilica. They have drawn a map of the sanctuary. They report there is a brotherhood who watch over the tomb and protect the corpse. We don't know the exact location of the sarcophagus within the church itself."

"Perhaps the saint does not wish to leave," said Nicephorus.

Tyun and the Factor ignored him. "Caliph Harun al-Rashid once sent a general to steal the healing corpse," said Tyun. "He could not find the body. He left the basilica frustrated and empty-handed. His ship immediately sank in a storm."

"The location of the tomb is not on that map?" asked Rollo de Bailleul.

"No." Tyun folded the map and slipped it back into his sleeve. "But we do know that there is an apparatus for the collection of the sacred slime, the *oleum martyris*. Often in these cases there is actually a system for piping in holy water or oil, running it over the blessed remains, and then draining it from the tomb. The priests decant it into small bottles for pilgrims to drink." Tyun smiled at Nicephorus. "This shall be our sign: I suspect the sarcophagus has a cock." When Nicephorus shifted his feet, Tyun clarified kindly: "A spigot."

"Do we use subterfuge or force?" asked the Factor.

"We assess. Our story—and you must ride on the same donkey, dreamer—our story, once we leave the port of Bari, is that we are on our way to pick up a shipment of grain in Antioch. We will be stopping for water and provisions every night or two. We will be asked our destination. Antioch, yes?" He looked sharply at the monk. "Do you understand? This is a necessary lie."

Nicephorus frowned.

The Factor insisted, "Brother Nicephorus."

Nicephorus was about to speak.

"We will keep him onboard, then," said Tyun. "He won't talk to anyone about our mission or his doubts about his dream." Tyun looked up toward his giant. "For the moment, let's invite Brother Nicephorus to stay in a pleasant room down by the docks for contemplation and prayer until we're ready to depart tomorrow morning. Perhaps he needs to stay under lock and key."

"There is no need," said Nicephorus.

"There is always need for prayer," said Tyun, rising.

The giant moved to take Nicephorus's arm.

. . .

St. Nicholas was born in the town of Patara, on the Lycian coast. The Roman grain ships came and went in the harbor. Up in the hills was a great temple of Apollo, where during the six months of winter, pilgrims came from all over the empire to ask questions of the oracle.

Though Nicholas was born when the empire of Rome was still pagan, we're told that he was a Christian from birth: as a newborn, when the blood was first washed from him, he stood upright on his own legs in the bath for two hours babbling Christ's name. As an infant, on holy fast days he refused to suck on either of his mother's breasts.

When he was a young man, Nicholas joined a monastery near the old city of Xanthos, half ruined since the people of that town had all burned themselves alive. The monastery was built outside of town, down a processional avenue, in the shadow of three abandoned temples half sunk in a marsh: one to Apollo, one to Artemis, and one to Leto, mother goddess of ancient Lycia. It was there in that marsh that Leto, we are told, angry that no one would let her take a cooling drink after she gave birth to gods, transformed the Lycian peasants into frogs.

Nicholas and his brethren took stones and capitals from those tumbled porticoes and raised up their sanctuary to the Christian god.

I picture his early life as quiet, cloistered, the only sound in that landscape being the complaints of cattle and the buzzing of cicadas. But the Vitae *of Nicholas all tell us that when he touched the stones of fallen temples, demons fled from him, shrieking in the air.*

One night during Nicholas's youth, as he was passing down a street in Xanthos or Patara, he heard a father talking to his daughters. "I do not have money for your dowries," said the father, weeping. "We are penniless. Therefore, you must sell yourselves to the men who come to port here."

Nicholas was appalled. He went to his parents' house and stole from their treasury a great quantity of their gold and he wrapped it up in three bundles as a gift. Each night for the next three nights, he tossed a bundle of gold through the window of that family's house: a dowry for each daughter. The father was delighted, though it is hard to sympathize with him. The daughters, anyway, were saved, and bought fine husbands, one for each of them.

Some believe that this is why pawnshops hang signs with three gold balls above their doors, for the three dowry bundles. Others say Nicholas did not throw the packages through the window; he tossed them down the chimney.

This story is what we recall in giving our children miraculous gifts from the saint: We shall not have to sell you. We will keep the world from you as long as we can. Soon enough, you will have to sell yourselves.

The room was hot. Once, at lunch, they unlocked the door to feed him jerky. Nicephorus looked down on the square by the docks. He did not pray. The closest things to cherubim were idiot flies circling his head. They landed in a reflection on copper.

They could not find the window, though it had no glass.

Cool night, and Nicephorus did not close the shutters. He did not want to feel closed in, though the door was locked. He stared out at the empty square. A small moon was on the sea. The great ships slept like whales, bobbing at anchor.

He could not sleep. He had not been outside of Bari since he was a boy, a novice at the monastery. Every day was a round of offices, a routine of blessings, the faces he knew. The families in the tall, narrow streets around the monastery, the monks themselves. People proud that prayer had become rote. Nicephorus prayed at known hours. He purchased food in bulk and kept accounts. Each day he ate the same soups, the same pulses. There was a terror in leaving that all behind, but Nicephorus was also thrilled. He thought about the seas he'd sail, the sawtoothed waves of oceans in illuminated Gospels. Saint Luke and Saint Paul had sailed to the ports of Lycia.

But he did not trust his own vision, the glimpse of the saint. He knew he—

There was a figure on the quay, walking alone.

It was the saint thief, cloaked and solitary. Nicephorus leaned forward and watched.

Tyun prowled along the ranks of tenders.

Another figure: very tall, but breasted. A woman, draped in a shawl, waiting by a stunted fig. The saint thief approached her as if they would pass each other. Nicephorus could not hear the whisper of their feet above the lapping waves. They stopped parallel to each other. They turned. Now they faced each other.

They were close enough for confidences.

Now they spoke. Their voices could not be heard above the restless surf, which said only, *Distance. Distance. Distance. Tomorrow. Change.*

They pointed. Perhaps indications of location. Perhaps negotiations enumerated in the air.

Then some conclusion was reached; abruptly, they kissed. Nicephorus watched, calculating: It wasn't Gallenice. Much too tall.

Then the two pushed off from each other. They both swiveled and walked in opposite directions.

Tyun went around a corner to the right and was gone. The woman walked to the left. In the confusion of shadows, Nicephorus could not make her out anymore. Still, he watched.

The room was getting cold. The monk lumped his feet one on top of the other to try to preserve their warmth. He wished for the eyes of an eagle.

In a few minutes, a ship's boat pulled away from the docks

on the promontory—it must be the woman—and rowed out toward a warship, a mammoth trireme dromon of two hundred oars slumbering on the deep.

Nicephorus marked its position.

In the morning, he was asleep on the pallet when the tavern owner unlocked the door and let the dogs in to wake him.

Shortly after Nicholas became Bishop of Myra, appointed by the Christian God in a vision, there was a drought in Lycia and a famine, or so the story goes.

At this time, there were three young scholars traveling together who stopped at an inn. The innkeeper apologized but said he had nothing to feed them. The three scholars said they would pay handsomely for a room where they could sleep, protected from bandits and slavering beasts. They showed the innkeeper the gold their parents had given them for travel.

So they went to bed, and the innkeeper brooded in his kitchen, bent low over his knees, and then he called for his wife, and they whispered, and they tied on their gray aprons and took knives and went upstairs, and he held the boys down and shoved straw in their mouths while she cut their throats. The innkeeper and his wife took the bodies down the stairs and drained their blood and then they butchered the boys, cutting them into steaks and rashers.

The Blessed Nicholas, so we hear, was traveling with his episcopal retinue, visiting the lonely village churches in the hills. He stopped for the night at the inn. He and all his deacons sat around the table and asked for supper. The innkeeper brought out a rich ragout, rare in a time of famine.

Nicholas and his retinue were delighted. They picked up bread to dip in the stew. They tore the bread with their hands. The sauce was rich and brown with fats. They dipped their bread.

Then Nicholas heard the angels speak. There was a light upon him. He shoved the table away from him violently. A bench tipped over as he rose and shouted, "Stop! Do not put a morsel of meat in your mouths."

He led the deacons into the kitchen. There, in a pickling tub, they found the bodies bobbing, the boys' eyes white as onions in the green brine.

The innkeeper picked up a knife and bared his teeth. Nicholas made signs in the air and unseen angels held the man's arms fast.

"Look at these children, these children!" wept Nicholas, praying to his god.

They rolled the vat into the dining room. Nicholas swept all the crockery off the table and laid the corpses out. Lovingly, he took out strips of meat and put them back upon the frames. The others, bewildered, helped, unable to match muscle and tendon, gristle and scalp.

We do not know the bodies we live in; our hands do not know by feel how to assemble the mysteries of our flesh. They were just bloody lumps heaped and misplaced on the long, grinning bones.

Nicholas, appalled at the dripping feast, fell to his knees and prayed again, as he might before dining at a full table; and as he prayed, the lumps of flesh began to move. They crawled and slithered sluglike to the places appointed to them, the joints and calves and cheeks. They circled the chest. The skin grew new. Nicholas's retinue gagged at this gory circus, but as they did, they started to whisper acclamations.

And then the full miracle was complete. The boys awoke. They were no longer shredded. They were whole and unharmed, though still basted. They rose refreshed from their slumber, oiled, scented with rosemary.

"Where are we? Where is the man with the knife?"

They went on their way with Nicholas, singing hymns to the glory of God.

This tale is told to show how St. Nicholas cared for the young and innocent. It reminds us also of this: There are those who would devour us; and worse, most of us live by devouring others without ever knowing our sin. We must watch what goes into our mouths and what comes out.

. . .

The sky the day they set out was overcast—so I have heard—but the launch felt like a festival nonetheless.

The monks of St. Benedict's processed from their monastery all the way through the city and out to the docks with crosses held above them and choristers singing chants in praise of Nicholas, Wonder Worker and Navigator, who gave gifts of gold and grain to the wretched and raised the dead from tubs of brine. Behind them marched Norman lords and Barese merchants, with the Factor, Rollo de Bailleul, at their head. There were cries of "Nicholas! Nicholas! Heal us! Heal us!" and many brought out their sick to be blessed by the side of the lanes. The faces of the feverish were pale and stippled with pox. They kissed the Abbot's hand, and he tried not to recoil. He made the sign of the cross above their spotted foreheads and hurried on.

The ships were at dock, surrounded by crowds. The hundred sailors of the *Dagobert*—Normans, Apulians, Lombards, Byzantine Greeks, a few Arab oarsmen—stood at attention with hands on their spears and the hilts of their swords. Forty oars bristled from each sleek flank of the war galley. The shields lining the gunwales were newly painted.

The assembled company were already being called the League of St. Nicholas, and the whole of Bari, it seemed, came out to see them off and wish them a swift voyage and a glorious return with the healing bones in tow.

The brothers of St. Benedict saw off one of their own at the docks, Brother Nicephorus, who stumbled out of a nearby inn looking bewildered and was led toward the docks by a sailor. Nicephorus and his escort pushed through the crowds to the *Epiphany*, a merchantman of two sails and only ten oars to a side, dwarfed by the mighty bireme warship that would carry the Norman Factor and his auxiliary force.

Friends and neighbors from the town (girls, husbands, wives) called out Nicephorus's name and waved and cheered, because he was the dreamer, and he would see places they would not. They sent their wishes with him over the sea.

"This way, dreamer," said Tyun, putting his arm around the monk to guide him on board the *Epiphany*.

Nicephorus, dazed by the shouting, confused by the arm slung around him, stepped unsteadily onto the plank and almost fell into the water. Tyun grabbed his shoulders and pushed him along. Wide-eyed, the monk looked around at the crew who stood at the ready on the decks. Piratical: of no professed country, clearly a rabble of misanthropes, cat burglars, toughs, and refugees from the laws of many nations.

That is no way to think of my companions, Nicephorus scolded himself. *Think instead of how much of the wide world stands upon the deck of this ship: men from scalding deserts and the cold, endless forests of northern birch. Men from cities without names in my language. All come together to seek the Blessed Nicholas's bones.*

At that moment, Tyun said to him, "What do you think of our crew, dreamer?" and unfortunately, Nicephorus answered truthfully: "I was just thinking how thrilling it is to be among so many people who come from so many places unknown to me: the deserts of the East and the northern steppe, and that one there looks like he's from underground," and when Tyun said nothing, but simply withdrew his arm in distaste, Nicephorus kept on babbling about mountain villages where the evening is clothed in Christ's majesty, and mighty rivers that cascaded down cliffs toward the seas. He eventually came to a halt. Tyun, and Reprobus, the dog-headed first mate, and Shchek, the Rus giant, were all staring at him.

The saint hunter pointed to the canopy at the rear of the vessel. "Go sit there. We'll be setting out soon. You don't need to move for a while." He stepped away. "Three weeks or so."

"Can I do something to," asked the monk, at a loss, "help?"

Tyun shrugged. "You seem utterly useless to me."

Miserably, Nicephorus walked down the full length of the merchantman, down the long aisle between benches as sweating sailors glowered at him from their oars. He reached the platform at the stern and sat in the shade of the canopy. A scanty overhang shaded the rowers from the sun. There was no room belowdecks but the hold, empty of all cargo, since there would be no real trade for the grain of Antioch. Nicephorus looked back at the docks, at his friends, at his city, at the people he knew. They waved silently, though the sound of the crowd was overwhelming.

Abbot Helias of St. Benedict's blessed the two ships with holy water, and there was an acclamation: "Saint Nicholas guide you on the waves!"

Then the rowers started tugging on their oars, and gradually, the two galleys swam out into the harbor until it was time to spread their sails.

Brother Nicephorus sat beneath the canopy while the men around him worked with skill and dexterity, urged on by barked orders from the dog-headed first mate. The voyage had begun.

Then the endless horizon, the ship pitching down swells. Nicephorus had never been to sea.

Supper was two biscuits. The cook was an old Turkish woman, thin as famine. She poured warm water on the biscuits to soften them. Tyun and Reprobus and Shchek sat next to Nicephorus under the canopy and ate.

Nicephorus tried to be gracious. "This is excellent," he said to the cook.

"It's biscuits and hot water," said Tyun, groping for lumps in his bowl. "We're always getting sick from the crap she serves us."

Nicephorus told her, "You did a fine job boiling the water."

"Musarat can't cook worth shit," Tyun said, chewing hard. "But she killed someone for me when it mattered."

Musarat herself said nothing.

Several of the sailors had been glaring at Nicephorus and his bowl. He tried to eat more unobtrusively.

One of the sailors called out, "Why does pretty boy get two biscuits?"

Tyun stared at the man and kept chewing.

"Why two?" The sailor held up his own bowl and pointed: "One." He jabbed his finger at his neighbor's bowl. "One. One. One. Down the line."

"Because pretty boy is the client," said Tyun.

There was no sleep at night. The deck rolled. Nicephorus was feeling sick. He was crammed between the Rus giant and an old, bearded Armenian ex-cavalryman with a white mustache like a currycomb. The Armenian slept with a torn blanket wrapped around him that reeked of horse. Shchek, it transpired, was a eunuch, which explained his stature, and in his sleep he cooed in treble. Nicephorus did not know how time could pass so slowly. When he was wakened yet again by the giant's sopranino snoring, he longed for a holy office to count off the hours.

The dog-man stood at watch with two of the men, scanning the dark horizon.

"It is clear you are not Christians," said Nicephorus.

"We are the very soul of the Nazarene," said Reprobus, scratching his ear with his toes.

"More than half of the crew performs exercises five times a day facing Mecca."

"Limbering up, I'm sure. The oar is a brutal mistress."

"Where are you from? Some pagan land . . . ?"

"The Land of Enfeoffed Dogs. We are deeply Christian. Do not forget that in the Gospels, it is said that a dog was in the manger with the infant Christ."

"I don't think that's in the Gospels."

"It is absolutely in the Gospels."

"I would remember a dog."

"Well, neither are the ox and the ass, but we all know they were there. Ass and ox. Alpha and omega. The dog wished to render service to your god."

"*My* god?"

"Ours," said the dog-man, looking under the spars at the sea.

Travel was slow. They hugged the coast when they could. Almost every night they put into port to replenish the barrels of water in their hold. They stopped at Brindesion, Corfu, and Zakynthos.

Occasionally the *Epiphany* was winched up on shore and beached for the night. Sailors went off into the stone towns to drink and find something better to eat. "Recall," said Tyun to his crew, "we are a merchant ship with a military escort on our way to Antioch to purchase grain." He shut his eyes. "Millet, say."

He then said to Nicephorus, "Not you."

"You are afraid I will tell the truth."

"The truth is so precious," said Tyun, "that it must be preserved in absolute isolation. The world is a dirty place, dreamer. Let's keep the truth on board."

The saint hunter rarely spoke at sea. All the easy garrulity of his pitches was gone. He strode the small length of the boat like it was his kingdom. He stood close to his men when he commanded them.

Nicephorus was uneasy. He could tell the crew disliked him, and that the Tartar restrained their distaste. At first the monk offered to assist with the work, hoping this would thaw the chill, but clearly he had no skill with ropes or oars. The men turned away without speaking to him. "Back to your cloister," he heard one say.

At night, the monk found himself watching the captain as he slept. Though Tyun's face was wide, his features were surprisingly delicate in sleep. On hot nights he slept wrapped only in an izar, his chest and arms bare on the reed mat. A muscle in his arm twitched, a response to some challenge in a dream. Distantly, onshore, dogs yipped and fought in empty alleyways. As the saint hunter moved in slumber to shift his body on the mat, to cradle his head, Nicephorus discovered he was glad the giant Rus was snoring between them. He did not want to roll into the captain when the boat heaved, and to find he touched the flesh that was sanctified in sleep.

And yet, in the day, Nicephorus found that Tyun often grabbed him in passing—handling his wrists, conking him on the arm, gripping his shoulder to adjust him, move him a few fingers to starboard, as if the ship were tight.

Nicephorus had no idea if it was a game, a tease. *Not worth the speculation.* He stared out at the horizon and concentrated on Trinitarian controversies. If Father, Son, and Spirit were all one, did they share thoughts? If so, why did Christ have to cry out for his god and father with his human mouth when He hung upon the Cross?

Nothing was steady. There were great troughs they slid into. The *Dagobert* pitched in the gray distance. Nicephorus had no sense of absolute up.

The *Epiphany* did not sit deep in the water. Spray shot over the gunwales. The rowers bitched and groaned when waves hit. They had only an overhang to protect them. There was a bitter wind.

Then, one day when they needed to put in to port and get more fresh water, the sea was becalmed. It was dead. The skies were blank with cloud. It was difficult to determine direction.

The *Dagobert* and the *Epiphany* sat side by side upon the sea. Sails were useless, so they had to rely on their oars. It was hard work, and the water was down to half rations. The *Dagobert*, with eighty oars, had to dawdle. The mariners of each ship stared at the others balefully over the gunwales. They were thirsty and irritable.

Nicephorus asked if he could row. Tyun would not let him. Then the monk had nothing to do except sit and concentrate on his thirst. The sky was flat and nothing moved, even when they rowed.

The sailors glared at Nicephorus and whispered.

"Why are they whispering?" Nicephorus asked Shchek.

The eunuch grinned with pointed teeth and said in his high treble, "They are deciding whether to pitch you overboard."

"What have I done?"

"All of this," said Shchek, looking from the *Epiphany* to the *Dagobert*. "A hundred and fifty of us out here because of your dream. Isn't Saint Nicholas supposed to help sailors?"

"He has saved many sailors during storms."

"Pray to him," said the eunuch. "We are starting to ask whether he favors you as you claim."

"I have never claimed—" said the monk, but stopped himself.

"You lied?" The Rus rolled his lower lip beneath his upper.

Nicephorus did not feel safe on board the merchantman. But when he turned to look at the *Dagobert*, cruising beside them, he saw the crew there inspecting him, too.

Each coiling of rope, each pull upon the oar, each yank of muscle, lanyard, tendon, sail: all of it justified only by an insubstantial dream.

He thought about the word "founder," and how it refers both to the man who begins an endeavor and to the cataclysm that capsizes it for good.

"Any word from your dreams?" Rollo de Bailleul shouted across the gulf between ships.

Nicephorus waved, as if he did not hear.

The next day, there was a ship upon the horizon that appeared to follow them.

Even when he still lived upon the earth, Saint Nicholas saved sailors with his miracles.

The stories are many: always a terrible storm, and the sailors call out the name of the Bishop of Myra, athlete of Christ—and then he comes through the air, cope flapping, and the waters are calmed.

In one, a boy's boat capsized, and as he went under and felt the sea rush into him, he prayed to Nicholas. The water filled all his chambers, but he still fought to repeat the name with blue lips.

Then he was transported. He was no longer in the maelstrom. He found himself standing, miraculously, on his own street. His neighbors came out at the sound of his coughing and spitting. His clothes were still dripping wet.

Or a crowd of fishermen far off in the Aegean would cry out to the Wonder Worker and he would come striding across the waves, head wreathed in flame, and where his staff struck the water, it threw off sparks. He would command the tempest to cease.

During these miraculous acts, the Bishop of Myra himself remained in his study or going about the daily business of his see. He was not aware of his own interventions. When asked, he would say, "I am nothing. Just a man."

Once a sailor who was knocked off his ship saw the saint descend and throw down his cloak, and it spread across the tossing waves, growing in compass until the ocean itself was flat brocade. The sailor, astonished, lay swaddled upon this sea of scarlet silk, which was stippled all the way to the horizon with stars and golden Chi-Rhos.

Thus, Nicholas became the saint of sailors, and from this followed the patronage of merchants and all who traded on the uncertain and treacherous waves.

The ship appeared on the horizon when they were in the strait between Crete and the Peloponnese. This was after the great age of the Cretan pirates—the island was now held by Byzantium—but there were still many other enemies at sea. Tyun and the Factor agreed that they should tack to the south and hope to find safe harbor at Kissamos or Chandax.

The wind was still dead, luffing the sails, so the men, for the third day running, were rowing, the long lines of paddles rising and flashing and falling again. They were exhausted and their throats were dry. With a distant ship apparently following them on the horizon, Tyun asked his master of ordnance to lay off his oar and instead prepare the mounted ballistae for engagement.

The master of ordnance was Tornik, the old Armenian ex-cavalryman with the currycomb mustache. He stared sourly off the stern at their pursuer. The artillery officer and the monk stood side by side. They squinted back over the flat sea at the bright smudge that pursued them.

"St. Nicholas saves sailors, does he?" asked Tornik.

"He does," Nicephorus agreed. He told Tornik a story of maritime peril. "When there was a feast in Heaven, the other saints could not find Nicholas because he was out on the Aegean in the midst of a storm, pulling mariners out of the sea."

"He didn't help us on land, at Manzikert," griped the Armenian. It seemed like a bitter, military thing to say. Nicephorus did not know how to respond.

He tried, "I'm sorry."

"Slaughtered," the Armenian said, "like the Persians and Arabs before us. Like the city of Ani."

They watched the ship in their wake. "A merchant?" said Nicephorus. He was trying to speak in sentence fragments, which he thought might make him sound hardened.

"She's military. A dromon. Trireme. Three ranks of oars," said Tornik. "She could overtake us if she wanted. She's waiting."

No land was in sight.

The ship followed them until evening, when Crete first appeared in the haze. Then the trireme started to gain on the *Dagobert* and the *Epiphany*.

The monk observed with satisfaction how the possibility of conflict brought out a new restlessness in their laconic captain. The man paced around the deck like a cat at night. He conferred with Tornik and Reprobus. He turned, pointed at the oncoming vessel, and shouted to his crew, "Venice!"

The monk could barely make out the pennant on the marauder.

"Drink—drink—drink," said the captain, and he ordered the final amphorae of scarce water to be served up to the crew.

"The last of our water?" said Nicephorus. "Shouldn't we husband it?"

"The men will be rowing hard and then fighting," said Tyun. "It's thirsty work. And if we lose," he grinned, "none of us will be needing water anyway."

The galleys unshipped their masts, laying them flat along the deck, securing them with rope to prepare for engagement, and in this, finally, Nicephorus could help, shouldering the weight with twenty others as the great timber came down.

Six men manned the ballistae, which bristled with quarrels. The rest resumed their rowing.

Still, the Venetian galley gained on them.

"Wait for it, boys," said Tornik. "They're almost in range."

The sailors prepared themselves for battle. They shrugged on quilted coats or wriggled into corselets of bone, hide, bronze, or iron. They fastened leather straps around their chests and tied on cummerbunds. They wound turbans around helms. Some wore the words of the Prophet on strips of cloth around their arms to ward off harm.

"Bring the ship about," ordered Tyun, "so we're facing them. No way we can outrun them."

In passing, he grabbed the monk's shoulder hard. "Don't worry, dreamer," he said. "It's two ships against one."

"What can I do?"

"Pray to Nicholas. Ask the athlete of Christ to protect us in the coming battle. The rest of us will piss out all that water now. It's going to be a long battle." Tyun grinned and yelled, "Everyone pass the bucket! Pass the amphora!"

Nicephorus was unhappy about the captain's earthy juvenility. The saint hunter looked gallingly handsome with battle lust in his eyes and a jaunty skew to his baldric.

The *Epiphany* had slowed. Half the rowers were dressing for war. The Factor's great galley came about to face the enemy, its port oars up and dripping while the two rudder men at the back struggled to insist upon the turn.

Individual mariners could now be seen on board the Venetian galley, roiling in their preparations.

"Fire!" Tornik ordered, and the ballista volleys began.

Tyun shouted, "Dreamer! Stop gawping! On your knees!

Pray to Nicholas!" He pointed. "No—aft, so you're not a target!"

There was a startling rattle—a thicket disturbed by some charging boar—and Nicephorus realized arrows were striking the deck all around him. He ran for the stern.

Once there, he took up his job of supplication. He dropped to his knees and began to call out Latin plaints. Next to him, Shchek glowered out at the enemy, eager for combat.

Nicephorus paused in his intercessions long enough to look up and see that the Venetian galley was bearing down directly on the *Epiphany*.

He would have panicked—*Kyrie (O Lord, who walked upon the waters, have mercy upon us) eleison*—except that barreling toward the Venetian warship was the Factor's mighty galley, propelled in perfect coordination by a hundred men rowing, its crushing spur headed right for the oars of the enemy.

Another minute, and the two great ships would collide, the *Dagobert* snapping off ranks of paddles from their shafts, and the Venetians would be left one-armed and stranded.

O Nicholas, protector of sailors, who struck sparks from the waves with your crozier, come to our aid!

But then Nicephorus heard, from twenty-five feet away, Tyun cry, "No, no, no, no, no, *no!*" and then shout a warning: "Greek fire!" Again, screamed at the Factor's ship: "Factor! Greek fire!"

Then Nicephorus saw it: a platform on the prow of the Venetian ship with a siphon of brass, a piping device manned by five men who swiveled the engine's mouth toward the *Dagobert*.

With a roar of detonation, it spat fire across the sea. Everything the fire touched erupted: spur, prow, oars, men, and water itself. Even the waves flamed luridly.

Nicephorus rose. He had heard of Greek fire but had never seen it.

Its composition was unknown. The Byzantines had discovered it; their emperors had demanded that the recipe should never be written down. When the chemical was concocted, no one person was ever allowed to oversee the whole process, so no one could know every ingredient—likely pitch and naphtha skimmed off tar pits near cursed Nineveh. Water could not wash it off, since it floated. Splash a victim to try to extinguish them, and the fire would just spatter, spreading.

The Venetians blasted streams of fire toward the careening *Dagobert.* Flames roared across the gunwales.

Nicephorus saw armored men burning, frantic demons with faces of flame searing in their coifs. They toppled into the sea, and the water around them burned. It was a vision of Hell.

On the deck of the *Dagobert,* men were bailing water onto the flames, which only spread them further. The Factor was shouting some kind of order, but no one could hear. The *Dagobert* drifted in a slow arc, propelled by only a third of its men.

The Venetians slid around its stern in its wake. Terrified, Nicephorus saw the awful spout swivel toward the *Epiphany*. It was a lion's head of brass, mouth open. There was a small spark of flame near the nozzle which would cause the fluid to combust. The siphonists pumped their bellows and prepared another blast.

"Dreamer!" Tyun yelled, suddenly at close quarters. In his hands was a bucket. *"When they hit us, splash it on the flames!"* The bucket was full of piss.

Nicephorus stared. The saint hunter shoved the sloshing bucket into his hands. Tyun demanded, "Think of it as a mighty aspergillum." He spanked Nicephorus on the cheek and pointed at the prow. "Go! 'Purge me with hyssop, and I shall be clean!'"

A shove, and the captain was off screaming at men to prepare for boarding. They were strapping on swords.

Nicephorus charged fore, and as he did, he saw the molten fire bloom. Between the rows of warriors rising from their oars like men grown from the sown teeth of dragons, he smacked along the deck, bringing back the bucket to hurl urine at the flames.

As fire touched down on the banister, it met the piss and guttered. Nicephorus was startled at the urine's potency. He sloshed the bucket up and down the gunwales, proofing the hull against attack.

The siphonists locked eyes with him. He was a challenge. They prepared another blast. Nicephorus blanched. His bucket was empty—it dripped between his fingers. He help-lessly watched the siphonists touch the flame to the brass lion's chin. But then at his elbow appeared a batty old sailor, holding a full amphora, grinning almost toothlessly, offering, "Wee?"

The monk tipped the man's jug and filled his bucket.

Another burst at the *Epiphany*, and this time a man fore was on fire: his jubbah burned as he screamed in fear. He waved an arm around and started to run, the flames trailing behind him.

No time for the bucket. With one hand, Nicephorus snatched the half-empty amphora out of the old soldier's grip and swung it—hurled it—it flew—it smashed against the flam-ing mariner—and the man was, blessedly, piss-wet.

Off starboard, the *Dagobert* burned. The prow was a column of greasy black flame. Bleary smoke curdled the sunset.

The siphonists were already working the pumps for another attack. Nicephorus picked up his bucket and turned to find Tornik. The old Armenian was wrapped in his horse blanket, firing off quarrels as fast as he could load them.

Nicephorus called to him, pointed: *"The brass tub!"*

Tornik looked, nodded. The ballista swiveled and fired.

The bolt hit the tub of liquid fire—punctured it. Then

another bolt. The siphonists were alarmed. They ran for sand-bags. They released pressure on the valve.

Nicephorus turned to put out small cowlicks of flame perking up along the deck.

But then there was a thump. The *Epiphany* quivered.

The Venetians had thrown down a plank and were boarding.

The first warriors leaped across the thwarts.

Tyun was in the midst of them immediately, his sword flashing. Shchek was at his side, piping, "In Hell! In Hell!" and jabbing with his spear.

Another plank slammed down between the ships, and soldiers marched across it.

Tyun turned to confront them.

The first: almost inhuman behind a muffler of mail and a nose guard, simply a set of baleful eyes, a longsword rising to slash.

They engaged, and Tyun felt the sick *thud* as his sword hit hauberk. Tyun had gotten too close. He was exposed.

He took a step back, but now three were upon him.

One swung a battle-ax and missed with his swipe. One toppled backward to avoid Tyun's swing. But the largest hacked down at the saint hunter's wrist—smacked his shortsword—sent it clanging off to the side.

Crouched, Tyun now faced two armed men, himself unarmed. They prepared to finish him. He looked around wildly: nothing to protect him, no room to maneuver, just his bare hands facing blades.

Abruptly, he had the sense the game was over. He found himself surprised: he had always slipped through before. But now he could feel the presence of the black gulf already waiting to swallow him. He did not want to be without memory.

A curiously high voice said, "Kill him."

They moved in on him. He fell backward on the deck.

I do not want to die a worm.

He wondered if the stars were lights or perforations.

A battle-ax swung down toward his skull.

And then a monk with a piss bucket was standing before him.

Nicephorus had blocked the blow. The enemy's ax dug deep into the bucket and held. The monk yanked the bucket, and the lodged ax swerved with it, dragging the warrior who still clutched its haft in his leathern mittens. The warrior stumbled—skated to the side.

Desperately, clumsily, Nicephorus danced one warrior into the other, and the two Venetians tottered on the piss-slicked gunwale.

Tyun grinned at him, a look of unexpected delight, as if he'd just discovered a player with a set of dice and a sack of dinars—someone unexpected in the game. Their eyes for a moment followed each other.

Then Tyun launched himself up and slammed into the Venetians with his shoulder. The warriors, already off-kilter, fell, yelping. But there, behind them, stood a towering warrior in a high, peaked helm, masked in chain mail, two hateful eyes blinking out at an unconquered world. A northern barbarian, a mercenary wielding a blade forged in the darkness of Scandinavian nights.

"The Benedictine, he is good with piss bucket," she said in an accent of fir-tree and slush.

"Every noble band of companions must have its specialists," Tyun said. Sideways, to the monk, Tyun hinted, "Mine is fighting with a weapon." He held out his hand; the monk lifted a fallen sword daintily and handed it to the Tartar hilt-first.

The saint hunter took it. He and the Northerner squared off. Everyone else backed away. The two figures, saint hunter and swordswoman, defined a circle of violence.

The air was acrid from the burning *Dagobert*. The sun fell aslant the channel and made helms blush the color of meat. The sea around them burned quietly.

"The Blessed Nicholas will not protect you," said the woman.

"Venice already stole one saint," said Tyun. "You hid Saint Mark in a cart of pork scrapple to get him past the Faithful. What are you planning for Nicholas? Tripe trough?"

They raised their swords to fight. Nicephorus prayed.

At their feet groaned wounded warriors.

Eye took the measure of eye. Two mouths, both frowning. Four feet circled. The Northerner darted, swung, feinted.

And then the air exploded.

The Greek fire projector, pierced by the ballista bolts, had just leaked into the brazier that warmed it. The naphtha had caught. In one moment, the lion head flared, blasted itself apart, and was no more.

The forward platform of the Venetian trireme burned.

Chaos. Towering flames. And in the midst of it, Tyun saw Shchek, faithful Shchek, who had made his way onto the Venetian ship, eager for battle. Now the giant was alone, spear raised. He peered back at the *Epiphany*, shocked that no one had followed him.

Orders were shouted. The enemy warship was backing away.

Their rowers labored. Their ship rocked from the explosion on its foredeck, the waves engulfing the lowest rank of oars, the oars hacking spastically at the chop. As the Venetians pulled away, boarding planks toppled into the sea.

Tyun called Shchek's name, then swore aloud, "Fuck!" On the deck of the trireme, Shchek was surrounded by puny swordsmen, like a beached and fantastical fish in his coat of metal scales. Haunted, he stared back at his own ship. His arms were limp at his sides.

Tyun yelled, "We will see you in Myra!" but nothing could have been heard above the roaring of flames.

A handful of Venetians were trapped aboard the *Epiphany*. Men surged forward to grab them. Hauled to their feet, the Venetians watched the trireme abandon them, pulling away to the east, toward Lycia. It left a trail of smoke.

The sun was red upon the deep Aegean.

"You saved my life, dreamer," said the saint hunter.

"It is God who spares us."

And to the subdued Northerner, Tyun said, "Never tell Nicholas who he should favor," as the cynocephale stepped in and disarmed her.

The *Dagobert* was damaged beyond repair. Its prow was blackened and would not hold for long. Many of the strakes were charred and popping. Ten of the crew had died from ballista bolts or Greek fire, and many more were wounded. The remaining sailors rowed for the Cretan shore as fast as they could before the hull lost its integrity entirely. It was a delicate operation: for each stroke of the oars, they feared the futtocks would snap.

It was dark by the time they came to the shore. There was no port there, just jumbled cliffs under the stars. The *Dagobert* slid into the shallows and grounded itself. At the first touch of the sand, the prow crumpled as if with relief. The ship staggered and heeled to the side. Cries went up as the waves rushed in belowdecks.

Mariners waded ashore with their arms raised to the sky.

Nearby, the *Epiphany* dropped anchor for the night.

Rollo de Bailleul came aboard to discuss plans with Tyun. "You have prisoners?"

"Several wounded," said Tyun, "and this one who we wish

had been." He pointed at the Northerner, who was tied hand and foot.

Rollo de Bailleul said, "That smell. Piss."

Tyun shrugged. "We saved ourselves."

There were campfires on the slopes defining hills in the darkness. The waves in the cove were gentle.

"We will have to proceed with only your ship," said the Factor. "The Venetians are pressing on toward Myra."

"We need to provision," said Tyun. "The men are thirsty."

"There is a stream," said the Factor. "Tomorrow morning we will sail your ship to the next town east of here. Restock. Revictual. Tomorrow afternoon, we set off for Lycia."

"Your men?"

"A few of us with sail with you. The rest can walk to Chandax. We don't have time to arrange for another transport."

"It would be weeks," said Tyun.

"They can find their way back to Bari. We need to move ahead, hmm? Fast."

Tyun nodded.

The Factor strolled aft to take in the damage. He found the irritating young monk, the dreamer, was at his side.

The monk said, "Sir."

Sailors were settling down to sleep on their benches. The Factor looked up to the North Star.

The monk said, "Sir."

The Factor came to the aft rail and ran his red hand over it. It was not unburnt. It reeked of urine.

The monk said, "Sir."

The Factor turned and laid his fingers on the brooch that clasped his own cloak.

The monk declared softly, "The night before we embarked, I saw the saint hunter meet a woman who rowed out to a ship in the harbor."

"My impression," said the Factor, "the saint hunter says yes to anyone with legs."

"It was that woman," said the monk, nodding at the trussed prisoner. "And the ship she rowed out to: that was the Venetian trireme that just destroyed your ship."

II

DISTANT WHITE TOWNS ON THE CLIFFS. BLUE SEAS. THEY ATE AN OCTOPUS.

As the ship sailed east, the Factor was surrounded by eight soldiers chosen from the *Dagobert*. He had brought aboard a gilded chair of command. He sat uneasily, ready for action, as if on enemy ground. The Factor and his retinue took up most of the captain's roost under the awning.

"I owe you my life," said the saint hunter, grinning at Brother Nicephorus. "I did not expect it from you, dreamer."

The monk did not smile back. "We all are full of secrets and surprises," he said.

Tornik, master of ordnance, asked Nicephorus, "Do you think she noticed when I pierced the brass tub?"

At first the monk did not understand the question, but then saw that Tornik considered the cook, Musarat.

"She could not have ignored the explosion."

"But does she know why the tank ruptured?"

Nicephorus smiled. "Would you like me to bring it up in conversation with her?"

Tornik picked at his mustache. "If it arises."

Night, and the ship rocked gently.

Though it was not discussed, the saint hunter arranged to

sleep next to the captive mercenary. The rest of the prisoners slept bound in the hold with a sailor sitting guard.

Nicephorus, waking, sat up to observe Tyun and the Northerner where they lay on the other side of the sleeping pack.

Several Norman guards kept watch by moonlight. In the prow, Reprobus paced uneasily, gnawing on a cuttlefish bone.

The prisoner had worked herself diagonal and her head was cradled between Tyun's arm and his side. In sleep, at least, Tyun did not reject this alliance.

It bespoke an intimacy.

This was a time for *sotto voce*.

"What does he gain," Rollo de Bailleul wondered, "by betraying us?"

"Money," said Brother Nicephorus. "I assume you paid him half in advance?"

The Factor looked down at the planking of the deck.

Nicephorus continued, "And then, whatever Venice is paying him. So if you think about mathematics, you offered him double Venice, and he got half of that from you before we left, which is already equal to one Venice, and then he gets the Venice fee too—"

"So that's just exactly what we offered him."

"Except Venice would pay him more now. So he'd get equal to your whole fee plus some. That's how I see it, Factor de Bailleul."

The Factor brooded. Something on the shore disturbed the seabirds, and the gulls rose, protesting in the dark, wheeling.

"The battle. Why would he engineer an attack against his own ship?"

"Your ship was destroyed, sir. This one was hardly touched. The Venetian warship wasn't damaged badly. Just the forward deck blew up. And it wasn't Tyun who made that happen. That wasn't part of his plan. It was someone else who suggested they rupture the tank."

The Factor considered.

Nicephorus insisted: "No one who boarded this ship died in the battle. When their ship retreated, they just stopped fighting. As if it was staged."

"He knows the Northern bitch. Whatever she is. Dane? Rus?"

"I've never been north to the frigid zone, sir. I confuse everyone who sails down the Dnieper. He does know her. He knows her well. They have an understanding."

"Why are we still the saint hunter's guests, then? Why didn't he leave us on Crete? What is he using us for?"

"Some further scheme?" Nicephorus looked back to where the captain lay, beautiful and supine in sleep.

"And when he is done with us . . . ?" the Factor mused.

"The crew could rise up. Thirty against ten."

The Factor considered: "How to proceed . . . ?"

Nicephorus appreciated being included in the Factor's strategic deliberations. He tried to think of some piece of knowledge that would be useful. He tried: "When Alexander the Great had conquered most of the world . . ."

"Ah. Yes?"

". . . and was marching through the Land of Darkness, where nothing was visible for days, and which was guarded by prophet birds with human faces . . ."

The Factor rolled his head in irritation and closed his eyes.

". . . none of the soldiers could see anything for weeks in that thick darkness. But Alexander ordered his men to pick up things they felt under their feet and carry them with them. They picked up shapes they couldn't see." Nicephorus looked out into the dark off the prow. He flashed his eyes sideways to regard the black, bulky outline of the Factor beside him. "When they came back into the light of day," said Nicephorus, "they looked down into their hands and saw they'd picked up gold and gems. Anyone who hadn't picked things up in the Land of Darkness started wailing and weeping."

"This is . . ." The Factor bowed low over the railing.

Nicephorus said, "We're walking without any guide through the Land of Darkness. We don't know where we're going to end up. But we've got to have faith to pick things up along the way. One day we'll realize some of it's treasure."

The Factor was already walking away.

"It's a good symbol, not just for now, but for life," said Nicephorus, louder, though apparently no one was listening or believed him.

Awake, Tartar and Northerner roasted each other.

"See?" said Tyun. "You're a fucking coward."

They were playing a betting game. Gunnlaug, the warrior, had to shake and toss the dice with both hands since her wrists were bound.

"You cannot bluff me," she said. "You have a tell like—eh—nun's climax."

"Ah, do I?"

These insults seemed to be less about corrosion than collusion. Their spite was a sign of their secret bond.

"As the sun sets," said Tyun, "your skin seems to glow—"

"Mmm."

"—with a greasy, unwashed sheen. Is that bear fat?"

Stripped to nothing but his sirwal, Tyun stood by the mast, his hips loose, his arm cast upward, as if by chance, to touch the upright wood, the black hair of his underarm flaring—but with a ridiculous consciousness of ease, as if he didn't know he was posing like a Roman marble. He was watching Gunnlaug down the length of the ship's aisle. Presumably hoping she saw him.

Pointedly, Nicephorus said, "You must miss Shchek."

"I do."

"He is also from the North?"

"Also? Yes, of course. Captured by the Pechenegs. They castrated him to get a higher price when they sold him to the Byzantines. The Byzantines hate to do the castration themselves."

"Poor Shchek. Poor child."

"Mmm. Even his name sounds like the slice of the knife," said Tyun carelessly.

"And yet you sleep next to the enemy." Nicephorus was stern.

"Let's hope someone's doing the same for Shchek."

"Don't be flippant," said Nicephorus.

Tyun now looked Nicephorus full in the face. He crossed his arms and leaned back against the mast. He said, "You know how it is, when there's a beautiful woman." He smiled unkindly. "You know how that is, don't you, dreamer? When you're around a beautiful woman?"

Nicephorus considered: Accuse Tyun? Tell him he'd seen the kiss? Demand to know what agreement still stood between him and the Venetians?

Too dangerous. Surrounded by the saint hunter's sailors. In the middle of the sea.

So instead, Nicephorus said stiffly, "One day the founder of my order, St. Benedict, thought naked thoughts about a woman he'd seen in town. Do you know what he did? He threw himself into a bed of stinging nettles to squelch his desire."

"He sounds like an irritating person."

Nicephorus admitted, "Those around him not infrequently tried to poison him."

Tyun walked away and called out for the men to trim the sails.

Nicephorus felt like an idiot.

"You not able to seize the Nicholas bones," Gunnlaug announced. "Venice is two day ahead. Crew of two *ousiai,* that ship: two hundred men."

"But we have the goodwill of the saint," said Tyun. "Dream boy there talked to him personally."

She sized up the monk. "Do not joke," she said, with a rime-frost of Baltic distaste. "Look—this man. You see he often dream of men who tell him secrets."

Nicephorus flinched, as if at an unwelcome revelation.

He did not dream of saints anymore, though, or the voice of Nicholas chanting orders through the northern snows like a Lapland wizard.

Instead, at night he saw the sailors and marines of Bari lit ablaze by the gouts of Venetian fire: how their armor, enraptured in flame, had still run, swinging arms with hands gloved in fire, even as the burning figures leaped into the unforgiving sea.

He had treated some of the survivors on the Cretan shores after the *Dagobert* had sunk. He'd swabbed burns in a paste of white lead and mastic. He'd apologetically held down men with a knee while pulling out the splintered shafts of Venetian arrows and dressing the wounds. The injured hollered with pain into the hot Cretan night.

Those left behind would have a difficult march over the rocky coast to the fortress at Chandax. From there, they'd have to await a ship heading back home to Bari.

Lord, he prayed frankly, *tell me this is not all my doing.* He conveyed to his omnipresent God, in images rather than words, the memory of the deaths, but also, anxiously, the grim faces of Norman investors, the chalk crag of Factor de Bailleul surveying the damage of the sunken ship and the shivering men on the cliffs of Crete. *If it is my fault that we are all here upon the sea,* he requested in the dark hours, *strike me with fire like those who burned on deck, and cleanse this ship of the curse of me.*

Musarat rarely spoke, and when she did speak, it was typically in pieties, scolding men for their blasphemy. Generally, she sat near her cooking tripod and mended sooty jubbahs for the Muslim boys on board. She didn't look up when the waves pitched or the wind rose. Her indifference to the activity of the ship seemed to be an artifact of her age, as if the schemes and excitements of this world were somehow behind her, and she were immune to contingency, already inhabiting another kingdom, one outside time.

Nicephorus tried speaking to her. "Ma'am, I appreciate how you always seem to follow your own path, regardless of how much noise the rest of us make."

She didn't even bother to look up.

"Like you're already inhabiting another . . . well, never mind that, but it was some battle a few days ago, hmm? Have you seen many battles like that on this ship?" No response. "Since you joined the crew?"

She tested the needle against her thumb. "Dinner when night," she said, and shook her head. "No now."

"Did you happen to see Tornik blow up that Venetian ship? With the bolts from his ballista?"

She looked up and peered down the length of the ship at the old Armenian soldier, who was resting on his bench. The ship was under sail and the waves curled like acanthus leaves.

"I only mention it," said the monk, "because it was delayed.

He shot the bolts and then, a few minutes later, the fire projector exploded. Some people might not even have noticed that it was him who did it."

"Yes, then," said the old woman, shrugging indifferently. "So I give him two biscuits."

The crew no longer sneered at the monk. They did not bother with him at all. Occasionally he lent a hand. He knew them now, and started to put together their stories: an Arab mercenary bored with tents and desert princes' campaigns; a Jewish caravan driver who'd lost everything to bandits; an emissary from the far court of the Khwarazmshah who'd decided he didn't want to deliver some bad news to an unstable emir, and took to sea instead; brothers from Merv seeking a fortune for their parents; a grizzled Sufi from Damietta who no longer wanted to think of past or future, just wanted to row in rhythm and pray and eat whatever fell into his mouth and sleep like one of God's beasts.

Nicephorus watched their faces and saw the Factor and his guards watching them too. The crew did not seem to know of any trap or betrayal pending.

Looking at the mariners as they strained at ropes or pulled on oars, Nicephorus found himself asking of each one: *When he is ordered to kill me, what will he do?*

Reprobus stalked the prow, unable to come to rest, as if he wrestled with some dark, hidden matter. The monk hinted, "You have seemed uneasy, since the battle."

"I am occupied."

"There is some secret anxiety that weighs on you?" Nicephorus pressed.

"Think, Benedictine. I am a dog-headed man on a ship marked with the urine of thirty friends."

The cynocephale continued his uneasy rounds.

Since the battle, Tyun had regained his garrulity. He seemed enlivened by the new challenge of the impossible task and by delight at his own survival; perhaps by the joy of deception. He talked rapidly at the phlegmatic Factor, as if still pitching the mission, hawking broth at a night-market, though the broth was a stew of dead bishop. He was boastful and crass in front of the Northerner, whose presence Nicephorus worried was the real source of the man's new energy. But now Tyun seemed more natural with Nicephorus himself, as if they finally were easy comrades.

"Are you from Bari originally, dreamer?"

"South."

Tyun waited for more. Usually, Nicephorus would go on.

"My father was a clerk for the grandees of Monopoli. Then later, after the Normans came, a goatherd. They sent us away, out of the city, to the plains. It was very flat."

"Did you like it?"

"There were sinkholes. My friends and I kept a list of the best things that fell into them."

"I see."

"Our favorite was a wandering acrobat in a bird hat."

"Fascinating."

"Everywhere we looked was a straight line."

"There are actually mountains in Lycia."

"I am excited to see them."

"You've never seen a mountain? Ever, in your life?"

"Once we visited my aunt," said Nicephorus, proud Apulian. "She had a hill. I saw that."

"A whole hill."

"We had—by the sea, we had cliffs. Where the plains ended," Nicephorus offered. "They were very wicked."

"Impressive."

Nicephorus was tired of Tyun's petty sarcasm. "And what about you, Captain? You don't talk about where you're from."

"I am insignificant," said the saint hunter, "and always will be. Some day, *inshallah,* I shall be insignificant and rich."

Nicephorus pounced on the "inshallah": "So you are a Mohammedan?"

The saint hunter's face grew flat. He said, "In my village when I was a child there were many gods. They were all over the place. But I was taken away from there, and as I got older, there were fewer and fewer. Once I reached Khurasan, there was only one left. And now, finally . . . they're all gone. I have none."

The *Epiphany* was tied for the night to a pillar that stood in the middle of the sea. The salmon sky lit an old hermit who sat upon the top of the lone pillar cross-legged, gazing out to the purple edge of the world and the court of Heaven beyond.

That was a night when they told stories. The theft of a lock of Saint Helena's hair, the liberation of the towel of Naaman.

Musarat was serving up a mutton harissa.

"Ma'am," said the monk, "I can't believe you'd ever really kill someone."

The old woman stopped circulating with her ladle and stared at him with distaste.

"I am sorry," said Nicephorus.

"One hundred seventeen roads to God," she said. "I take one."

"Do you mind if I tell the story?" Tyun asked her. "She saved my life."

She did not turn around to face him as she shrugged. She headed back amidships.

"Eight years ago, I was in Isfahan," said Tyun. "It was just Reprobus and me. We were hired by a theologian visiting from Nishapur to find a sacred book."

"*Regarding the Lightning of Unbelief,*" said Reprobus.

"This mullah told us it was in a particular house down a particular alley in a particular quarter of the city. So we began to watch the place."

"What the captain means," said the cynocephale, "was that he insisted I sit for two days behind some trash in the alley, so my head might pose as a street dog. How I thought witheringly of your strategy as the local pack arrived to challenge my suzerainty."

"Someone threw you scraps. So, what Reprobus discovered was no one lived in this house but an old blind man."

"And," said Reprobus, "he would often importune passing wayfarers and ask them to assist him to his door."

"And then," said Tyun, "then they would go into this house, supporting him, and would not come out. So, I decided to see what was going on. I walked through the souk near that alley several times one day until the blind man heard my voice and my accent and came over to me. He said, 'You sound like you are a visitor here.' And I said I was. And he asked me where I was from."

Angling, Nicephorus asked, "What did you tell him, Captain Tyun?"

"The truth," answered the saint hunter, without pausing. "One should only lie if it will make you a profit. And he said to me, 'I am an old man who lost my eyes in the wars, and the sun is hot today. Will you assist me a few streets away to my home? God will reward the pious.' So he put his arm around my shoulder, and I helped him down the alley."

"Everyone else who went through that door disappeared," Reprobus said. "But you thought somehow you, by dint of genius, would be different."

"I'm left-handed. My sword hand was still free." He smiled at Gunnlaug, who was listening with sullen Norse attention, propped up against a bulkhead. "We get to the door. The blind man opens it and I usher him in. It's all going according to plan. I'm inside the house, ready to ransack the place for this book.

"Then he clamps his arm around my neck and throws me sideways, into this pit just inside the door. There's a pit right there. A deep one, too."

Even the Factor's guards were engaged now, leaning forward in their formation. The Factor alone looked severe and unamused on his lion-headed chair.

"I almost fell in," said Tyun. "I would have, if I hadn't been expecting a shove. But I was. I swiveled and danced on the edge, and then I pushed him into the pit instead. He toppled in and started shouting for help. 'Murder! Murder!' I rushed to search the house for the book of lightning, unbelief, whatever. The problem was, it wasn't really a house. More of a warren for Ismailite assassins. They were using the old man to lure rich foreigners to the house, then he'd throw the visitors down into the pit and they'd break their necks and his henchmen would rob the bodies. Because only foreigners were disappearing, no one asked questions.

"Now here I was, running through this den of thieves—I really cannot stand thieves, you can never trust them—and I could hear the assassins stirring in the hidden tunnels under the house. Several of them climbed up a ladder and I could hear them coming for me, so I hid in the kitchen. I hid behind a sack of lentils. I was starting to wonder about the mullah who hired us. How did he know the book was there? Why did he really want us to go in there? Did he know that it was a trap? Was there any book at all? At this point, I saw this old woman—the widow, it turns out, of a brave *ghulam* foot soldier from the army of Khurasan—and she's tied by her ankle to the brick oven, and there's a dirty little pallet they let her sleep on, and she's staring straight at me where I'm crouched behind the lentils.

"Then three assassins came into the room, three killers trained in mountain fastnesses for deeds of utmost brutality, and they started yelling at her, asking where I was, and I saw her move her hand toward—"

At this point in the story, there was a voice from the sky. *"Silence!"* it demanded.

Tyun jumped. He looked up. The Factor touched his heart with his fingers. Tornik crossed himself clumsily. Nicephorus rose to his feet, ready to see Nicholas, flying thaumaturge, descend from the clouds.

"Be—quiet!" enunciated the voice from over the mast.

"I believe it is the stylite," the cynocephale explained.

Indeed it was the ascetic, yelling from the top of the pillar.

"Hail, lonely servant of the Lord!" called the captain. "Can we not regale you with a story of adventure to pass this night away?"

The scrawny man called down, "I have made my home *on a pillar in the middle of the sea.* Do you think I want to hear your clack?"

At that, outraged sailors rose to their feet and started to shout back up, and Nicephorus bade them to respect the man's sacred mission ("He is a holy man, please—please, he is holy!") and Captain Tyun and Reprobus argued over whether the pillar was Doric or Ionic.

Then a voice broke through the whole fracas: "Captain Tyun! No more! *No more!*"

People fell silent.

It was the Factor. There was shock at his fury. He pointed

his finger. *"These fucking jokes! Your fucking secret smile when you talk about thieves! All of it!"*

His guards had formed a box around him and were drawing their swords.

Nicephorus noticed he himself was outside the box. The sailors were still on their feet. Some were looking at their weapons.

"This juvenile *bullshit*!" snapped the Factor. "What are you waiting for?"

"Factor?"

"Try. Kill us. Try. We will hack up every fucking man on this ship and sail it to shore ourselves."

Gently, Tyun said, "What is this?"

"The dreamer saw you," the Factor announced.

Tyun turned with a sweet smile and serpent's eyes and said, "Saw what, pretty boy?"

Nicephorus steeled himself. "I saw you with the Northerner late at night on the docks in Bari," he said. "I saw her go out to the Venetian ship, the trireme. And I can't help noticing, I mean, if you look at it, I can't help noticing that in the battle, your own ship didn't take much damage, and none of the people who boarded were killed, but the attack stopped before—"

"Because the Greek fire projector exploded," said the captain. "It exploded. Exploded." He made a blossom with his hand.

"So what I want to know," said Nicephorus, "is what you were talking with her about. Why were you talking with her on the docks, the night before we left?"

Tyun was still smiling, but Nicephorus could tell it was simply a rehearsal of the muscles. The con man was worried. "Easy," he said. "I was delivering a message to their captain."

The Factor leaned down under his lion-headed chair and

took up his sword and scabbard and drew forth the sword slowly.

"I was telling them no deal," Tyun said. "Because you offered me twice as much as them."

"Then," the Factor accused, "you waited to see if they'd offer you even more to betray us?"

"No waiting," said Tyun. "She immediately told me to go shit in my own mouth."

"You asked her, though," said the Factor.

"Of course I asked her," said Tyun. "I am a man of business."

"You kissed her," said Nicephorus.

"Goodbye," Tyun clarified.

"And you swear," said the Factor, "that it was a negotiation, but you still pledged loyalty to Bari when we left the dock that next morning?"

"I swear to the Lord God of Sabaoth."

"You are an unbeliever," said Nicephorus quietly.

"I swear to the gods of my people. I swear by all the bodhisattvas and the devas and the Asuras and the Trinity and the Trimurti and Mohammed (peace be upon him) and the saints and all the company of Heaven."

"He is swearing to the dead air," said Nicephorus.

"Dreamer," said Tyun, "I imagine your head as a catkin about to blow: an ugly lump bristling with dainty, feathery little instruments and devices that burst out in a flurry, spread everywhere, and do no one any good."

The Factor did not lose the thread. "So you swear: no relation with this woman except negotiation?"

"Are you asking," Tyun said, "if we've fucked?" He put his hands together. "Yes. We have. After I met her in Venice, the Northerner and I fucked for some days. This," he said, indicating the prisoner, "is not how I would wish things turned out, but she should not have tried to kill me."

"Fuck you," said the woman. She held up her bound wrists. "This man, he is scum."

"Point with the fingers of both hands at once," Tyun suggested. "It makes it easier when you're shackled." He said to the Factor: "I can promise I am still in your pay. The Northerner and I are done. I am yours. My men and I are firmly pledged to collect the corpse of the Blessed Nicholas for Bari." The saint hunter crossed his arms.

"These Venetians: They outnumber us," said the Factor. "You and your girlfriend . . ."

"Since the attack," said Tyun, "my strategy has changed. We have hostages. We can use them. That, Factor, is what we will do. That is why they are worth keeping."

"You've been sleeping next to her," said the Factor. "Playing your stupid games. Dice." He shook his head. "I don't trust you."

"Nor I you," said Tyun. "But you will keep your guard at the ready, and I will no longer go near the lovely Gunnlaug. Since the dreamer seems to want to keep an eye on me, I'll sleep next to him instead. Are we happy?"

So, trapped somewhere between anxiety, misery, and excitement, Nicephorus found himself twenty minutes later lying beside the saint hunter on a reed mat, facing resolutely away, unable to sleep, feeling the man's warm breath tickling his neck.

In a whisper no louder than a midnight sigh, the saint hunter murmured, "Do you feel safe now, dreamer? Do you feel safe with me beside you?"

Nicephorus did not move. He shut his eyes. He felt a finger gently rub across the stubble of his tonsure in slow circles. "Where I come from, everyone wears their hair like this," said the saint hunter. "You remind me of home." Tyun moved his hand down from the monk's head to his waist, and left his hand casually crooked against the cincture, as if it had fallen there without intent.

The night was dark and long.

When the dawn came, the ascetic on the pillar was standing with his arms spread to greet the sun, and one leg raised and pointed at the northern pole.

The ship came to the Dodecanese Isles, white in the blue of the sea.

The glare was overwhelming.

"Yet," said the Factor quietly to Nicephorus, "we still must squint to see. We still travel through the Land of Darkness, hmm?"

The Factor's guards took watches of four hours, rotating sleep carefully so six were always awake and armed.

The Genoese at Rhodes told them the Venetians had passed through two days before.

Captain Tyun did not go near the *Epiphany*'s Venetian captives. They were fed down in the hold and allowed only a few minutes each day to parade around the deck and shake out their limbs.

Once, while they were on parade, the Northerner called out to Tyun, "Mutiny! Kill this Bari Factor! I promise: Venice, she pay you when we in Myra!"

"You don't have that kind of authority, blossom of the northern summer," said Tyun, and turned back to his work.

The monk had taken to sitting near Musarat, the cook. She seemed safe, or at least indifferent. She took his modest help for granted. She asked him to cut up fish, and he did, deftly.

When the galley was under sail, Tornik would join the monk and Musarat. His pretext was talking with the monk. Tornik and Musarat never spoke to each other directly. Musarat rarely spoke at all.

At first, only the monk would talk; so, to put the other two at ease, he would tell stories of wonders he'd read about, stories of travel: The Arimaspoi, one-eyed people of the North. The mirror of Alexandria, which burns ships with refraction. The adventures of the Argonauts, who sought the Golden Fleece. ("They would never think of killing one of their own number," he said by way of example.) The hidden tomb of Solomon, glittering with gold. The coffin of the Prophet Daniel, which was fought over so fiercely by two sister towns it finally had to be encased in crystal and hung on chains off a bridge exactly halfway between them, where it impeded the fishing.

He was good at ancient yarns, and soon others came to listen. He was aware there was a utility in his storytelling: *As long as I speak to them in the manner of a person with a past and a future,* he thought, *they will not agree to kill me.* When he noticed Tyun listening, he spoke more softly.

Tornik would not even look up at Musarat's eyes. The monk asked him helpful questions, things that might make the old cavalryman appear to best advantage. In this way, they aired Tornik's life story, though the Armenian was a terrible storyteller.

In his middle years, Tornik had found himself without a wife (she had died) and without kids (they had gone off to seek their fortunes in Trebizond, on the Black Sea) and so he had fallen in love with a horse. The horse was named Akritis. He bought the horse excellent barding and himself riding armor and spear and sword and mace and bow and joined the Byzantine cavalry. He sold his family's house in Ani because the armor and the horse were expensive, and he was sent off in a cohort guarding a mountain pass at the Cilician Gates, which he did for years, happily with his horse. At night, standing near the campfire, he would lean against Akritis's flank as he chewed. He would sleep by Akritis's side.

Akritis had a thousand winning ways. The horse understood silence and the blank moods of men. And in battle he knew Tornik's will before Tornik did himself. The horse was noble and an excellent tactician, a brave and passionate warrior.

"You can't love an animal," said Tornik, "until you've killed alongside them."

In the years of Tornik's youth, the Seljuk Turks had swept out of the Khazar steppe with their flocks of thousands driven before them, and they had, to the astonishment of the world, defeated all the walled and settled cities. They swarmed the battle elephants of Persia and brought them down. They took even famed Baghdad, seat of the great caliphs. The Seljuk Sultan demanded to be crowned with the ancient diadem of Persia and invested with seven robes representing the seven realms of heaven and earth. Before many years passed, the Seljuk Sultan was proclaimed master of the known world at Friday prayers each week in pulpits across the deserts and the mountains and all the way to the distant sea.

The civilized nations did not know what to make of these Turkish invaders, who were accustomed to living in tents scented of lanolin and mutton, but who now wandered through the empty, tiled pleasure palaces of the emirs they'd defeated. It was whispered they barely knew how to use chairs, let alone sit upon the throne. Their sultan could not understand pastry. The Seljuk Sultan and the Caliph of Baghdad glowered at each other from their palaces across the city's central square.

The Seljuks burned the Armenian city of Ani and slaughtered everyone in it; the streets themselves were blocked with bodies. When Tornik heard about this, hundreds of miles away at his garrison post, he mounted his beloved Akritis and rode off to a lonely place, and when there was only the horse to witness his sorrow, he wept. He thought of people he'd known—his cousins, his sister's family, his sister herself—all slaughtered. Sitting on the back of his horse, arms useless at his sides, he sobbed like a child, thinking of those streets and markets and courtyards now blackened with smoke, of the white, torn mountains above the massacre. Akritis stood firmly beneath him, as if the horse recognized Sorrow and stood at attention while it shuffled past before them.

That night, Tornik had a dream that Akritis was attacked by a mighty lion, and that the lion's claws tore the horse's flesh into strips, and he saw the horse buck and rear and then die. Tornik woke up. He felt disaster nearby. He got up and went to check on his beloved steed. Akritis stood deep in the shadow. The horse watched in silence until his friend approached, then whickered. Nothing was wrong. "But I knew then," said Tornik, without explanation.

The Turks gnawed their way west into the Byzantine Empire. When the Emperor called for a force to assemble to stop them, Tornik volunteered. He was sent north with his horse and joined a great column of tens of thousands marching under the imperial banner. They confronted the Seljuk Sultan, Alp Arslan, and his small army at a town called Manzikert, near Lake Van.

Alp Arslan stood on a hill overlooking the two armies and fired three arrows into the air to announce his sovereignty. And so the armies, one winged like an eagle, the other a crescent, met upon the rugged plain at Manzikert.

Mounted on Akritis, with hymns sung all around him, Tornik marched into battle.

It was at this point that Tornik's story always came to a halt, because he would insist on adjudicating the battle, now more than fifteen years done. The Emperor of Byzantium had everything in his favor. Yet he lost disastrously. He lost everything. Tornik was still smoldering with rage at the impossibility—the incompetence. *It was ours to win.*

Tornik would sketch out the battlefield using whole-wheat paximata as the mountain and some millet for the Turks, and then he'd start arguing about tactics: What was the Emperor thinking, sending off a whole division to another town right before the battle? Was the rearguard just incompetent or did they actually betray the Emperor on purpose? When the Seljuk cavalry retreated, were they actually scattering or were they trying to draw pursuers into an ambush? When the Emperor sailed with his troops from Constantinople, a mottled dove flew down and landed in his outstretched hands. Any beardless hoplite could tell you he should have strangled it right there and counted whether there were more dark feathers than light. Who sets out on a military campaign with that kind of augury?

Nicephorus noted that while Tornik described Manzikert in painstaking detail, it was always from above, as if he'd seen it with the archangels. The cavalryman was arguing with someone unseen. He got more and more petulant. He circled again and again around the same points. He was arguing with history itself, which once had been wind upon a plain, and now was fallen stone.

He argued this way, Nicephorus realized, and did not speak of his own experiences—the saddle, the arrows, the glint, the swords of the enemy—because in this battle, there at Manzikert, must have been where Akritis, his beloved horse, had died.

Never mentioned, always present.

Once Nicephorus realized this, Tornik's dull descriptions of the marching order of the infantry or the incompetence of the retreat seemed throttled with poignancy. The monk no longer interrupted to try to skip the story forward. He just listened. Musarat, too, was still. She couldn't have understood Tornik's schematic diagrams of cavalry battalions (his terminology was impenetrable), but she must have heard the weeping behind it, though his face was dry; he merely touched his mustache with his hand and fell silent.

It was implied that in the fray, Tornik was captured.

The morning after the battle, Tornik saw the Emperor of all Byzantium led on a rope by a slave into the presence of the victorious Sultan of the Seljuks. Tornik and the other captives fell upon their faces in the dust in sorrow. Sultan Alp Arslan spoke kindly to the Emperor, and then asked the Emperor to get down on his knees, and he stepped on the Emperor's neck. Alp Arslan slapped the Emperor across the face six times to signify defeat, and then helped him to his feet, and the two of them went into a tent for watermelon, which had been brought from Bukhara on a bed of snow.

"Fell upon our faces in the dust," Nicephorus heard, and thought: *Not mounted.*

The Seljuks released most of their prisoners a few days later, once agreements had been reached. Free, dazed, Tornik wandered away from the army. He disappeared into the hills. No one would notice his absence: with news of the loss against the Turks, Byzantium sank into civil war. The Emperor was shaved like a monk and blinded. The Turks spilled across Anatolia and everything was chaos. In any case, Tornik could no longer be a mounted archer. He did not have a horse, and he had no means to buy another.

Yet he dragged pieces of the padded horse armor with him. He could not give it up. He served as a mercenary, carrying Akritis's barding folded, tied with rope to his back. A few years passed, and he went to sea because he hated the land, he hated plains, he hated mountains swept with dust in the late afternoon.

Passing by Tornik's bench, Nicephorus saw the felt headpiece for the horse armor bound up with its tassels and stowed. It was scraped brown and threadbare with age.

"I am sorry," said Nicephorus. Tornik rowed and did not respond. "Alexander the Great gentled his horse Bucephalus and loved him so well he built the horse a tomb."

Tornik thought about this for a long while and then said, "I knew as soon as I had the dream of Akritis's doom . . ."

"You can't trust dreams."

"Can't you, dreamer?"

"Well, that—that's not. The dream did not come true. Akritis died heroically, in battle."

Tornik kept rowing. "The sultan who defeated us, his name—Alp Arslan," he said. "His name, in their language, means 'Great Lion.'"

The *Epiphany* came at last to the islands off the coast of Lycia.

Brother Nicephorus leaned against the railing, watching the bright isles pass. Ancient cities, long extinguished, stood on the hills of low scrub. A few columns, an empty agora, an apse split by an oak.

A hut built in the shell of an old temple; by it, a shepherd stared at the passing galley from where he sat on the plinth of something forgotten. The terns wheeled above him. The sheep nuzzled the laurel that furred the steps. One of the brothers from Merv raised a hand to wave. The shepherd did not wave back.

Then the ship came to a narrows where the crumbling walls continued down into the turquoise sea. Leaning over the deck, Nicephorus could see the wrecks of houses and granaries beneath the shimmer. The galley glided over mosaic floors from the age of Rome's strength: a man wrestling a lion while fish skated above him, the school snapping away from the ship's sliding shadow.

Nicephorus wondered if these towns were sunk in the general Flood, when Noah rode the waves, or if there was some other calamity of which he did not know.

Among these ruins, the little islets and molten outcroppings themselves appeared to him the basilicas and citadels of even older empires, cities from before the dawn of humankind, before the Fall, blurred turrets and waxen keeps towering over the strait.

"Like it?" said Tyun, who was by his side.

"It is miraculous," said Nicephorus. "To think of the impossible antiquity of the Earth. Imagine the ancient history of this world. Look at these hills of rock and think: it has been six thousand years, six thousand long years, since the Earth was formed molten in the Creator's hands. And since then, empire after empire spread here. The kingdom of giants. The Greeks. The Persians. The Romans. Byzantium. We are passing over their dining halls and marketplaces. We are so blessed to walk for a while in this place, before we too are covered with silt."

He looked up to find Tyun was eyeing him with skepticism. "That's what you were thinking? In your actual head?"

"Yes," said Nicephorus, adjusting his habit.

"I was thinking it was too hot," said Tyun, looking up at the sun. "And how much goddamn treasure must be waiting to be discovered down there." He pointed at the paving stones that passed beneath the prow.

"That's it?" said Nicephorus.

Tyun grinned proudly. "Somewhere in one of these bays is a statue with eyes worth more than all of Antioch. That's what I'm thinking." He tapped his skull.

"Then I'm sorry for you," said Nicephorus, and crossed to the other rail as if he didn't want to be followed.

Tyun watched him go, frowning in confusion.

· · ·

When they anchored by the old lighthouse at Patara, Nicephorus pointedly did not tell Tyun that Patara was St. Nicholas's birthplace, or where the Apostle Paul had once changed ships on the way to Jerusalem, Acts 21:1.

He did inform Tornik. "This was St. Nicholas's birthplace."

Tornik looked at the port and nodded. "Ah. So it is. So it is," as if something had been revealed.

Patara was a village of muddy huts in the reeds, a swamp growing in the ribs of a columned city that had not flourished for four hundred years.

"Before that, it was a holy city dedicated to Apollo," Nicephorus said. "There was a huge temple to him, one of the most important in the world." He could tell Tyun was listening now. "Supposedly, Apollo spent his summers in Delphi and his winters in Patara. In their sleep, his nuns would dream of the future."

The next day was tense. They would arrive at Myra's port by afternoon.

They rowed between the islands. The air was hot and windless and drowsy with the churr of cicadas. They could smell sheep.

"The Venetians have already been there for two days," said the Factor. "They must have the body by now."

"Have faith, Rollo de Bailleul," said Tyun. "You have hired me. You will get your sacred corpse."

"We do not have the men to storm the basilica."

"If we slipped in by night, we would not need them."

"If we do not steal the corpse by day," said the Factor, "no one will know that Nicholas is ours. All of this will mean nothing. Hmm? We must have the light of heaven shining down upon our deed. The world's eyes open. Christendom must be awake."

Tyun bittered his mouth. Went off fore to check rigging.

They came to the harbor. The storerooms and fisheries and churches were stacked upon a hillside. As they navigated the river mouth's waters, they passed other ships at dock. Stevedores were dragging merchandise up out of holds with winches. Bait baskets rose and fell in the waves by the quays, drenched, then dry, full of sparkling snails. Turkish watchmen in felt caps stood on old walls, keeping an eye on commerce.

There among the masts was the Venetian trireme at rest, its foredeck scorched.

"Fuck," said the Factor. "They have two hundred men. Who knows what they've done by now."

"Not much," said Tyun. He grinned.

The Factor frowned at the arrogance. "Two days is all the time needed."

"Look around their ship," said the saint hunter. He skirled his fingers in the air.

On the docks, surrounding the trireme, were soldiers, city guards at ease in their posts.

"I took the liberty," said Tyun, "of sending word to Myra by merchant ship a few days before we left, warning them that a Venetian trireme would come to harbor here and that if the harbormaster boarded it, he would find it was filled with iron implements for the cracking-open of sacred tombs."

Nicephorus did not understand. "But you might have been part of their expedition."

"And I would still have been arriving in my own ship. This one, not that one. Either way, whatever city was my master, I figured their warship would best serve as a distraction."

"You might have told me sooner," said the Factor.

"Then you would not have learned a lesson in faith."

During the great famine when the Blessed Nicholas was Bishop of Myra, three ships came to dock at the harbor there, transporting three shiploads of grain from Alexandria to Constantinople at the Emperor's orders.

The people of Myra were starving, and so Nicholas went down to the docks and spoke with the captains, requesting, "Sell us some of your grain."

"We cannot," they said. "We have orders to deliver this cargo to the Reigning City."

Nicholas pleaded his case, saying, "If you do this kindness for us, you shall be rewarded by the Most High."

The captains had heard of Nicholas and his holiness—or perhaps, by "the Most High," they thought he meant the Emperor Constantine, who, though he had recently seen a Christian cross flaming in the heavens, would otherwise have been scheduled at death for his own ascension and godhood. Regardless, after long argument, they assented. For one long day, they unloaded the wheat into Myra's civic granary.

"Now our ships are empty," said the three captains. "Are we going to continue on to the Emperor's port with nothing?"

"Have faith," said Nicholas.

"So we sail in a dumb show of delivery?"

"If your ships were full of grain, then there would be no show of faith, and no reward."

Exasperated, the three captains sailed onward to Constantinople, their route swift because their burdens were light.

When they arrived, they found their holds were full of wheat, and even as they unloaded it, their ships were brimming with more. All three captains became rich men. And Myra was fed in the days of the famine, and its people flourished, and thanked the Blessed Nicholas for his miracle of wheat.

The granary at the port of Myra, built in the days of Hadrian, still stands, a testament to Nicholas's ministry. So Myra was saved. I am not sure what they did about the famine down the coast a few miles at Antiphellos or Phoinike.

God's mercy is infinite—an infinite eye—which, seeing all, favors

*none, and makes no particular distinction in quality between those
who eat and those who starve.*

Reconnaissance was necessary. In the afternoon, Tyun asked
several of the crew to set off into the city to eat and drink and
collect intelligence. The questions at issue: *Who controlled the
city now? How was the Church of St. Nicholas protected, since the
invasion of the Turks? What was the attitude toward the Venetian
ship?*

"Go out and do business," said Tyun.

"Needs?" said the Factor. "For the heist."

Tyun looked from face to face. "Three donkeys and a sack
of niter."

He assigned Tornik, as cavalryman, to procure the donkeys.
"Check their gums and their instep. Whatever it is you do."

"The niter," said Tornik.

"Go to a leather tanner. Follow your nose." To Reprobus
and Brother Nicephorus, he said, "The three of us will go to
the market square, provision the ship, charm the vendors,
drink, and ask questions."

"The dog-man? Ashore?" said the Factor. "Can't expect him
to go unnoticed."

"I can expect him to distract and provoke conversation,"
said Tyun. "Unlike, for example, the ruddy-faced features of
Gaul."

Nicephorus was pleased and excited to be included in this
trinity. The three of them walked up the broad steps from the
docks and through the storehouses. Around them rose the
tombs of the great, the dead of distant generations set high
on pillars, sarcophagi held to the sky, mausoleums built like
temples to remind all who came to the shore of the generosity
of patricians who'd paved the public ways. The port of Myra
was a small town in itself, with domed chapels, a muddy agora,

and a murex factory where half-naked men sat in darkness, cracking snails with clippers to lift out glands for the royal purple. Light queered the dye.

The monk, the saint hunter, and the dog-man passed the murex huts. The air was thick with the smell of mucus and brine, the tapping of little chisels. Snail divers were hauling baskets up from the docks, shouting to each other.

"The granarium," said Nicephorus in awe. He crossed the agora to touch the stone wall. "Here the Blessed Nicholas multiplied the seeds of grain." He placed a second hand on the limestone. Tyun snapped impatiently and kept walking.

The road into the city itself was dry and dusty and the cicadas razzed invisibly in the bushes all around them like spleen. They saw two members of the crew, Hisham and Rif'at, the brothers from Merv, walking ahead, and slowed to avoid them, so they would not be associated.

"Very quiet," Tyun observed, glancing at the local sights: the dried mud of an untenanted sheep pen; an empty courtyard where wooden pulleys and tangled rope gathered afternoon dust. "This road should be swarming."

"I feel visible," said Reprobus, regretfully.

"Keep your hood on and your ears back."

They passed a group of three Greek women out shopping together with baskets. All three had their striped shawls pulled over their faces like veils so they could not be seen and assessed. One, noticing Tyun, said something to the others, and they crossed to the other side of the road, short, short, tall, all disdainful.

At the wide market street, Tyun placed orders for provisions: several chickens, twice-baked loaves, barley, Ahwaz sugar, too much millet, and barrels of watered-down wine.

A row of houses was nothing but blackened hulks, emptied by flame when the nomads invaded. Tyun was busy dickering with someone over weights and measures, and so Nicephorus meditated on the fire, the assault, the holocaust, the weeping. It must have been a terrible night. Pray God there was no one inside when the torches were set to the beams.

The monk closed his eyes and attempted to concoct the disaster, which was a frequent spiritual exercise of his. *It is our duty,* he thought, *to imagine the suffering of all; for God is outside of time, and so should we be in weeping for the sorrows of others; as on a church wall, Jonah stands upon the ship and lies within the belly of the whale and dances under his woodbine all at the same instant, standing next to himself. The world is never young and never old.* The refugees still tumble out of their burning homes, gagging on smoke, and are met by the invader's sword. The father still weeps that the child is lost inside. Then he is slain. There is no safety, though now the sun is bright above the hazy fetches and the plateia is full of pigs.

In a taverna with a low ceiling—none of them could stand—which smelled of tallow lights and garum, they sat cross-legged on the dirt floor and waited for the grim-faced Myrans to warm. Tyun was carefully expansive, ready to offer drinks, but no one seemed interested. They assumed, from his face, that he was some form of Turk. The dog-man was clearly a monstrosity.

So the three sat in isolation. Nicephorus drank retsina, a Byzantine wine from piney casks, which reminded him of his father. He said that exact thing out loud: that retsina reminded him of his father, which was the kind of inanity they were reduced to for an hour or so, there being a general air around them of misery and suspicion.

To make conversation, Tyun said to the monk, "So do you know many things about temples and histories? Like that temple of Apollo in Patara?"

"I have read many of the stories of travelers and historians," said Nicephorus. "I like to catalogue the world's oddities."

"Do you know where that temple of Apollo is? Has it been plundered?"

Nicephorus frowned. "No one knows where it is. It was once a site of prophecy for the pagans. They would come from all over the Aegean. Now it is under the reeds and the silt of the river."

"So, unplundered."

Leaning forward, Nicephorus insisted, "God hides secrets around us to remind us that the world itself is a marvel."

"If this Nicholas job doesn't work out," said Tyun, "maybe we can poke through the swamp, find a few gold figurines."

"That is all you think about when you hear of the passing of lifetimes and empires?" Nicephorus pushed his cup away from him. With some combination of disappointment, accusation, and pity, he said, "You're a salesman of miracles, Tyun— but you can't see the wonders waiting all around you."

Tyun flipped him the fig, and they all sat there, silent, hot, and cross, while the patrons surveyed them with open dislike.

The place cleared out entirely when two Turkish soldiers came in. Excuses were made. The tables emptied. People rose from the dirty mats and rugs on the floor. But the Turkish soldiers bowed toward Tyun, and he smiled, which he figured they would appreciate, being conquerors and strangers.

He called out to them in their language and went over to sit with them.

The cynocephale said to the monk, "It was a mistake for us to come ashore. I should have kept my snout on board." Reprobus lifted his bowl of water to his lips. "Tyun needed to remove himself from the Factor for the space of an hour or two. The Factor is leaning on him."

Nicephorus waited for explanation.

Reprobus said, "Tyun has planned all along for an elegant

heist, an affair of felt shoes, lockpicks, grappling hooks, and the silence of night. An hour when even the monks do not rise to sing their offices. It was his wish for the guardians of the church themselves to remain ignorant for weeks that the corpse of the saint had been taken.

"The Factor, though, is demanding a frontal assault. Forty men marching to the gates of the Church of St. Nicholas, armed with spathion and paramerion, sword and saber, paying off the guardians handsomely or holding them at sword tip, taking the body in broad daylight and casting off as soon as possible."

"That," said Nicephorus, "does not seem . . . tactically wise?"

"His people favor frontal assault. Corfu. Dyrrhachium. They are a hungry, but not a subtle people."

"Has Tyun agreed?"

"Unhappily. But we do not have forty men. Not even thirty who can be spared. Do you also wish some crawfish? The scent of good food, after the long tyranny of Musarat's brutal and impoverished assays, distracts me."

The Factor wandered through the streets with one of his bodyguards, irritable at the open suspicion of the populace. "I do not trust this Tyun at all," he said. "Methods. He is a thief. He will sneak in by night. Snatch. Steal. Leave us behind. Is that a man?"

It was a question about Tyun; but also, as soon as spoken, he wondered about the shape behind them that skulked in the cornered shadows of late-slanting sunlight.

He murmured to his guard, "Followed."

Tyun returned full of news. When the Turks had ridden into town and seized the region, the citizens of Myra had fled up into the mountains. The city had been empty except for the proud (few) and the wretched (many), who stayed on to witness the plunder.

The Turks had settled uneasily in the hills just outside of town, grazing their flocks and watching over the city with a sharp eye. Some of the Myrans had returned after a few weeks, when they saw they would not be massacred. Others in the mountains gave up on their homes and set out to the west and the north for the cities of Ionia, the Cyclades, and the Troad. The Turks were indifferent to who came or went, so long as there was no resistance, and they could graze their flocks.

The old Byzantine militia still kept peace in the town, overseen by the Turkish garrison. They had heard a rumor, delivered by a merchantman coming from Bari, that a shipload of Venetians planned to steal the Blessed Nicholas. When the Venetian ship arrived, the harbormaster had gone aboard, and indeed, he had found tools for breaking and entering: crowbars, pickaxes, grappling hooks. The Byzantines had set a guard around the ship and would allow only one or two men off the ship at once. The Venetians did not seem pleased. (The Turkish soldiers laughed, one toothlessly. Tyun laughed harder.)

Nicholas? His shrine was outside of town. The Christians no longer came so often from far away to visit it. They seemed worried about the Turks. The Turks had agreed to spare the sanctuary, so long as the priests paid double the jizyah tax on unbelievers. This Nicholas, peace be upon him, was a holy man, and it would do no good to offend him. He flew through the air. He helped the fishermen and merchants. The sea looked wide; who did not want a name to call out when the swells grew tall?

Nicephorus asked Tyun, "Where did you learn to speak their language?"

Tyun looked at him curiously. "I lived in the Great Seljuk

Sultanate for twenty years," he said. "I was sold there when I was eight or nine."

At this, Nicephorus said gently, "I have not heard your story."

"I haven't told it. It's the usual story of a handsome rogue."

"A small village in the hills," Reprobus explained for his friend, "peaceful, cows lowing, butterflies landing on the ivy. And then the raiders, the reavers, coming through with fire and sword. You have heard the epics."

"The barbarians," Tyun agreed. "The night of the raid, my parents and my brother died. They were old enough for the sword. I was seized. Sold, I don't know where. I didn't speak any language but our own. I assume it was Kashgar, maybe Khotan. I remember the high ramparts of earth. I was eight." His voice was light, conversational, glib. This was a bit that he and the dog-man did.

"I am sorry," said Nicephorus. He wished to say something consoling. He tried, "The cruelty of conquest."

Tyun grinned, delighted. "No—no. You misunderstand me. We were the barbarians. We came down out of the hills. A whole army. My father was a soldier. My mother, my brother, and I were in the army's train. We were on a border raid."

"You? From what kingdom?"

"Why ask the name? It will mean nothing to you. For a Latin, it will just sound like a name from legend."

"You are right. I will not know it. But your concealment means something."

Tyun shrugged. "We called ourselves the Great Empire White and Lofty. Help?"

Nicephorus nodded solemnly. "To know you."

"I don't want to be known."

"I know."

"In our country, you could be put to death if you did not shave the middle of your head. In the neighboring country, you could be put to death if you did not shave the sides of your head. So we were always at war. We crossed their border. My father rode down out of the hills screaming on his horse and firing his arrows. I don't know what happened to him. My mother and brother and I were at the camp when we were seized. They were killed. I was sold. I ended up in Khurasan, the chattel of a small-time trickster."

"And that is where you learned your trade?"

Tyun smiled. "As soon as I could be taught to speak again. I remember our first score. I was sent crying and sobbing into a stranger's house. I ran through the rooms wailing about how my father had beat me and also taking note of what was there to steal. I hid behind some woman's legs. It was not acting, that first time: My boss had actually pounded the shit out of me. He ran in after me, screaming and yelling that his damn son this, his damn son that, and the husband and wife who lived there tried to quiet him down and stop the abuse. While they were distracted, I lifted a couple spoons and a faience bowl.

"My boss dragged me outside again and once we were out of earshot, he scratched my head like he actually liked me and we went out to sleep by the tombs and we ate well, though he was a stingy bastard."

"These are awful lessons to learn. Deception. Greed."

"I know. About a week later I went back to that house to apologize. I told them I felt terrible. I burst out crying. I spilled everything about my crooked boss and how he'd bought me. I begged them to forgive me, and they did. They forgave me. They told me I could stay there with them until they found me a place where I could serve."

"See?" said Nicephorus, leaning forward. "There is kindness, Tyun. Not everyone is hard. Not everyone betrays."

"True, true," Tyun admitted. "So that night I got up in the dark and I went through the house and took everything of value: candlesticks, the wife's crappy little jewelry—they were not rich people—and I went out and met my boss, who was waiting by the door, and we ran off to a small village and lived well there for about a week and a half before we had to go into the city and steal again."

Nicephorus shifted uneasily on the dirt floor.

"That was a typical scam for us," said Tyun. "But we got bolder with it. Back then, the great Seljuk emirs and maliks and the sultans often did not live in the palaces and capitols they conquered. They would set up their courts outside the walls in a city of military tents, the *mu'askar*. We robbed the court's ministers and *katib*s blind. Sob stories. Scams. Outright theft. Snipping through felt walls, cutting through leather. It was an education. Over the years we got platters, bowls, ladles, chased helms, the trumpets they blew their fanfares on . . ." He smiled, recalling fixtures of brass.

"Was it your master who taught you to search for sacred relics?"

"Yes," said Tyun. "That's how he died, in fact."

Reprobus chimed in: "We were seeking to claim a feather from the wings of the cherubim."

"We did not expect the violence of their glory," said Tyun. "The wheels within wheels. Buzzing. The old bastard was sheared apart from neck to hip."

Outside, it was getting dark, and the Factor and his guard fled through the small lanes of Myra. It had been a large and prosperous town. Now houses stood empty, abandoned. Whoever followed knew when to hang back. The Factor would linger, waiting for a figure to appear, but there was no sign of a tail. Perhaps a nervous fantasy?

Then, moving again in some little paved byway, they'd hear footsteps behind them, timed to match their own.

They were lost, and the half-empty streets of the town enfolded them.

"Now you," said Tyun, pointing at the monk. "More retsina? I want you drunk."

"There is no need. I will speak freely," said the monk.

"Of yourself," said Tyun. "That is generous." He poured the wine. "Have you always been, you know, holy? With God and the Virgin and whoever?"

"There is a story," said Nicephorus, and looked down at the plaited rug they sat on, so thick with dirt it was almost muddy. "I was once dead."

Tyun was delighted by the teaser. He reached out and took the monk's wrist and shook it and urged him to tell, tell.

Reprobus watched them both, and there was the wisdom of the wolf in his eyes.

Nicephorus was born in the town of Monopoli, south of Bari, when the whole of Apulia was part of Byzantium. There was only one midwife in the town, and she served both the low and the high. The day after Nicephorus was born, the same midwife assisted in the cubiculum of a woman known for her fine taste, the wife of one of Monopoli's grandest shellfish magnificoes. She gave birth to a baby girl. Perhaps Nicephorus and this child of wealth would hardly ever have met, except to glimpse each other passing through archways; or perhaps they would have been friends, companions, meeting shyly by the countinghouse where Nicephorus's father worked for hers, later holding hands in the blind alleys where the laundry hung. Their story was never written, for there was a fever at that time, a prelude to the pox, and it killed them both, girl and boy.

Nicephorus, days old, died, scarlet in the face. His parents wrapped him in a sheet and laid his infant body in the grave.

It was a small town; the two mothers, sharing midwife and grief, could not help but meet. They were at the church. They had shared a midwife and had heard each other's stories. The wealthy woman clasped the clerk's wife. Those around them avoided them, for the curse of ill luck on infants was thick and catching. This was a dangerous concentration.

The two women began to meet during the day to talk of their sorrow. One weaved, the other spun. There was a friendship between them, born of sadness. Their husbands did not entirely approve. The two mothers spent hours in church upon their knees together, praying. They walked barefoot together to visit holy shrines built in caves by the sea. They spoke about how the boy and the girl, if they had lived, would have fallen in love and one day married. It was meant—the Fates and all—if the shears hadn't clipped off the babes' threads so quickly.

There is no sorrow so deep, no way to turn the head once that has happened, the death of your child. But in time, the women even smiled together at some shared pleasantry.

"You know this how?" said Tyun.

"My mother," said Nicephorus. "But everyone watched them. Everyone knew."

This warm companionship went on for many months. Perhaps a year. And then a holy man came to town. He was of deep sacredness, and the black-winged wheatears would settle around him like the Holy Spirit. The worms would rise out of the ground to greet him.

He heard that a poor woman had lost a babe and was broken because of it.

He went to pray with Nicephorus's mother and as they spoke, he was struck by her piety and reverence. She went daily to pray in the church for the soul of her son. She saw the angels at midnight when she was crying.

"To the poor shall all be given," said the saint, and he went to the ossuary and knelt by the bones and asked to be locked in the tomb all night. He said he would keep vigil by the body of the defunct infant. The sexton closed the door to the crypt behind him and set the lock upon it. Through the watches and hours of the night, the holy man called for mercy on the babe, and his prayers were answered.

The next morning, when he was let out, he held a dirty cloth, and swaddled in the cloth was Nicephorus, wailing as if newborn, full of life.

"He has been chosen," said the hermit and, kneeling, gave the boy back to his mother.

The mother said something rapturous like the Magnificat.

That evening, the hermit was asked to visit the house of the wealthy woman. She sat upon a divan.

"I have heard," she said, "you can raise the dead."

The hermit said, "I can do nothing for the rich."

"A hermitage need not be bare," said the wealthy woman. "It can be a foundation that attracts the faithful from all over greater Apulia and the Murge."

"The rich do not need miracles," said the holy man. "The accrual of rent from those who can't pay it is miracle enough."

"I have always understood that a martyr's grave, though to be longed for, is best enjoyed in one's own good time," she said.

"Those who lay violent hands on the holy rarely swell later with healthy heirs."

"I hear Herod had eighteen children."

(With a hand cupped to an ear:) "Is that an avenging angel?"

"So I am denied grace because I am rich?"

"You are granted grace *because* you are rich. Be thankful for what you have. There is so much more for you to atone for."

Thus the hermit was allowed to depart from the port of Monopoli and to wander on, and the wealthy woman was filled with fury and bitterness. She could not bear to see her friend's new happiness.

Nicephorus's mother couldn't hide her joy at her boy's resurrection. She wanted to share each new darling kick and squeeze. But she did not want to cause her friend unhappiness, so she avoided her entirely. And the wealthy woman noticed she was being shunned. *You were my friend? And now that you have what you want . . . ?* Like that.

She and her husband began a campaign against Nicephorus's family. It is not hard to destroy reputations in a time of unrest. Byzantium and the Normans were tussling over the port of Monopoli, where Nicephorus's father was a clerk, and the town passed from hand to hand. Stories circulated that the father of the dead boy, the resurrected mite, was zealously loyal to one side or another or perhaps to neither and knew the secrets of Egyptian poison—a concoction so powerful it had to be compounded while blindfolded. The new governor turned him out of the gates and told him he was lucky to be leaving town with his life. "We have found a post for you in the countryside." Nicephorus's father discovered he was to be deployed as a goatherd. He and his family were assigned to a beehive hut in the middle of a drab plain, beside some olive trees recently broken in a storm. He did not own his own goats. Boys of twelve performed the same job and gave him tips on how to milk. "Bump the udder first." He did not enjoy throwing rocks at walls with them.

Nicephorus grew up in the flat plains between Monopoli and Bari, and though they were featureless—largely horizon, grass, broken rock, and dwarf olives—he found much to wonder at. His mother would say to him, "Look out at the clouds, and how they roil and turn red like Armageddon. Never forget that your life is a wonder. You were dead, and now you live. Never forget that there are miracles everywhere, and you are only present in this world to see them once."

But his father became more and more bitter. The man could not stand the cold in their hut in wintertime, the chill rain that blew in off the sea, or the sickness of the goats that lived with them; and though Nicephorus's mother would not stop praising the old hermit and sending up prayers for him, Nicephorus's father increasingly suggested that it had not been a miracle at all, but that the risen Nicephorus was actually the hermit's own brat.

"The miracle is," he said, "that an old buzzard like that could actually convince someone of childbearing age to fuck him."

His anger got louder and could be heard echoing across the rocky pastures. The goatherd boys stopped talking to the little family in the hut of stone.

Another year went by, and Nicephorus's father neglected his flock. Goats were disappearing: stolen or eaten. Nicephorus's mother took the child on her shoulders and walked the dusty fields, trying to scare the strays back home.

When she returned one day to the beehive hut, her husband was sitting on their pallet in tears. He reached out his hand for the boy. "I love him," he said, "but he is not mine. He is not ours. He will always be a stranger."

Nicephorus's mother lit into her husband. He did not believe in miracles, she yelled. He needed to have faith, for what could be more real and solid than the flesh of the son standing before them? A boy chosen by God to live, to come back from the dead, a boy destined for divine work?

The father nodded. He stood and was still nodding. He nodded while he ducked down and left the hut. He walked off into the rain. The mother hugged her son. She whispered to him how much she loved him, and how much his father loved him, too. "Don't listen to him. Don't listen."

The father, out in the rain, came to the bluffs at the edge of the ocean, and then kept walking over the edge.

The cliffs in that place were spiked tufa and wicked, clawed.

After his father's death, Nicephorus grew for years on the plains of Apulia, playing lazy games with the other kids, doing whatever work was needed so there was goat cheese for the great men of Monopoli.

When he was ten, his mother said it was time for him to take up the mantle and habit of his divine purpose. She sent him to the Benedictines in Bari.

"Remember," she said, "you will be behind the monastery walls. But do not shut the gate on life. You have being in this place, a body to move like a puppet, for only so long, and I have seen it lie limp and cold as a doll. While you inhabit it, watch for the glories, my son. My son."

Weeping.

"My son in this life."

"That is my story," said Nicephorus.

"Thank you," said Tyun. "It is good to hear the stories of others." He reached out and put his hand on the monk's.

"It is," said Nicephorus.

"When you know someone," Tyun said, "truly know someone, it is easier to use them." He tapped the back of the monk's hand, pinched the skin hard, and rose from the mat to leave.

It was the hour when lonely men stand on their roofs and look toward the sea. In other houses, children were chasing each other around courtyards, shrieking, and stone and distance muffled them. Girls rattled wicker trays of carob pods. On the city walls, a Turkish soldier called out the evening prayer, and in their homes, old Byzantine men muttered the holy Trisagion. The rim of the sky was still blue.

Tyun, Reprobus, and the monk walked cloaked along the

main highway from Myra down to its port. The monk seemed sour and silent; Tyun and Reprobus, watchful. It was almost the time of curfew.

They were passing by a synagogue when they heard a hiss. They turned. Two figures stood in the dark arch of the door.

"Factor," whispered Tyun, and walked to them.

"We are followed," said Rollo de Bailleul.

"By?"

"They will not show themselves. They walk like a thought, like a suspicion. Not like a man."

Tyun walked out into the road. He cautioned the others to stay put. He followed the road back a bit, up a rise, and surveyed the town and the harbor.

He flicked his fingers to indicate motion. He began to walk.

The others joined him, looking around them into the dark alleys.

"We cannot afford a fight in the street," said Tyun.

"What were you looking for at the top of the rise?" Nicephorus asked.

"An oblique angle."

He turned abruptly and they were in a cramped lane between whitewashed walls streaked with mud and lamb shit. He led them in a line. The dog-man went last, walking half-backwards to watch for their pursuer.

Tyun stopped them all abruptly, holding out his arms.

Yes: behind them, two footsteps too late.

It was confirmed. Then Tyun took off running. The others, startled, followed. They clattered through small plazas where chickens ran, astounded, from their path. Down a narrow staircase.

The faceless footsteps followed them.

Nicephorus feared what could not be seen.

They turned a corner; there was a wall.

A small yard, the blind end of the alley.

Tyun yanked them each, one by one, around the corner but kept slapping his feet on the hard ground, stomping, as if he ran. He and Reprobus pulled out their knives.

The figure flew around the corner, expecting a long jog, and found himself trapped. Tyun grabbed him and slammed him back against a mud wall.

It was a scarred man, a mercenary.

"Oh, him," said Tyun. He turned to the Factor. "He's a Venetian."

The Factor's guard drew a sword and held it to the man's throat.

"Not necessary," said the Venetian. "My lord wishes to parley."

"You followed me," said the Factor.

"To learn," said the Venetian. He pushed the guard's blade up and away from his throat with his thumb. "He'll meet you in the old baths. No one will hear us."

"Mmm," the Factor agreed. "Go."

So, another sub-rosa meeting at old baths. The building was in ruins. They met in the tepidarium. It had been some centuries since Byzantines had attended lectures there after a long, collegial soak. High on the walls, there were still the remains of frescoes depicting the different states of water in the form of nymphs. The Barese Factor, Rollo de Bailleul, stood under Ice. He glared across the rotunda at the Venetian commander, a stringy, bechinned teen nobleman in black, who posed and vaunted at the feet of Brackish.

Neither leader spoke. Each one waited for the other to break the silence. The first words would give away the game. Strength. They stared across the dry pool in mutual dislike.

The Venetian youth sneered, pouted, shook out his excellent hair.

At the Barese Factor's side stood the monk, the saint

hunter, and the dog-headed man, who all waited for the Factor's word. Nicephorus's hands were greasy with sweat.

At the Venetian boy's side stood an old priest of evil counsel—bald, and clearly enjoying his own ophidian stoop—and a ribboned herald. A herald seemed a strange choice for a secret meeting in occupied territory, especially a herald dressed in stripes like a Phrygian fancy man; Brother Nicephorus suspected that the Venetian princeling's strategic thinking was not entirely developed.

In the vaults beneath the floor, water dripped.

Rollo de Bailleul evidently decided to assert primacy by beginning: "We have captives. Four men and the Northwoman. If you wish to—"

"Uh!" cried the boy, as if just spitted. "I will not speak to a Frank."

"You will speak to me, and—"

"Uh, the accent!" said the boy, scrunching up his eyes. He turned and said in Venetian to his herald, "Tell the Norman I would rather speak to the dog-man than him."

The herald said, in broad Greek, "Patrizio Matteo Tradonico will only speak to the dog."

"You little Venetian shit," said Rollo de Bailleul.

"O—did you hear—did you hear that?" said the Venetian princeling, wincing. He scrubbed at his ears.

"With your permission, excellent Factor," said Reprobus, stepping forth from his spot beneath Mountain Tarn (a maiden of distant distraction, holding cedar boughs). To the Venetian boy, the cynocephale said, "Patrizio Tradonico, if you will pardon the rude gibbers of one who bears no human tongue, I am pleased to serve as herald." He held up a steadying paw to restrain the anger of his Norman employer.

The youth—perhaps of nineteen or twenty green, patrician summers—clasped his hands and said, "Ah! The dog's bark is better than the Norman's growl."

"You fucking—"

The youth held up a finger. "You shall not speak that way—
you will not talk that way to a prince of the Republic, scion of
one of the Twelve Apostolic Families, descended of the first
Tribunes of Venice, *ad gloriam rei publicæ mercatoris*. Dog-man?"

Reprobus bowed and said, "I am Reprobus, exile; my sire
was Biscuit Major; my dam, Daisy; my litter is of the lineage of
Fang-Fang, creator goddess and Foundation Bitch. The thin
silver cord of life is tenuous for the captive Venetians in our
custody. Their lives hang on our goodwill. They sway in the
merest breeze like men on the gibbet. Judging by the veins
at the temples of our excellent Factor, I'd say their survival
is unlikely. However, you have one of our own in tow, the Rus
spearman Shchek, and if the—"

Matteo Tradonico stuck his chin up in the air. "What are
your demands?"

"How good and pleasant it is for brothers to live together in
unity. We pursue the same goal: liberation of the holy myroblyte from his entombment; his expression to a wider world,
where the perfume of his undecayed orts may enliven all
Christendom. Yet we have reason to suspect that the guardians of the sepulchre might not share our broad and generous
vision of St. Nicholas's future."

Matteo Tradonico crossed his arms and once again tossed
his lively and carefully unregulated locks.

Reprobus said, "We of the League of St. Nicholas assumed
that after we secured the saint, we would be able to make our
exit with the help of a war-dromon and its doughty marines.
However, as you may recall, our military escort was incom-
moded by the unprovoked violence and venomous pyrotech-
nics of the Most Serene Republic. Therefore, we would be
interested in augmenting the numbers of our little force with
a few of your finest, in return—"

"This is not on."

"I assume it would be awkward for a prince of your antique lineage to return to the dreaming lagoon empty-handed. Yet you have no means of fetching the saint on your own. Myra watches you. You shall not stir from your ship in any large number. Yet, if you assist us with some muscle, we can assure you of at least a limb of the Blessed Nicholas. You choose, one of four."

"A leg or an arm? That's it?"

The Factor was also outraged. "You can't just barter away a leg!"

"Yet I do," said Reprobus. "We will yield up a precious leg of the athlete of Christ if you assist us in the liberation. And if you do not aid us, nothing. You will remain trapped on your ship, surrounded by Lycian guardsmen and the Turkish garrison, and you will return to the waiting Republic without so much as a knucklebone to rattle in your feretory."

"There is no deal," the Factor announced to them all. "I will not collaborate with this cunt."

Reprobus folded his paws together neatly and bowed to both parties. "There is a moment in any noble parlay when the two negotiators must turn half-away from the table and whisper. It appears we have reached that moment. Let us converse." Having said this, he went into a huddle with Tyun, the monk, and the furious Factor.

On the other side of the tepidarium, under tawdry maiden Brackish, Matteo Tradonico swiveled and grabbed the cassock of his pet minister. They spoke closely.

"Factor de Bailleul," whispered Tyun, "you want a show of force at the tomb. You want to overwhelm the basilica. We need soldiers. If you will lay the matter in our hands . . . ?"

The Venetian princeling called across the echoing chamber, "Dog-man of Bari." He had a look of stupid cunning in his eyes. His hands were spread wide and visibly empty of weapons. He said, "Tell us your plan and we will assist."

"Ah," said the cynocephale, "so after all, one *can* teach an old Doge new tricks!"

He regretted it even as he said it.

When the Venetians had left the rotunda: "You are outrageous, dog-man!" hissed the Factor to Reprobus. "This is no deal. We're not going to yank a leg off the body of the saint for those murderers. We'd be stricken with blindness before we made the Peloponnese."

"Of course we won't," said Tyun. "Reprobus did right. The kid thinks he's going to con us. Once we use his heavies to break open the vault, and once we get the body back down to the port with enough show of force to stop the Turkish garrison or the local militia from blocking our escape, and once we trade prisoners—then we'll deal with Venice. We know what we're doing. I assure you: the saint, intact, will be ours, Factor."

"Does this seem," said Nicephorus, "as if we are perhaps not removing Nicholas *willingly*? Of course, we wouldn't want to *kidnap*, to *force* him to—"

"We'll hand over the dreamer's leg instead," quipped Tyun, grabbing at Nicephorus's knee, nipping at the thigh, and Nicephorus was rattled and swerved and staggered, hopping.

The Factor watched them carefully.

Above them, the sallow nymphs of stream and steam and pickling brine looked down, mildewed by their own native moisture, as we all are, eventually.

Early morning. Gusty.

Incoming breakers roiled against the river's outlet, smacking the gunwales of boats.

At each slapped report, a Venetian slipped off the trireme

and dove into the bay. The sleepy guard on the quay, posted to give warning if the Venetians made a move en masse, heard nothing but rhythm.

Bobbing, their heads in a line, ten Venetians swam along the jetties toward the estuary. Bait baskets floated in ranks upon the waves, emerging, immersed, weltering with spiny snails. The heads of the swimmers rose and sank behind the bait. They worked their way toward the *Epiphany*.

On board, Tyun was cooking something up over a newly lit flame in Musarat's brazier, stirring niter and sugar together as they browned.

"Who will marry Musarat?" said Tyun. He held up her hand by the wrist. He spoke almost in a whisper.

Black shapes climbed over the rails.

"If you—I," said Tornik, "could. If it's needed. I would be pleased to . . ." He didn't give a verb.

Musarat looked unmoved.

Brother Nicephorus could feel his heart beating within his chest, and thanked his god that he was alive here, in this moment, undertaking this liberation. Everything around him seemed heightened: the bitter smell of dead fish on the wind, the keening of seabirds as they woke, the glow of morning lamps from the agora up the hill. The apertures of sense were thrown wide by anxiety, and he was happy, grateful.

I am here once upon this Earth, Lord, and you have given me such avenues to breathe deeply, to be.

He looked at Tyun and saw his own anticipation reflected. The saint hunter was pouring the sludge he'd cooked into clay candle-molds, coaxing the batter into tubes, applying wicks. The candle molds were marked with the cross.

Tyun smiled at the monk, a shared recognition, almost glee. He stood and reached out and rubbed the dreamer's arm. "Vow of silence," Tyun said. "Until you learn to lie. Yes? You're one of those monks that doesn't talk."

"Silentium magnum," Nicephorus promised.

"See, that's already talking," said Tyun, and reached out and pinched the monk's lips shut softly with his fingers.

They disembarked just after noon had passed. The fishermen were bringing in the morning's catch.

The Venetians, dressed blandly in Byzantine tunicas, filed off the *Epiphany* first. Two carried sacks with picks, sledge-hammers, crowbars, bound up so they wouldn't clank. Down the docks toward the mouth of the harbor, their trireme stood silent, offering no trouble to the sweltering town.

The Factor's eight bodyguards and ten of Tyun's sailors, dressed inoffensively in robes and cloaks—though their swords were concealed in a couple of sacks—came next. With the Venetians, the Factor, the monk, Tyun, and the patrician boy, that made just over thirty. Reprobus and half the crew stayed behind to guard the ship and watch the captives.

As Brother Nicephorus was about to step onto the gang-plank, Tyun handed him a sack.

"What's this?"

"Tools. Carry it."

Nicephorus opened the sack. It was a human skull and some snapped ribs and femurs. "Mother Mary," he said.

"I know. They'll look better when they're wet. Like river stones."

"For what?"

"Substitution, when the Venetians get greedy. Sling them on your back and don't think about them."

"Whose are they?"

"Yours, now." Tyun gave him a shove forward.

"What grave did you rob?"

"I know a little monk who does not understand the meaning of 'silence.'"

The Factor and Matteo Tradonico were standing unwillingly side by side on the quay.

The Factor said, "You will get your captives when we return."

The playboy winced and patted his ear. "That voice. That Gaulish bellow. Too early."

Tyun took the bag of bones back from Nicephorus and tied it to the third donkey. The other two donkeys were kitted out for riding, with fancy rugs laid across their backs, glittering with metal eyelets.

"We are ready, Factor," said Tyun. "Let me say one final time that a more delicate operation stands a better chance of success."

"Leave delicacy and trickery to the Greeks," said the Factor. "The sword is raised. It must drop."

Saint Nicholas, Bishop of Myra, died on the 6th of December, angels clustered around his bed, faces upturned like petals to the sun.

That day was marked in red and celebrated through the centuries.

On St. Nicholas's Day, Getron and Euphrosina, husband and wife, went with their son to pray at the altar of the saint. They did not reach the shrine, however. They found the village besieged by Cretan pirates. And in the chaos as they fled, their son, Adeodatus, fell behind and was seized and dragged off in a coffle.

The mother's song of weeping is preserved:

Alas—alas—alas—Why do I live, when my son is gone?

Why did my miserable father beget me?

Why did my miserable mother bathe me?

Why did the wet nurse feed me her breast?
Why didn't I die before I met this sorrow?

Adeodatus was taken to the court of the Amir of Crete, who, noticing the boy's resemblance to Ganymede, made him a cupbearer. Amir and servant boy held theological debates on the nature of God.

For a year the abducted boy Adeodatus and the Amir of Crete sparred on the nature of the Deity while the child poured wine from a ewer.

On the next St. Nicholas's Day, the first anniversary of the abduction, father and mother, Getron and Euphrosina, went to pray to the saint for their missing son's salvation. And the saint, idling in the clouds, heard their cry.

Adeodatus stood by his master's side, pouring Euboaen wine. He lurched—was snatched up—found himself dragged into heaven by the hair—and was teleported across continents—across the wrinkled seas—vertiginous—appearing in his own father's farmyard, by his own father's gate, with a napkin still draped over his left arm to wipe the rim of the Amir's cup.

He was welcomed with stark unbelief, then sobbing, then singing.

His story is still recalled for this reason: Remember, when you are trapped in this life, that often whatever liberates you, whatever transports you, must drag you by the hair to yank you free.

Bless us, St. Nicholas, Navigator and Thaumaturge; show your generosity to our fallen race through intercession with the Most High; show us your bounty, as you have granted bounty to the city of Myra, warmed in the hills around your sepulchre, the sweet aisles of orangeries and the orchards of pears and, higher in the hills, the olive groves buzzing with the million-voiced cicada. Shower benedictions upon us, shower them as freely as the scented storax drops from the branches of the Lycian sweetgum when it is gnawed by the worm, and give to

us as openly as you grant these fruits, this incense, this healing balm, to the hawkers and salesmen in Myra's agora, across
which your pilgrims pace in their procession.

The column of thirty-some, heads bowed in piety, made
their way across the market square between the costermon-
gers. At the head of the company an old, wealthy couple rode
upon donkeys: the husband with a white currycomb mustache
and beard, the wife veiled in her shawl, both dressed in rich
dalmatics striped with bands and panels of silk embroidered
with pilgrims' crosses, Persian roundels, flowers of Eden.
Behind them, perhaps their two sons: one blunt and rocky
in the face, pitted, a little scarred, perhaps forty, the other
a black-haired stripling who practiced sneering in his bed-
room. Behind them, a monk, hands folded, eyes down. Then
an entourage of lesser pilgrims, retainers, clients, servants, all
in sober dress. And in the rear, their barbarian guard: Tartar,
perhaps Oghuz? Something steppe, at the very least, and East.

They passed through the city's agora and marched onward
until the houses grew squat and lonely, surrounded by toppled
wattle pens. They continued out, past farms and orchards.

At last, in the afternoon, they came to the domes of the
St. Nicholas Church, which had not yet then been sunk in
sediment, but still stood bright and tall among the plane trees.
They passed through a gate into the compound. The fountain
in the courtyard was dry. The two elders climbed off their
donkeys and a servant tied the animals to a post. The little
procession reassembled and moved on to the church's great
doors, and the barbarian servant scurried forward to knock
for his masters.

In the door there was a smaller door. It opened. A deacon,
a Guardian, bearded, peered out.

The older son said, "We are here for the balm of the Blessed
Nicholas."

It was not, Nicephorus noted, an untruth.

"Peace be upon you," said the Guardian.

He shut the small door, and then the large doors slowly swung open, and the cool of the church floated out to the courtyard.

The sharp white light of sun on limestone seemed almost blinding. Within, as the pilgrims entered, the dark was soft as satin, deeply piled, lit only by candles, friendly, musty, ancient, painted with rich murals. They stood in the entranceway.

"Where do you come from?" asked the Guardian.

"Ephesus," said the older son. The younger said, "Someplace better."

"My parents," the older son pressed on, "want to pay their respects at the tomb of the Blessed Nicholas. My father has a bilious cancer. Wishes healing."

The mustached father, coached, said stiffly, "May the Wonder Worker have mercy upon me!"

The mother, veiled: "Amen, amen, amen, amen, Jesus, amen." She shook her head.

The deacon smiled. "All are welcome at the Blessed Nicholas's shrine."

He led them into the naos, the sanctuary. Three windows lit the apse, one each for Father, Son, and Holy Ghost, though all were white and empty, without feature. Distinct, but of the same substance. The light cast by the Trinity transcribed a cupola with four ancient pillars that stood in the center of the sanctuary—perhaps the remains of some earlier shrine. The light would, in the course of a day, crawl across the sacred chamber like God Himself making the sign of the Cross. The floors were dazzling mosaic, the ceiling tiled with gold and all the company of heaven. Martial saints in Byzantine armor held up their sacred swords; the Son of God died and was raised again; Mary wafted to heaven; the Four Evangelists butted heads; the Lord God Sabaoth held the world as a sphere. At his side was Nicholas himself, draped in his bishop's omophorion, bald and cranky, carrying a ship in one hand and an anchor in the other.

Nicephorus saw Tyun taking stock of all the side chambers: sarcophagi lined up, each one potentially holding the saint, if he was not hidden beneath the floor. Tyun's eyes flicked up to the clerestory, looking, presumably, for catwalks, hidden galleries, places he could hook a rope. Nicephorus found himself wishing it were just the two of them breaking and entering by night.

Since when, he wondered, *have I been so drawn to burglary?*

The four Guardians of the chapel stood before them, all with equal beards. "Do you wish to pray?"

Tornik looked to Tyun for stage direction. Tyun nodded slightly, so Tornik said, "Yes."

"Bow before the altar," said a Guardian. He pointed.

Now that Nicephorus was confronted by the deed itself, and by the basilica itself, the floor upon which, he supposed, the Blessed Nicholas himself had processed seven hundred years before, he was full of doubt. The church was solid; a dream was a flimsy thing, and God and angels peered down upon that sanctuary with sharp interest.

The Factor himself seemed a little awestruck by the majesty of the place. He stood awkwardly before the altar, as if uncertain how to talk to it, how to address a stone that might be a god. Tornik, supposedly the father, hunched miserably beside him.

"Monk," said the Factor. "You could—pray?"

"I will say a litany for the saint," said Nicephorus gratefully, adding in silent prayer: *Show me if we are here rightly. Do you wish to leave with us?*

"Tell him," said the Factor, pointing at the monk, "tell him where." He looked around the sanctuary. "Tell him where the tomb is. He will pray beside the tomb. A litany."

"The whole of this space is infused with the divine

Nicholas," said one of the Guardians, describing circles in the air with his hands. "We do not speak of the place where he lies, for so many have come to steal him: emperors, kings, generals, and caliphs. All have failed, for this is his home."

Now you must intervene, insisted Nicephorus. *You cannot simply watch.*

"Pray," said the Factor to the monk. "Father wishes you . . ." He pointed inelegantly at Tornik, who was touching his own elbows a lot and blinking at the ceiling.

Nicephorus padded to the apse and faced the altar. He began his litany in Latin:

"O Bishop of Myra, born of Patara,
O patron of sailors, friend of children,
O Thaumaturge and Wonder Worker . . ."

As he chanted, he could feel the thieves around him relax; there was a protocol, somehow. Permission was being sought.

"O Nicholas, who spared the condemned from execution,
Who raised the butchered boys from their vat,
Who gave gifts to the three weeping daughters,
Who still shows mercy without restraint
And through generous acts, does—"

Then Matteo blurted out, "Where is he?"
The Guardians looked startled.
Matteo demanded, "Where have you got him?"
"His spirit infuses the whole sanctuary," repeated the Guardian. "Any who pray at the altar are—"
"But I mean the actual him," said the Venetian. He paced around the sanctuary, peering at all the sarcophagi in the side vaults. "What?" he said. "People must want to know!"

"His holy essence is contained in these phials," said one of the Guardians. He pointed to a table with many delicate glass bottles, elegant as water drops. "Which may be purchased after your visit."

"And where do you get it from? The oil?"

"Brother," said the Factor heavily. "Let's pray."

"No!" squalled the Venetian. "We came to see the saint!"

"He's not like a side of beef at the butcher," said one of the Guardians. "He walked across the sea."

The boy pushed his way past one of his disguised guards, which was unwise, since the man audibly clanked. Everyone turned and stared.

Nicephorus had a terrible feeling that things were about to go awry.

"You're not pilgrims," said a Guardian.

"We are pilgrims," insisted the Factor.

"You've come to steal the body. We heard—"

"Liberate," said Matteo, pulling out his saber. "We are great and bold, and he likes us more. So where?"

"Many have searched, none have found," said a Guardian. "Harun al-Rashid—"

"Shut the fuck up and show us the box!" said Matteo, holding the tip of his saber to the holy man's neck.

"Matteo Tradonico," said Tyun, warning, and at the same time, Nicephorus groaned in protest.

But the pretense was dropped. More swords were unsheathed.

Matteo Tradonico said, "There. The weak are astounded."

"Quickly, now," said the Factor to the Guardians. "We'll get what we want and be gone. There won't be any blood. Time for the saint to leave. He was yours for seven centuries. Time for a change." He drew forth a silk bag from his mantle. From the bag he took out a pretty carved box of ivory, and opened it. It was full of gold coins, Byzantine solidi, thin as foil. "Payment," he said.

The most serene of the Guardians said, "What do you think could possibly be as precious as the blessed corpse, our treasure? The dome of his skull is worth more than a crown."

"We will take the body anyway," said the Factor. He held out the coins again. "Payment. Here."

"The people of this city would have us hanged if we took your bribe. St. Nicholas is our confessor, our protector, and our joy. He is our city's symbol, the source of Myra's pride, the tale we tell the world. We will accept no money to betray our brethren, our neighbors, and our families. There is no gold that glitters bright enough."

"Then you're going to fucking die," said Matteo Tradonico, who did not have a practiced ear for rhetorical niceties.

Three of the Guardians looked pale as death at the sight of blades. One was about to cry. "You can't," he said. "God won't let you."

Nicephorus could not stand the scene—innocents threatened, brigands by the holy altar, swords out and held on the horizontal, the twin edges of the blades sharp with light. To see a bared sword in the sanctuary of the Wonder Worker filled him with outrage and a little terror. He looked to Tyun, who seemed as astounded as he was.

Tyun saw the monk's look, the plea for order to be restored, and he nodded. He said, "All right. We're going to do this quickly—"

And he was about to move into action when there was a slam at the back of the sanctuary.

Everyone looked up.

"Hello?" called a man's voice. "We're here to deliver the funeral cakes!"

Everyone shifted. Swords went under cloaks. Matteo Tradonico kept his pressed into the back of a Guardian.

A long line of mourners entered the church carrying candles. The first five of them were women paid to weep. They filled the church with ritual wailing. Behind them came the family, a whole clan, two by two. Nicephorus was astonished by their numbers. They kept pouring in. They cried for mercy upon the soul of Eumathios, father, grandfather. The men all wore their ceremonial swords, fitting for the funeral of a hero.

The company of thieves and their four hostages stood absolutely still as this pageant unfolded. Nicephorus could barely breathe. Tornik had grabbed his sham wife's hand.

The mourners snaked up to the apse and turned to the right and trailed, two by two, into a side vault. Now that Nicephorus looked, he noticed a new body there laid out in an old sarcophagus: a corpse in a winding sheet, covered in flowers and locks of clipped hair, hundreds of locks of hair, curls and tufts of black and white and blond all over his body, as if death were not extinction, but a transformation into the race of wild men, lighting out forever into unknown forests.

A woman whose misery was honest and uncompensated stepped to the side of the sarcophagus and bellowed, "Nine days! Nine days since we wound him in his sheet! Nine days since we sealed his eyes shut with ribbon against the entry of imps! Now we come, O Eumathios, to place the cakes upon you!"

A man, perhaps now paterfamilias, approached the Guardians.

The Baresi and the Venetians shifted warily, gripping their swords beneath their cloaks. The man came up and said conversationally to the weepiest of the Guardians, "Gabe, thanks so much for letting us come by." In the side vault, the woman was leading the family in a funeral chant, everyone keening about the bosom of angels. "Look, if it's okay, could I get that letter? Thea is really getting jumpy."

"Sure," said the Guardian. "It's in my cell." He gathered his skirts in his hands and prepared to float left.

"It would be a shame," said Tyun, "if you missed any of the mourning. The . . . laying of the cakes?"

Matteo Tradonico said, "You might really regret it later."

Tyun said soberly, "People only die once."

Matteo Tradonico nodded. "Sometimes quite dramatically."

"Well, I call that very thoughtful," said the paterfamilias. "But it's okay if you slip out for a mome, Gabe. You've written up the letter, right? You have it written?"

"Mmm," the weepy Guardian confirmed: "It's written."

"Great. We have to get word over to the Thessalonike bunch. They don't even know yet. So?"

"I'll just head up there to my cell for a second," the Guardian agreed. "Letter's on my stand."

The mourning woman, a daughter maybe, cried, *Let him be numbered with Your saints in glory everlasting!*

"Gabe," said Tyun, grasping the Guardian's shoulder. "Gabe, you told me you were heading into town later this evening. You could bring the letter then?"

"We're here," said the paterfamilias. "Might as well give it now. You don't want to go into town later. From here to there it's crawling with the Turks today. They saw us processing out here with the swords and they got antsy. They're waiting outside to escort us back."

"The Turks," said Rollo de Bailleul.

"Oh yes," said the man, rolling his eyes. "Whole posse of them."

Everyone stood awkwardly for a while, each of them, in their own way, meditating on the fashion of their own death. The daughter and her daughters took out kollyba cakes and placed them on the father's body, laying them on the wads of hair and flowers. Hymns were sung.

"No letter?" said the paterfamilias.

Matteo Tradonico pressed the tip of his sword into Gabe's back.

"Not right now," gasped Gabe.

The door at the back smacked open again. A Turkish soldier peered in, outlined in golden light. He called out, "The family goes now. Curfew!"

The mourners shot the soldier dirty looks. They tossed the final few oatcakes into the sarcophagus. They bowed briefly in prayer.

Then the conspirators and their victims stood still as a mosaic while the mourning family processed out, two by two, the paid mourners once again screaming at high volume, hoping for tips.

There was a silence.

The saint thieves dipped their weapons and withdrew them from their cloaks and the folds of their robes and from behind each other's backs.

And in the silence, Nicephorus realized: *Now there is nothing to interrupt the miracle. We shall see him in the flesh. He shall be before us. We shall learn if he wishes to come with us.*

We shall learn if my dream has his blessing upon it.

"Now," said the Factor. "Business."

Matteo Tradonico told his men, "Search the nooks." He shook his saber to indicate "all around."

"No," said the Factor. "Four of you, out. Stand guard."

"Are you doing ordering?" said Matteo Tradonico. "I think I'm better at ordering."

The Factor selected four—two Baresi, two Venetians—and jabbed his finger at them. "One. Two. Three. Four. Lookouts." He had a voice of command. They headed out to the courtyard.

Tyun reached into the wide sleeve of his *qamis* and pulled

out the map of the basilica he'd been sent by pilgrims. He shook it out and consulted it. Then he delivered assignments, nodding to his men, pointing through arches, "Rif'at, north side aisle. Hisham, south side aisle. You, Norman, mole, squint, the apse. I'm particularly interested in what's under the dais, those steps, the synthronon."

The monk went to his side and peered at the floor plan. "The corridors to the south," he suggested.

"Mmm. Asymmetry. Good thought."

The company spread through the church's chambers and methodically, chamber by chamber, inspected the walls, the floors, the sarcophagi. Nicephorus wandered among the soldiers, looking for signs of reverence in stone. Several of the tombs were ancient, pagan: putti with doused torches, the deceased at funeral feasts, sphinxes, centaurs, griffons' heads. He did not like the glowering of bishops' councils in the narthex: over each arch, armies of ecclesiastics standing in judgment around the cross, their faces ashen as the dead, their beards drawn severely into frowns, their eyes glaring and accusatory.

He could hear the echo of argument from the sanctuary.

"You are taking what belongs to the city of Myra," said the gravest of the Guardians, "when we have just been conquered and don't even know what nation we are of. Myra remembers what it is only because we have this gift of bones and flesh, sacred to us, so pilgrims come to us from far away and tell us who we are."

"You'll tell us where you hid him!" said Matteo Tradonico. "Or look! Look what this sword can do!" He brandished his sword and then swooped it around in wide, energetic arcs like he imagined a hero would do. "And!"—demonstrating more swooping, up and down, teeth gritted. "And this!"—and at that he knocked against the little table with phials of oil on it and said, "Oh, damn!" while they all collapsed and one rolled off and hit the stone floor.

Everyone looked in horror at the little bottle with its sacred liquor rolling back and forth on the tiles. It wobbled to the center of a mosaic vortex and rocked until it was still.

Tyun, thinking quickly, announced, "A miracle! Unbroken!" He picked it up and held the fragile thing in the dying evening light coming through the three windows. "It is the saint's will!"

"Stop this farce," said the grave Guardian to the Venetian princeling. "It's obvious where the tomb is, child. Look for the spout. God won't grant you the body, though."

Nicephorus felt distaste at it all: the Venetian boy's idiot boasting, the bearded deacons' pleas. *Make your will known, Wonder Worker. In some sign.* Two side chapels to the south were dedicated to military saints who even in heaven were armed.

But the southern corridor he'd pointed to on the map—this was promising. For one thing, the door was locked. One of the Venetian soldiers saw him fiddling with the latch and the lock, came over, and kicked the door open. Nicephorus winced at the noise.

The room was dark. Without being told, the soldier went to fetch a lamp. He and Nicephorus went in together. The air was damp as caves.

It was a burial chamber with niches for sarcophagi on the north wall. The ceiling was arched and low. At the far end, they could just make out a door that must, according to the plan, lead back outside. Nicephorus and the soldier paced along the corridor, reading the frescoes on walls and on arches. It was all there. Not the history of Christ, his death and resurrection, but scenes of Nicholas's life, his doings at sea, his scolding of demons, his gifts of gold thrown through a window, the Council of Nicaea in the moment before the blessed Wonder Worker punched Arius the Heretic in the kisser.

And there, on the south wall, the spigot: a brass fixture in the shape of a dove that would vomit forth fluid when the cock was turned.

The monk reached out and touched it. He turned the tap.
A single drop of sainted scum fell through the air and landed
on a greasy spot on the floor. Quickly, Nicephorus shut off the
bung before another drop fell.

He went to the door of the burial chamber and called out
to the sanctuary, "I think it's here." As he said the words, he
felt a shock go through his hands, for with that declaration,
he knew he had set in motion a new desecration.

"There!" said Matteo Tradonico, and grabbed one of the
sacks with iron implements from one of his men and wrestled
the pickaxes and crowbars out of the sack and handed them
back to the man who had already been holding them and said,
"Go on!"

The whole horde came, prodding the Guardians along with
them. Their torches guttered in the burial corridor. Nicephorus pointed to the brass dove. The Factor nodded and spread
out his fingers.

Then, the awful chipping and hacking at the plaster wall
where the spigot came out.

"You have damned us all," said a Guardian. "We will be
killed by crowds. By our own neighbors."

The wall had upon it a scene of St. Nicholas praying with a
father and mother for the kidnapped boy, Adeodatus, who had
been taken to the far court of the amir. The pickaxes bit deep
into their robes. The father was now faceless. A chip flew and
Nicholas himself was without arms. His hands, in prayer, lay
on the floor.

"It won't be there," said Tyun. "There's more to it. Priests
love a good obfuscation."

More blows. Clouds of plaster drifted in the candlelight.

The whole crew gathered around the desecration. For
twenty minutes, the soldiers hacked away.

There was a hole. The men paused. They peered in.

"It's just a pipe," one said. "The wall's solid."

"Shit," muttered the Factor.

"We'll knock down all these fucking walls if you don't tell us where that pipe goes," said the princeling.

"It'll take forever," the Factor griped. "Someone's going to notice the noise. Even out here."

"Just tell us or we'll raze your fucking church to the ground," said Matteo Tradonico, "so there won't be a—a—a pillar to piss on!"

Nicephorus spoke up. He looked, though, at Tyun. He said, "You don't have to knock down the walls." He pointed all the way across the gallery, to the other half of the same scene from Nicholas's life: Adeodatus, the kidnapped boy, weeping at the court of Crete. "I suspect it is behind there. The power of the saint binds the two places. The boy is conducted along that route, through the ether, back home. Perhaps the saint's ichor flows along the same course." He saw that Tyun grinned at his ingenuity, and he was giddy.

The soldiers walked to the scene of Adeodatus at the court of the amir. They knocked on the wall.

"Hollow?" said the Factor. One nodded. The Factor said, "Break it down."

Desecration again. This time, the amir and his court gutted, smashed as time smashes princes and principalities, and a boy defaced, Adeodatus, son of Getron, until he was less than a corpse.

The plaster was thin. There was a really big hole now.

There lay a sarcophagus behind the wall. It was fine and ancient: thick, curling acanthus scrolls on its side, fish scales on its lid, and plumbing going down into its roof and coming out its base.

The four soldiers with their picks and metal bars fell to their knees before it.

Nicephorus sneaked a glance at Tyun; then he too kneeled in reverence. Tyun looked upon the dreamer with a certain affection, but the monk's eyes were closed in prayer.

Nicephorus's eyes flipped open when he heard the grating of stone. Matteo Tradonico and five others were trying to drag the lid off the sarcophagus. "Come on! Come on! Come on!" cried the Venetian, pretending to strain at the weight so the others would pull harder.

It was not easy. It had to be slid toward them out of the recessed nook. Tyun took out chains. "Stop, stop. Put these around the rim and pull."

They did. They couldn't budge it.

"Let's—" began Tyun, but Matteo Tradonico had seized a sledgehammer from one of his soldiers and, with a triumphant caw, brought it down on the scaled lid. Again—again—and with each blow, another cry of anger at being thwarted by stone.

The lid finally cracked. Matteo called over his soldiers. They bellied up the pieces, heaved them to the side, scrabbled for more.

And with that, the tomb of St. Nicholas, Navigator and Gift Giver, was open to the air.

Reprobus and the sailors uneasily played dice. It was getting dark. Fires were lit in houses and in yards above the harbor. The dog-man and his crew spoke quietly in Arabic.

"It is your turn, *qaid*."

But Reprobus's nose was twitching. He abandoned the game and stood. He looked out across the black river.

"Myrrh," he said. "Do you smell it?"

He walked to the railing and took in the night. "They have found him," he said.

. . .

The box was full of dark, welling oil. It steeped the basilica in its scent.

The Venetian boy was ecstatic. He held up both his hands. "We got it! We're favored! Look!"

He plunged his hands into the pool. Nicephorus let out an involuntary yelp. The Guardians hissed in horror.

The boy was actually climbing into the sarcophagus like he would into a bath his nurse had just warmed.

"Take off your shoes!" said Nicephorus, appalled. "At least take them off!" (Thinking of Moses, who did not dare to keep on the sandals of exile when he met the burning bush.)

The boy plunged himself down into the saint's oil, pulling up handfuls and lapping it up. It splattered between his fingers. His face was greasy, running with it. It poured down his chin.

Now we are gone, thought Nicephorus. *The column of fire. His face will melt. We will all be blasted.* Nicephorus was still on his knees. *What have we done?*

"Get your ugly little bitch of a—" said Tyun, but the boy was already dunking himself in farther, patting the floor of the coffin with both his hands, looking to seize the bones.

Maybe poisonous air, thought Nicephorus. *It's not Biblical but I've always wondered why there wasn't more of it.* The myrrh's perfume was thick in the room. *Or mudslides.*

The boy's movements were more frantic. "No!" he cried.

And *Aha!* thought Nicephorus. *A fitting death—piscine! Divine tentacles.* The tousled locks would disappear behind the rim. A final gulped cry for help.

"No!" said the Venetian again and swore in the language of his city.

He stood up, running with oil. His clothes were drenched.

"There's nothing in here. There's no body," he whined. "It's just oil. *There's no fucking body!*"

Tyun and the Factor stalked over to the sarcophagus. They peered down into its depths, holding lamps.

Tyun turned to the Guardians. "So it's not . . . ?"

The solemnest Guardian now looked smug.

A half mile off, there were torches. A town on the move. The only evening left was small and charred on the horizon. The rest was night. Fields hissing.

The basilica was dark now, except for candle flames. In the sanctuary, the three windows were gray and cast no light.

In the burial chamber, the Guardian, standing like a preacher in the rubble, explained, "There is no Nicholas. Nor was there ever, perhaps. The stories are confused. Once a week, we pour scented oil into the sarcophagus. The channel is there, just above where you hacked. Behind that corbel. We take out the stopper and pour oil into the sacred coffin. Pilgrims come. We fill their unguentaria at the tap." He said, "We have our asceticisms. We perform our offices. We are punctilious in our service. Our worship of the divine. At the center, there is a void. Emptiness. An empty tomb. That is what all Christians long for: to find the stone rolled away, and nothing within."

The thieves stood astounded.

He said, "You may kill us, but you will get nothing more out of us. There is nothing more to give."

"The Blessed Nicholas?" said Nicephorus, rising to his feet, thinking of the monks of his order dying in monastery beds, the people of Bari marked with pox.

The Guardian shrugged. "Perhaps there was a bishop once,

at the time of Constantine. Perhaps there was a sea god, half-remembered. He is nothing but a bundle of folktales. Perhaps there was a man and stories were told about him. But perhaps there wasn't." He turned and started to walk away toward his hermitage. "Now I am tired, and I want to go to bed. Tomorrow, we have to hire plasterers and stonemasons. We must continue in our devotion to the empty mysteries."

Everyone watched him, listening to the lazy slap of his sandals on the stone.

The Venetian boy still stood, half-drenched, in the bogus saint's sarcophagus, like he'd just been dunked.

The other three Guardians hurried after their leader.

"No!" protested the Venetian boy. "No, no, no! You don't leave! Look where I am!"

The solemn Guardian wearily turned. "It is time now for sleep," he said. "Except for all of you. For you, it is time to die."

And that is when they all heard the doors to the sanctuary burst open, and a cry of alarm. The people of Myra flooded into the church, their swords drawn, ready to kill to defend their saint.

*O*NCE, SHORTLY AFTER THE DEATH OF SAINT NICHOLAS, THE EMPEROR OF BYZANTIUM SENT AN EMISSARY TO negotiate the delivery of his body to Constantinople. The corpse was already rumored to weep its holy ichor. The Guardians of the basilica refused to give the relics up. They would not even show the emissary the remains. The emissary spent the night in prayer to the saint, begging: if he couldn't fulfill his mission and return with the whole body, at least grant him some small token which he could kiss. The next day, when the Guardians permitted the emissary to lower a ladle through a hole in the lid of the sarcophagus to draw forth oil, the man's wish was granted: there was a yellow tooth floating in the scoop. The emissary grabbed it. The Guardians pretended not to see it. Perhaps they had placed it there themselves, some fragment stolen from an ossuary.

When he was alone, the emperor's emissary kissed the tooth. He pressed it to his lips, this remnant of another mouth. He placed it in a golden box. He planned to take it back to Constantinople.

But when he left his chamber for a few hours and returned, he found the golden box sitting in a pool. The tooth had not stopped sweating its oil. Sacred myron doused the box and ran down the table linens. The emissary opened the box, fished out the tooth, and wrapped it in cloths to sop up the excess liquid.

The cloth immediately got soaked. It didn't help at all. Like a nightmare, the tooth kept bleeding oil and the box brimmed with it, overflowing. When the emperor's emissary woke up in the morning, the table was streaked and the floor was puddled. Everything was stained.

Nicholas had appeared to him in the night. "I gave you my tooth to kiss," said the Wonder Worker. "Now return it. My body must remain whole."

And so the emissary of the Emperor of Byzantium returned to the Basilica of St. Nicholas of Myra and yielded up the tooth in its golden box. He never saw the body of the saint, if there was a body, if there was anything in that tomb at all other than oil, yellow as sunshine, green as the ocean depths, in which something might tumble and float free.

Saint Nicholas shone like a beacon for his people.

Ranks of citizens filed into the sanctuary silently, holding their swords, their spears, simple fists. Just outside the great doors, the church courtyard was packed with hundreds more, and there, struggling, in their midst, were the League of St. Nicholas's four lookouts: battered, bleeding. They had tried to shout warnings. Angry men swarmed all over them, dragging them down. One of them was held up by his arms. He could not even lift his head.

In the funerary corridor, half the thieves froze and the others sprang into panicked action. Tornik seized Musarat's hand, as if this were a time for a husband to lend strength to his wife. She shook off his fingers, glaring at the door that led back into the sanctuary.

Tyun drew his sword from his baldric and dashed out to the sanctuary to see what was happening, a brother from Merv on either side of him. The Factor followed with two bodyguards.

The crowd stood silently. The four Guardians stood on the steps of the dais, all four pointing into the side chapel at the burial corridor. Tyun and the brothers came to a halt, confronting two hundred angry citizens at the back of the church. The Factor faltered at the sight of them. The faces of the people of Myra were furious, creased in hostility. Their silence was not comforting.

The mourning paterfamilias came forward. "Yes, them," he announced to the crowd. "As we were leaving, I saw they had swords and—instruments of destruction."

More townspeople stepped into the church. They wanted to get a swing in when the battle started.

"Ladies . . . gentlemen," said Tyun. "This is such an impressive crowd. What is a greater blessing to every citizen than a strong community, the support of our fellow man? The speed with which you came together this evening truly should be a lesson for other towns and villages—and not simply how a town gathers for false alarms and the whims of overwrought mourners, but for festivals, processions, the summer haying, the weddings of your loved ones. What brought you together so rapidly?"

"I went to the city square and shouted," said the paterfamilias.

Another man stepped forward. He pointed upward. "The beacon," he said. "We were told if the lamp ever lights on top of the dome, someone is trying to bust into the tomb."

"The beacon," said Tyun, nodding. "The *beacon*. An oil lamp, I presume." He turned to the Factor—whose face was stark with panic—and explained, with the air of the professional, "Wick down a chimney into the sarcophagus. Flint ignition. Weight trigger on the plinth. Or perhaps that wall with the spigot. That's where the deacon directed us."

To the crowd, he said, "So sorry you all came out. There was no need. Really. No need. We are done with our commission." He clapped his hands together and turned to the Factor. "That should about do it, shouldn't it, sir?" To the rest: "Orders from the Pope in Rome. To check on the saint. Because of the Seljuk invasion."

"You are from the Pope?"

"In nomine Patris et Filii et Spiritus Sancti."

"Do you have documents?" the paterfamilias said.

"We do," said Tyun, "somewhere."

"Mmm. You have a bull."

Tyun might have been able to lay his hands on some bull, had the Venetian princeling not sloshed out of the funerary chamber at that very moment, dripping with defiled myrrh. He held up his sword and crowed, "La Serenissima—forever unconquered!"

The crowd began to move forward—not in a rush, but step by step, warily, inexorably, as if pushing the weight of violence ahead of them. They would not be stopped. They surged steadily toward the treasure seekers near the altar. Hundreds against seven.

The Factor and his toughs backed away, swords drawn.

It was a defensive retreat.

Tyun's gabbling delay in the sanctuary had done its work: the rest of the band had time to scamper to the far end of the burial corridor—hacking at the lock on the far door with a pick—the hasps bending, snapping.

Nicephorus heard Tyun's valiant blather. He stood nervously by the Venetian soldiers, ready to flee out the far door, asking himself, *Is it my place to flee when others remain behind? Or does friendship demand some sacrifice . . . ?*

"This," said one of the soldiers, and handed him a military sling. Nicephorus looked at the sling in his hands, bewildered. "Rocks!" the soldier shouted, heaving his pickax against the door. The monk bent to gather some rubble from the battered walls to launch.

Then the noise of full assault, a mob enraged. Metal against metal.

Nicephorus looked up. The Factor ran right past the open

door to the burial corridor, his two men following, then the brothers from Merv, the stripling prince loping behind them, drizzling oil—all of them barreling by, heading off into an unexplored wing.

This did not seem auspicious.

Tyun? I did not see him. He must be holding the crowd off.

The hasp cracked off. The door swung open.

The night.

The first of the mob had reached the door to the burial corridor. A single Venetian kept them at bay, swinging his short sword. As Musarat and Tornik ducked out, Nicephorus, desperate, turned and cupped a chunk of marble lid in the sling. He wound up—memories of boyhood pranks—thinking of David and Goliath, David and Jonathan—and released. The rock flew and smacked into a weaver. The man staggered backward, bleeding from the face. Nicephorus blanched at the man's pain. *What have I—*

But it was too late. The crowd was pouring in, screaming in anger at the dim sight of vandalism, fallen plaster, the ragged channels of pickaxes hacked through the stories of their city's saint.

Tyun has fallen, thought Nicephorus. *Gone.* But the monk was out the door and into the night.

The little band of thieves found themselves outside the basilica, in deep shadow. No torches anymore. Their leaders gone. The crowd was just thirty feet away, still roiling in the courtyard to push into the church's ceremonial portals.

Nicephorus took off into the dark fields behind Musarat and Tornik.

On the roof of the dome burned the warning beacon, a spurt of flame from the teat of salvation.

A donkey galumphed past, his packs sagging on his haunch.

"Hey! Donkey!" hissed Tornik, but it was in his own language, and the donkey failed him as all beasts of burden would, after the death of Akritis.

Scampering up a rise. There was dust in their lungs.

"Everyone scattered," said Nicephorus. "Where's Tyun?"

Tornik shook his head. They ran along a village wall, crouched.

"I've got to go back," said Nicephorus. They could hear the sound of something—melee? pillage?—echoing from the church. The mob was loud, shouting, some of them moaning, crying out to the saint pitiably, finding his sarcophagus, of course, empty.

Tornik shook his head again. "Not back," he said.

Hooves. They ducked.

Two mounted Turks had seen them. Just fifteen feet away. One hung back, an arrow nocked. The other drew his sword.

Nicephorus could not believe his adventure would end this way, in such disaster: flight, confusion, a Saracen blade. He halted and discovered his legs were wobbling with indecision.

"Thief," said the Turk, pointing with his blade. He pointed to Nicephorus, Musarat, and Tornik.

His face, beneath his cap of fur, looked disappointed in his victims, even as he called for their execution.

When the crowd swamped Tyun, there was only one way to flee: up the ciborium. Four pillars supporting a little cupola over the altar. Swinging his sword wildly and jabbing to keep the mob at bay, he shimmied up one of the pillars, clenching it between his thighs. He'd need both hands, though, if he was going to pull himself up on the roof of the cupola.

There were hands below; they reached for him. He hacked at them; they darted back. He lunged upward—threw one arm bent double over the lip of the brass roof, elbow clenched for purchase.

Brass roof? Gold leaf? Regrettably, no time to peel back some foil and check.

Heaving: his head over the lip. He'd dropped his sword. *Fuck.*

Free though, now, to climb. We lose a weapon, we gain a new dimension in motion. He kicked at hands, swung his legs, half rolled onto the roof of the cupola. He was up.

They bellowed at him from below like rioters at the hippodrome. He was already craning his neck, assessing the chains that held up the wheel chandeliers.

Tyun leapt, grabbed, swung. He racketed through the heavens. Christ Pantokrator welcomed him with open arms and hands spread across the dome of stars.

He missed the little arched window into the upper gallery *(shit)*, kicked himself off the wall again for a wider swing, shifted his weight sideways to add arc, flying over the faithful, their arms raised toward him.

I guess this is what it's like to be a god, he thought. *Airborne, but the little bastards on the ground won't stop raising their hands in need.*

Too far—left of the window. His knee smacked the wall with a jolt. He swore. Almost dropped. His hands stuttered. His body was hanging awkwardly from the chandelier. If the pendulum stopped swinging, he'd end up suspended helplessly above the congregation.

Once again, he flew out over the crowd, spinning through the tessellated heavens.

One last chance. He kicked his leg into the air, shifted his weight as he swung, spun the wheel. *O Fortuna* . . .

With a grunt, he caught the edge of the window with his foot, and his careening came to a stop. His whole weight hit. He locked his foot against the embrasure. His ankle spasmed.

His foot started to slide. The rim of the chandelier bit into his fingers. He could no longer think. He could barely breathe. People were running for the stairs.

The Turkish soldier prepared for a decapitation. It was a ghoulish scene: the village wall, gray under the dome of heaven, the deadbeat grasses trampled in tufts, the distant light of torches near the basilica and the warning flame standing like a seraph above the outraged sanctuary. Distantly, the sound of a mob screaming.

In your bosom, Lord, thought Nicephorus, and wondered if he should close his eyes. No, open. We must face the blade that takes each of us, alone.

Then, a miracle: Musarat, usually so silent, spoke. She spoke at length, as she never had before, snapping out some kind of rebuke to the sentries in sharp Turkish. Nicephorus, of course, could not understand a word of it.

She scolded the soldier. "Child: what are you doing? Threatening an old woman and her husband. Do not dare hold that sword toward me. Do not *dare.* Your mother is weeping."

The soldier was shocked to hear his tongue. Uncertain, he said, "There are thieves in the night, madame."

"So protect us. We have traveled many hundreds of miles—hundreds—to the shrine of this holy man, this *wali,* this friend of God (peace be upon him), to pray for blessings from him and from all the prophets as we approach our final years. And you would murder us in a cow pasture."

"The Christians say you are here to steal the body of the friend of God."

"Not us. *Eyvah!* You are looking for the Venetian boy in black. He ran." She pointed vaguely at the Taurus Mountains. "There. Child, I would not stir the bones even of a Christian saint. I would not. I still have my hair. Do you think I want to

lose all of it in great hanks? No. Go chase the thief. Find the
Venetian boy. Go, go—do the work of these Byzantine foxes,
as if they were your masters."

The soldier apologized: "It is our task to keep the peace."

"So you will murder an old man and woman with your sword
and your bow? In the name of peace? I have just heard your
father disown you. I have heard him say your name and spit
on the ground."

And so the scolding went on while Nicephorus and Tornik,
ignorant, watched in wonder as the arrow was reluctantly
un-nocked, the sword sheathed. Three minutes more of the
harangue and the sentries were backing away on their horses
and offering to escort the venerable couple safely back to the
docks. They offered Musarat a horse.

While she struggled to mount with the steadying hands of
Tornik and the soldier, Nicephorus announced he had to go
back to the basilica.

"He is one of the priests there," Musarat explained in Turkish. Tornik nodded at the monk in approbation. One should
not leave a friend to fight alone.

Nicephorus bowed before them all with his hands clasped.

He watched them amble off together, flanked by sentries.
He saw Musarat take in her fist a pinch of Tornik's cloak, a
gesture of a half-century's connection, and the dear children,
of course, and more sweet years to come sitting side by side
in the arbor by the shores of the Euxine Sea. They processed
together into the darkness.

Nicephorus turned back toward the flame that lit the night
as the angel's sword had done when Adam and Eve were first
cast out of the Garden.

Tyun hung in the heavens. His left foot was hooked tenta-
tively on the window's frame.

He didn't have long. Down below, a bearded Guardian was pressing through the furious mob to get to the winch that would lower the candelabra.

Slowly, slowly—in full sight of hundreds—the saint hunter began to bend his locked knee, muscles straining, quivering, pulling himself toward the window. He grunted with the effort, grimaced.

So many people watching me agog, he thought bitterly, *and it's such an ugly face I'm making.*

He extended his other leg, the right one . . . gently . . . terrified he was about to slip and swing out above the crowd again. His right foot gingerly touched the window frame and scraped along the plaster. He slipped it around the corner.

He gasped, a belted, half-muffled cry.

He was more firmly anchored now. He started to edge around the chandelier, hand over hand. The metal rim scraped at his fingers. He avoided the candles.

Then he was there, right next to the window into the upper gallery. One try only to flip himself through the arch. If he slipped and fell, he'd break himself on the mosaics before the crowd could tear him limb from limb.

The chandelier jolted. The Guardian was lowering it.

Tyun lunged forward.

Through the window, rolling on the sill, dropping, stumbling. Knees cracking on the pavement. Hands slapping stone. Elbow bruised.

But he was in the upper gallery.

There were footsteps clapping up the stairs.

He tried to get up.

His knees were in so much pain he could barely stand, and the crowd would be upon him again in a moment. Swords, knives, a mace. *Surprisingly delicate, bones.*

He scrambled a few feet on all fours, then ricocheted off the wall, which forced him up into a crouch.

Somehow, he was vaguely upright and running. Someone was behind him.

There was a door. He tossed aside its crossbar, opened it, and was out in the night, up near the domes, the warning flame sputtering above him. He slammed the door shut behind him. As fast as he could, he started limping down the stairs into the hermitage courtyard.

Bottom of the steps, and he was beside the church, frantically searching for a way out of the compound.

Someone was clopping down after him: three men, all armed.

Tyun bolted for an archway that led into the dark. Through that arch, and he'd be out on the scrubby plain: latitude to run and to hide.

Checking his pursuers, he reached the arch and grabbed the pilaster.

Then someone stepped out in front of him, a huge guy with a sword and no shirt.

Fuck and who joins a church mob shirtless?

Tyun had only a dagger left, and it was sheathed in his boot. He felt soft and penetrable. The blade of the sword swishing in front of him spoke of slices, wounds, veins, meat. *Fuck.*

Tyun paused warily, backed just out of range, but people were coming at him from behind.

The shirtless man growled and plunged forward.

Tyun prepared for the impact.

It did not come.

A *snap* from far off, and the shirtless man toppled, stunned, hit by a rock.

Launched from where? Someone out beyond the arch?

Who gives a shit? Tyun charged.

Then he was free in the night, running on wagon ruts, dry grasses all around him. His knees complained, but he'd put off pain till later.

"Tyun!" It was the monk behind a tamarisk bush, holding a sling.

Tyun veered and the two of them sprinted, side by side.

Tyun realized he was grinning. Fun to run with the monk.

And he was alive, still alive.

The fields that night were full of fugitives and search parties. Men with torches and lanterns hunted through the lanes and climbed stiles into paddocks, kicking their way through cow-shit to check each stable and shed.

Tyun and Nicephorus could see the lights bumbling through the landscape from where they rested, panting, hidden behind a stone threshing floor up in the hills.

"They're all around us," said Nicephorus.

"You, dream boy, are a wonder," said Tyun. "I could kiss you."

Nicephorus made no sound but a glottal stop, waiting to see how literally to take the subjunctive.

Tyun peered out into the darkness toward the bay and said, "I wonder where those bastards hid the corpse."

"There is no corpse," said Nicephorus. "My dream . . ."

"There's a corpse, dream boy," said Tyun. "Priests. Obfuscations."

"Where?"

Tyun blew out air between his lips.

"We've got another chance," he said. "We'll find the damn thing. This is exciting."

"No," said Nicephorus. "There is no healing corpse of Nicholas."

"Of course there is," said Tyun. "No one's been smart enough to discover it until now. We'll be the first."

"No, Tyun," said Nicephorus. "We've already lost one ship. Who knows where the crew of the *Epiphany* is? My dream was nothing. A dream."

Tyun took out a glass bottle. "I told you people that you need *faith*." He peeled away at the bottle's wax seal with his thumb. "Drink? I'm parched." The wax came off in a strip. He pulled out the glass stopper and handed the bottle to Nicephorus.

Nicephorus was about to take it when he realized what it was. "The Nicholas ichor?"

"Holy water and oil. Might as well," said Tyun. "We need the luck." He raised the bottle. *"Dii propitii."* Gods, be kind. He took a swig.

The monk was astounded. He stared at the saint hunter.

Tyun made a wry face. "More oil than water." He prepared to hurl the bottle out into the night, then paused with his throwing arm cocked. "Sure you don't want to try it?"

Nicephorus hesitated. "I guess there is nothing holy about it."

"I feel stupendously blessed right now," said Tyun. "Drink, and no one can catch us. This drink is a fucking apotheosis." He handed the bottle to Nicephorus.

Nicephorus looked down at the *oleum martyris*, the sacred fluid, the healing balm he'd come so far to find. He raised it to his lips. It smelled of myrrh. He tipped the bottle up and drank, gagged. It was thick, greasy, floral.

"No?" said Tyun.

Nicephorus swallowed and coughed.

They sat side by side, backs against the threshing floor, and watched the torches wander in the night. Nicephorus held the bottle near his chest like a roadside drunk. Tyun absently fiddled with the wax, rolling it into a ball, pressing his thumbnails into it.

"You're the chosen one," said Tyun. "The holy man revived you."

"Don't mock me."

"I'm not. You're an excellent person. A good person. You came back for me."

Stubbornly, Nicephorus said, "I don't know why."

"Let's pretend it's not because of my brutish beauty."

Nicephorus frowned. He took another drink, forgetting, and once again coughed. "What about the others?"

"Some of them escaped. Some of them will get the shit beaten out of them. The world has cudgels and cutting-edges." He tossed the ball of wax from hand to hand. "But we'll be the ones to find the body."

"There are people dying of the pox back in Bari."

"So when we find it, Bari'd better pay us well. I think the price is going up."

Nicephorus goggled. "You're still ready to betray us for money?"

"This is not a hobby," said Tyun, staring at him steadily. "Not a pastime."

"Over here!" crowed a voice about thirty or forty feet away. "I heard a cough!"

And so the monk and the saint hunter were off running again.

A Norman knight, alone in a dovecote. Secret chain mail, a sword held at the ready, in a dark that whispered with unsettled birds. The walls were punctuated by bricks of blue night, each flecked and sparkling with mica stars.

People were outside, hunting through the farmyard. The Norman cringed behind the door. Through the gaps in the walls he watched them pass.

He no longer knew which way he should run back to the harbor and the ship. The smell of cowshit was so strong and so familiar he should be able to lift it aside like a brown tapestry and step out safely in his father's farmyard in Saint-Lô.

The door to the dovecote slammed open. He was behind it, so it slapped him hard. His sword was trapped in the jamb.

They were all around him, grabbing at his coif and his flesh. He dropped the sword as they pulled him over, toppled him like a chess piece. A kick in the face. Blood and teeth.

The pigeons lifted off in all directions at once, a mirage expanding on the grassy plain.

Tyun and Nicephorus darted down a lane, gravel spitting under their feet. Torchlight was behind them.

There was a doorway in the high fieldstone wall. They fell sideways into it.

They were in a yard. Lots of sheep. They pressed themselves back against the wall until their pursuers passed. Footfalls sprinting. Calls: "Down here?" and "There were two of them!"

Nicephorus made as if to move, but Tyun grabbed the monk's cuff and pulled it hard against the stone to stop him from bolting.

Then he saw what the saint hunter saw: There was a child sitting on a wall facing them. She was perhaps six and had eyes like a goat's.

She watched them both. One lone call, and the citizens of Myra would flood into the yard and be upon them.

Nicephorus set a kind, conspiratorial look on his face and raised a trembling finger to his lips.

The child swung her legs and bumped her heels against the wall she sat on. She was clearly fascinated with Tyun's brocade coat, rich, though smudged with dirt.

Tyun gave a wink a try.

The child did not smile. She had been shorn of her hair.

The footsteps in the lane passed by. The girl waited for silence.

Then she asked them, "Can you fly?"

Tyun whispered, "Not right now."

"Have you seen the golden halls?"

Tyun nodded. He tried, "I walk there all the time. He sleeps in the corner."

"What?" said Nicephorus.

Tyun gave him an agonized look.

"Is it warm in the clouds?"

Nicephorus said, "Oh, honey, you think we're angels," and Tyun rapidly intervened: "And we are. We've come in secret."

Nicephorus did not like the deception. He frowned.

Tyun said, "We walk among you unawares. We heal and kill with a touch."

She said, "Angels are beautiful men."

"We certainly are," Tyun agreed.

"I'll get Mim and Bamp."

"Please, child," said Nicephorus, shaking his head.

"They won't be able to see us, as adults," Tyun explained. "Only the pure of heart."

"I'll tell them you're here. They'll make a church in the lambs."

"Let's not do that," said Nicephorus. "We will be gone."

She watched them for a while from atop her wall. Someone ran past, crunching.

When the footsteps were gone, she said, "Angels do arms like this," and she held her arms stiffly like an icon.

"They do," Nicephorus agreed. He gamely assumed a hieratic pose.

The girl said, "Angels put one hand on their head."

"Do they?" Nicephorus asked, but he put his hand behind his head like a halo. He wondered whether this was participating in a lie.

"Both angels do," she instructed them.

Tyun raised his hand to his hair.

She told them, "Angels stand on one leg."

Somewhat unwillingly, they each raised a leg. For Nicephorus, the right; Tyun, the left.

She advised them, "Angels hop in the mud."

On one leg, they hopped. Sheep shit spattered their hems. Tyun looked sour.

She said, "Angels rub their bellies."

The two men did. Nicephorus nodded kindly at the child.

She said, "Angels lift the other leg too."

The men obediently shifted, right leg to left and left to right.

She corrected: "At the same time. They lift both their legs up."

Tyun and the monk looked at each other.

She insisted, "Angels lift all their legs."

Tyun said, "In Heaven—"

She clarified: *"It's called flying."*

Tyun scowled, pushed himself lightly away from the wall, and turned to leave.

Staring at Tyun's eyes, the girl opened her mouth as if a scream were frozen there. He hesitated. She sat there on her wall, bouncing her heels in lazy rhythm, her jaw yawning, her lips taut.

"Don't do that," said Tyun.

It was the wrong tone to take. The girl stuck her chin out more.

"Angels are helpers," she said.

"Yes, they are," said Nicephorus. "In a thousand little ways."

"Milking," said the girl.

Nicephorus agreed, "Of course," mainly to hide Tyun's hissed "Fuck."

"I used to have goats," said Nicephorus, conversationally.

The girl pointed to a ragged archway, as if she were the angel, casting them out.

The goats met them at the gate. There were eleven of them, and they were excited for feed. Nicephorus walked among them, clucking, touching their foreheads.

The girl skipped along the top of the wall so she could watch the milking.

Tyun headed over to a single goat standing sequestered in its own stall. "I'll do this one," he said.

"Tyun," said Nicephorus. "No."

Tyun knelt next to the goat and felt for the teat. "Just grab it?" he said.

"Don't," said Nicephorus. "Billy."

The goat kicked and Tyun swore—"Shit!"—and hopped backward on one leg, as the angels do.

Nicephorus led a goat to the stanchion and fixed its head with a loop of rope. He said, "Where's feed?" and the girl pointed. He tossed a handful down in front of the doe. She began to eat, screwing her lips one way and the other. The monk took a bucket from the corner and set it down under her udder. He wiped the udder with the back of his sleeve. This was something he knew. He pinched the teats and pulled.

The rhythmic hiss was ancient and familiar. His childhood: *Do this, and you are a good boy, Niko.*

Then the voice of an adult: "What's happening out there?" said a man.

Tyun and Nicephorus froze.

The girl stared down at them balefully.

Then she called out to her father, "I'm just talking to the angels."

Nicephorus, panicked, half-rose from the stool, ready to run.

"They ready to fly me to Paphlagonia?"

The girl said, "They're helping me with Piggly-Goat."

"Okay, honey duchess," said the father, and they heard him walk away.

The girl pointed at the pail.

The angel Nicephorus turned back to his work.

. . .

A half an hour later, Tyun and Nicephorus were making their way through sheep.

"We don't deserve escape," said the monk heavily.

"Don't be drab. That fucking goat," said Tyun, slightly limping. "My shin is bleeding. My skin is coming off in a scroll."

Sheep bumbled all around them on the plain. The night crickets were sawing in the grass.

The monk said, "We went in with deception on our lips and swords in our hands. 'He has scattered the proud in the imaginations of their hearts.'" He looked bleakly out across the dim plain where search parties and thieves stumbled in circles in search of each other. "And there is no healing balm. There are no sacred bones."

"There's a balm. You drank it. And there are bones. Trust me. They're just better hidden. And remember, I didn't want to go with swords in our hands. That was the fucking Factor. I wanted to go in at midnight with ropes, pulleys, a ladder, a bag of sand, a small turtle, a candle, a brass hand, and the sticky wood of the *dihq* tree."

Nicephorus swatted him on the chest.

Tyun was about to complain when he saw where Nicephorus pointed.

Standing on the horizon were four horsemen, black against the night. On a rise, they surveyed the valley.

"Down," Nicephorus whispered.

The monk and Tyun sank amidst the sheep.

Restive, worried, the sheep shifted. Tyun and Nicephorus crawled with them.

The horsemen were armed. Nicephorus could not make out the weapons, but along the rims of the mounted bodies there were projections, spikes.

The monk and the saint hunter stayed low and wormed along the ground.

Legs a forest by their heads. "Like Odysseus and the Cyclopes," said Nicephorus.

"Why would you say that right now? Why do I need that information? Are they watching us?"

"I can't see."

"Good. Stay still."

They paused, breathing heavily.

Nicephorus was not used to danger. He had known it previously only when the Normans had taken Bari, stalking through the streets, and the monks of St. Benedict had clustered in their sanctuary, waiting for the conquerors to make their determination about whether the chalice and paten and pyx were worth the curse of homicide and theft—whether fire and the sword were necessary to bring the holy order and its house into submission.

Five minutes passed. Maybe ten. Nicephorus's elbows dug gradually into the sod.

He had the awful desire to shout. To end danger and deception with something clean and truthful and loud. To bring everything down on their heads.

He started to lift his head—just as a lookout, just to see.

Tyun reached out and put his hand on the monk's tonsure. He held the monk's head down in warning.

There was something strange in the pressure of that hand on his stubbled scalp. Nicephorus turned to look at the saint hunter; as he turned his head, the hand, immobile, slid, and so was on his cheek.

The monk found Tyun staring at him as if more frightened of him than of the four horsemen upon the horizon. Tyun's hand pressed hard against his face, affirming.

They remained that way for a time unknown. This triangle: the bristling figures on the knoll, the monk, and the treasure hunter—treasure hunter and monk on hands and knees except for the one hand that rested upon a face in a gesture that had ceased movement—an ancient bas-relief depicting a Hittite rite of worship now forgotten, but once filled with deep significance.

They crouched together amidst the flock.

Nicephorus could not stand the touch of the hand upon him anymore. It was too desired to be welcome. The need to break the silence grew in him. It would be a relief to scream. Scatter the sheep. An end to all uncertainty. *We are poised precariously,* he thought, *as a spinning knife on a table edge.* Sometime it must fall.

The crickets counted off the seconds as they had done since the beginning of the world.

Then Nicephorus twitched: "A-ya!" said a voice. And at that, the figure—triangle—the men on the ridge, Tyun on his knees, Nicephorus blessed—was broken. The secret couldn't be kept; their presence couldn't be hidden.

The four horsemen were making their way through the flock, pointing at the interlopers.

Rollo de Bailleul was irate that in their escape from the basilica, the Thunderer in High Heaven had somehow stuck him with the Venetian brat and two of the little shit's northern Longobardian guardsmen. They were ducking through derelict farms. The whole area had clearly taken the brunt of the Turkmen attack the year before: houses were deserted and the doors torn off their straps. Weeds were growing out of feed piles.

"Over this hill and I think we should see Myra," said Rollo de Bailleul. "We'll skirt the western edge of the town. Find the river. Follow it downstream to the harbor."

"Woe to anyone who tries to stop us," said Matteo Tradonico, and flicked his sword against the bared belly of the night.

"Mmm. Woe," said Rollo de Bailleul. He started to plod up the hill. The moon was now bright enough that he could see that the large mass on their right was an old watchtower, blackened with recent flame, striped with courses of brick and stone.

"Have you ever exiled anyone?" Matteo said. "I've exiled three." They climbed between jagged spurs of karst. When there was no answer to his question, Matteo tried, "I hold audiences behind a mask. I just sit there and don't speak for a while, when people come to ask about mercy or alms or Dalmatia or something. That gets them frightened. If you just look at them. It's something I've learned to do." The Factor's silence dissatisfied him. He said, "I arranged a marriage for Tarquino Contarini. Do you know who he is? The Contarini heir. One of the Apostolic Families. I set up a marriage for him with this woman from Genoa by writing letters and sending horsemen. I guess you could say I play a pretty important part in the whole Republic. I guess you could say that."

The Factor had frozen. He held out a blocky hand. He gestured at the tower above them.

There was a watchman standing up on the battlements, peering down.

The Factor hissed, "Manned."

Matteo Tradonico crouched. "Did he see us?" To his guards, he said, "Freeze."

They stood stock-still. It was too dark to see the face of the watchman in the tower.

"Byzantine or Turk?" the Venetian boy wondered.

Rollo said, "Good chance a Turk will turn us over to the Myrans anyway."

"He hasn't called out," whispered Matteo. "To summon anyone."

Rollo could hear the Venetian kid's hot breath. He considered whether he should kill the little shit. It would be easier to make it back to the harbor alive alone. No one back in the lagoons of Venice would ever know. The deed would be put down to the infidel.

The problem was the guards. He couldn't take on all three of them at once, boy and two soldiers. He wondered if there was discontent. He could offer a couple of good posts back in the governor's palace in Bari.

Enemy territory. This was a rare instance where to be one man was better than a force.

He suspected the Venetian's two guards, at least, were thinking the same about him—rival of their lord, untrustworthy, unnecessary.

The four of them stood without moving under the moon on that rocky hillside in the shadow of an outcropping, each doubtless contemplating the murder of the others, watched over from above, all of them, by the figure in the scalded tower.

Rollo had a son the Venetian's age. He was off in Sicily, training in arms. A better boy. Wide-shouldered, brave. Hungry but, unlike this mooning puppy, silent. Right now, battered by the flats of blades, hammered by his peers so his iron would be true. Shaped in the forge of youth. His mother would cry when she saw him next.

Rollo did not know if he could kill the Venetian boy without guilt, given the similarity of age and station, though the distance between this meeping cub and his own son was so great that their similarities just made him despise Matteo Tradonico even more.

No action, though, was possible, no movement, just the guilt-wracked questions while the black shape peered down from the tower.

The watchman shifted, suspicious that something hid in the lee of the rocks.

The crickets trilled in awful fullness. A demand, an order from the thick night itself: *Move. Do your violence. We are all waiting.*

The patrician boy's breath was coming faster now. He was frightened. Rollo wished to kill him with just a quick jab. To be free of this lumbering presence.

He carefully looked upward at the figure on the tower.

There was no way they would all four make it back to the harbor if they were together. Something had to be done. If the archer on the turret would take down one of Tradonico's guards, Rollo could risk an attack on the other.

The moon had moved since they had stalled. Strange how something that seemed so fixed could shift so quickly while men stood motionless on the turf below. The shadow of their outcropping was fleeing inch by inch. Their legs were now in blue.

The head of the figure swiveled. The watchman faced them directly. They were seen. There was no question.

The silence was acute now. None of them moved, but each waited for the others—the black figure above them waiting too, acknowledging roles of predator and prey—and all knew that it was the time to strike, that there would be a shout, arrows nocked.

And then, at nothing—at no obvious cue—the boy Matteo released a loud wail, enraged or desperate, it wasn't clear. It rose, keening, clean and awful, in the night. Rollo hurled himself toward the boy, to cover his mouth, but Matteo swerved away from him, pivoting, as if the warrior in the boy's limbs was separate from whatever child in him yowled.

Rollo looked to the tower.

As they all peered upward in horror, they saw the watchman's head quiver at the cry of the Venetian child. Startled, it lifted off the warchman's shoulders, the whole skull kicking free, and flew.

Rollo hissed.

The head winged its way out toward the pine and cedar forests on the hills, crying as it flew.

A guardsman touched his face and breast and said the names of Holy Mother, Father, Son, and Spirit.

"Fucking owl!" the princeling swore. He yelled after the bird, full voice, "I'm going to hack the shit out of you! If I can, if I can—"

"Quiet!" growled Rollo and smacked the child hard enough to send him sprawling against the outcropping.

The two soldiers were on either side of him immediately, swords out, ready to kill. Matteo was crawling to his feet, holding the back of his skull. Rollo could not fight all of them. They waited for commands.

"Let's walk," he said, to assume continuity of mission. "Still three miles left over enemy ground."

Matteo watched the Norman turn. They climbed the hill.

Matteo kept watching.

The four horsemen parted the sea of sheep and trotted toward monk and thief. The wool was silver under the moon.

"Turks," said Nicephorus, so Tyun raised his hand and, in Turkish, called out a hello.

"You are who?" they called back.

"Looking for my donkey," said Tyun, pointing at a donkey trailing behind the four Turks. It was indeed the expedition's donkey. It still wore its saddlebags, though they were half uncinched and sagging to the side.

"Say 'donkey' again," one horseman demanded.

Tyun said, "Donkey."

"You're from Khurasan?"

"That is exceptional," said Tyun, putting his hands together. "Yes, I grew up in Khurasan."

"This is your donkey?" said another one.

"It is."

"These bags are yours?"

"They are."

"So the bones are yours."

"The bones," said Tyun, remembering the bones.

"What are they saying?" Nicephorus pressed.

Tyun translated, "They say the infidel priest should keep his mouth shut at this delicate juncture." Then, to the four horsemen, "Not originally."

The horsemen circled around them, the donkey trailing behind. The horsemen were apparently shepherds, but among the Turkish nomads in those troubled days, there was little distinction between shepherd and warrior; they were armed.

"You are the one who stole the bones of the *Aziz* Nikolaos."

"The Christians are looking for you," another said. "Very unhappy. They want to murder you."

The four horsemen watched him closely. They had their hands upon their hilts.

Tyun weighed his options. Beside him, Nicephorus stood defiantly, expecting martyrdom.

"The Christians are looking for me," Tyun admitted. "But you found me. God has smiled upon you. I don't know what good deeds you have done today, but now your reward is here." The thief smiled widely and spread his arms. He exclaimed, "You can kiss the blessèd skull!"

"Ah!" said one of the horsemen.

"This man Nicholas—very holy. You've heard. Now you can press your lips to the forehead. This infidel priest will say the sacred words—that's why I drag him around with me. You will be protected from everything, every illness, every cough, every broken bone, all catarrh, mumps, for at least a year. And here is the thing: All I ask is that you give us something to eat, some water, and safe passage back to the docks. God Most High does not wish any payment for the sweet manna of miracles. No silver or treacherous gold. Only one night's hospitality."

The four horsemen considered. "Our friends can kiss the skull too?"

Tyun pressed his hands together. "Bless you for spreading the blessings."

A horseman shrugged his assent. "They are eating a sheep over there." He pointed.

"I thought I smelled it on the wind!" said Tyun, delighted.

Three of the horsemen led the monk and the thief and the donkey over the hill and into the broom.

One stayed behind to watch the flock.

"Where are they taking us?" Nicephorus asked.

Tyun said, "Mutton."

So: shepherds abiding in the fields, watching over their flocks by night.

Tyun was thrilled. The evening was really turning around.

Ten Turkmen settlers, servants of the Seljuks, were eating around a bonfire. They had slaughtered a sheep, stuffed its skin with the meat, and buried it in the coals some hours before. Now the juices were rich and the flesh had simmered and was soft and yielding and the air smelled of onions and fat.

"They are serving us supper?" said Nicephorus. "It smells delicious."

"It has been cooked in its own skin," said Tyun, "as we all are, eventually. Perhaps before we begin, you could say a quick grace in Latin?"

Nicephorus bowed his head before the assembled and gave thanks to the Lord Most High for the banquet laid before them, though he faltered a bit at the *"et in saecula saeculorum,"*

when he noticed that Tyun had ransacked the donkey's saddlebags, taken out the old skull they'd been planning to use to
trick the Venetians, and was holding it with both hands high
above his head, eyes closed in reverence.

Then, for some reason, the shepherds, chuckling and prodding each other, daring each other, approached one by one
and kissed the dusty pate.

"I see," said Nicephorus.

"Eat up," said Tyun.

"Will this actually help aches?" asked an old skeptic with
tired braids, pointing at the skull he'd just kissed.

"Who knows," Tyun admitted. "Christians."

The skeptic laughed. Few teeth.

They were given mutton and dry *yufka,* and they sat by the
fire. And while they ate, a shepherd played on the two-string
lute, and they asked Tyun questions about Khurasan, and they
bitched about their Seljuk overlords. Then they passed around
the *kimiz* and all drank until an old duffer called for a dance.

Soon they were doing a circle dance with a lot of stomping in time with a drum, and the rhythms were giddy, and
they asked Tyun and his pet unbeliever to join in. Tyun drew
the monk up by the hand and the two of them tried to follow the steps of their hosts, though Nicephorus explained
he had of course not danced since his novitiate. An old man
spun between them and galloped off, snaking his arms in the
air and trembling his fingers. The lutenist strummed and
thumped upon the dutar's chubby belly. The shepherds went
in circles, faster and faster, and paused and made signs as if
they shot a bow at the sun and then squatted and kicked out
their legs.

Nicephorus was surprisingly good at kicking out his legs.
He got low to the ground. They all applauded him. He could
not help smiling.

Then the circle all joined hands in a woven ring, so Nicephorus found himself holding hands not with the treasure hunter,
who danced beside him (joyous and intoxicated eyes), but with
the next man along, the old skeptic with a sly look and dry,
splintered braids. And yet his arm nuzzled his friend's body as
the circle stomped around the fire—and they bowed, and they
kicked—and the ring of shepherds raised their clasped hands
and dropped them, describing a protective circle, a charm of
mutual balance and reliance, as if to say: *Chance—Fortune—you
cannot throw us over.*

Under the moon and the circumscribed dome of heaven
they spun, their arms across each other's chests.

The dancing was over, except one old man who promenaded in
the dust. The drummer had stopped drumming. He was singing a long, sad, quavering song about how sweet it had been
in the old grasslands, chasing gazelles with eyes like almonds.
The lutenist played slow, wandering figures and watched the
other shepherds fall asleep by the flames.

"When I am old," said Nicephorus, "I want to be like that
man. There's something in him that still remembers youth."
The old man shuffled and turned in his dance, and though
there was no strength in his kick, there was the comfort of
eighty years spent in a familiar body. "Of course," said Nicephorus, "I won't be dancing. My Order doesn't allow it."

"You danced just now."

"I was dancing for survival."

"You are a strange one," said Tyun. "Like the blessed Abu
Bakr praying, 'Make the world wide for me, O God, and then
give me the strength to reject it.'"

"That is right, I guess," said Nicephorus, chastened.

Tyun fiddled absently with the wax that had sealed the

bottle of St. Nicholas's oil. He said, "I'm surprised to find that you are actually entertaining."

"I think I am."

The old man had left the circle of firelight, walking off into the scrub to piss.

"You enjoy things like this."

"People dwelling together in friendship."

"I wish you could see New Year in Nishapur," said Tyun. "It's fantastic. People dance in the streets in masks, disguised as goats and deer, and everyone burns lamps in the houses and bonfires in the streets. People sprinkle water on each other to wash off the dust of the last year. Kids make fake brides out of old crap and put them on the roofs and play flutes for them."

"You wish I could see it?" Nicephorus smiled at Tyun.

"It's a wonderful party. A great time for pickpockets." After the joke, he frowned. "My master's maxim: 'Wherever there's joy, it's a good place for pickpockets.'" He jabbed his thumb into the wax.

"Do you miss him?"

"Miss him?" said Tyun incredulously. "I hated the fucker. He was mean, stingy, cunning . . . We'd be there in the crowds, and he'd be telling me to steal things from people who were just . . . singing or laughing or swinging their kids by the arms. Even when I made him money, he never gave me a single dirham. He never fed me. I had to actually steal food *from him*. The crap he used to make me do. Crawling through windows. Throwing poisoned meat to guard dogs. And if I didn't do it, he'd slap me around. He was twice my size. I couldn't fight back. I hated him."

"How long were you with him?"

"Until I killed him," Tyun said. He rolled the wax into a ball between his palms.

"Yesterday you and Reprobus told me he was dismembered by a cherub."

"What?" Tyun looked at the monk with barely concealed pity. "That was yesterday."

"I didn't know."

"I was with him for five or six years. I have no real idea. Just a blur of thefts and embarrassing grift. I'm his son, his nephew, a thief he's just caught. Then I'm hiding in a well in a courtyard for five hours. I'm climbing up on a roof and I'm shivering with cold. I'm watching other kids play and he's whispering to me that I need to befriend them so I can get inside the house and slip the family's prized Changsha teapot into my sleeve. Then spend the night hiding in a midden pit. 'Go on, play with them.' I hated the fucker.

"I broke that teapot, by the way. I fell. It was as thin as paper. He beat the living crap out of me. I couldn't do grift work for a week because of all the cuts and bruises. It made people suspicious."

Nicephorus wished to say Tyun's name, to put his hand upon his wrist, but he knew it would just irritate him.

"The end of it . . . Listen to this, man of many sorrows. Some small-time wazir paid him for an act, an entertainment for some guests. Me and a girl. I was twelve or thirteen. After a banquet, after the sweets were served."

"Tyun. That's hell."

Tyun smiled faintly. "Don't worry. It didn't happen." He tossed the wax up into the air and caught it. "I couldn't." Tyun realized that he had meant to play the story for rough humor to shock the monk, the usual bullshit, something about size, but he found he could not. In that moment, he thought of Syrian apples and Basra peaches and the peeled pistachios the company had laid out before them—fingers, their mouths. Tipping back their heads to sip sweet rosewater cordial. Smiling lips, old men scratching white beards. They all washed their hands in succession and waited for the performance.

While he negotiated how to land the anecdote gracefully,

he threw the wax again and grabbed it. Nothing presented itself. He said, "I was in front of them all." He shrugged. "They served Syrian apples and Basra peaches and sweetmeats made of honey and wasps. I . . . under other circumstances . . . it wasn't . . ." He groped for a joke.

"Tyun," said Nicephorus. "No. Don't."

"He beat me for that failure, too. And that night, while we were guests in the wazir's palace, my master told me he wanted me to slit the wazir's throat while he stole the platters and the golden ewer and the basin the guests had washed their hands in. I told him I'd never kill. He said, 'Don't you hate him? He's the one who hired you. Then he laughed right at you. The whole room. They all laughed at you. Doesn't that make you angry?'" Tyun sat forward, putting his elbows on his knees. "So I agreed. I agreed to kill the wazir and we both went to sleep for a few hours, and when I saw my master was really asleep I got up and took my knife and held it to his throat. He woke up and started to talk to me gently about how we were about to be rich, so rich we'd never have to steal again, and there would be lamb tail and sweets for me every night. And I told him I was going to kill him."

"What did he say to that?"

"He said, 'You aren't a killer, Tyun. You'll never be a killer.' He smiled at me. I thought it was loving, as if to say, 'You're still a sweet kid after everything I've taught you.' But it wasn't. He was mocking me. He said, 'You're not a survivor, Tyun.' So I said, 'You don't think I'll kill you?' and he said, 'No, Tyun, you can't. It's a power I have over you.' And I said, 'I can,' and he said, 'You won't,' and so I showed him. I shoved the knife right into his throat. His eyes got wide and he started choking and bucking on the mat and blood and . . . I don't know. I got up and kicked his face and his ears for a long time. A long, long time. He cried out, but he couldn't make a normal sound.

It felt great. I kept kicking and kicking his skull until he was done moving.

"Then, just like he'd taught me, I jiggered the shutters and climbed out on the roof and shimmied down into the street, and by dawn I was a camel boy walking with a caravan to Merv."

The lutenist had fallen silent. The crickets were the only music, and the fire crackling, dying. Tyun shoved himself away from the monk. He was intent on the wax. Most of the shepherds were asleep.

"Tyun," said Nicephorus. "I talk now as I would talk to anyone, not just to someone who I . . ."

Tyun looked up at the silence. "Who you . . . ?"

Nicephorus began again. "I am sorry for that child. I wish I could speak to him."

Tyun frowned, tossing a little dust into the fire. He said softly, "He was fine. He worked, occasionally he still grifted, he made many good friends. Eventually he met a dog-man from the mountains of the east, and they decided to conquer the world together."

"Thank you for telling me."

Tyun shrugged. "You wanted to know."

Taptuk, the old skeptic, who'd been watching them, limped over and said, "You are chatty with the Byzantine."

"'Seek wisdom even amongst the unbelievers, as though it was a lost camel.' I would like to thank you not simply for the food, but for the music and for the dance, which have reminded me how to feel joy."

"'Cheerfulness is the marrow of friendship.' You should sleep now. Right by the fire, where you can be warm. You will have a difficult day tomorrow. Of course, in the morning we must turn you over to the Myrans."

Tyun sat up straight. "You can't be serious."

"They want their saint, and they'll give us trouble if they don't have it." Taptuk smiled kindly. "Plus, Azmat tells us there is a reward for the body."

"Ah! Aha!" Tyun exclaimed. "What if it's not *Aziz* Nikolaos? This skull? Not really?"

The skeptic did not change his smile. "By the waters of Zamzam! Then you will have lied to us, which would be a terrible sin and insult to us all."

He stomped and rolled on his bad foot back to his place, settled down by a log, and pulled his cap over his eyes.

"It seems," said Tyun to his friend, "that it's another evening for feigned sleep and giving people the slip."

An hour later, when the shepherds were all dozing, Tyun and Nicephorus got up and untied their donkey and were a full hill away before someone started to shout.

A mansion in the grasses. The remains of ancient pillars and pediments, now part of someone's decaying villa. An orchard had been burned. The trunks and muscled branches were dead-fingered and distressed.

"It is not long before they figure out which way we went," said Tyun. "They have horses." He raised his hand to knock on the villa's great gate. "Will you lie this once?"

Nicephorus offered, "I will remain silent."

"You can't remain silent." Tyun grabbed the monk's neck with one hand and, half-joking, strangled him. Half was not joking. "Look, you can say whatever the hell you want—speak the truth, even—but say it in Latin. Agreed?"

Tyun turned and knocked. It was a ghoulish haven: The windows and other entrances were blocked up haphazardly with brick, perhaps from when the Turks had arrived six months before. The door was surrounded by crosses roughly painted on the plaster.

Tyun squinted back at the road. "I think I hear hooves. Oh, come on." He hammered harder, then stepped discreetly behind Nicephorus.

"It is well past midnight," said Nicephorus. "Nobody may be awake."

But just as he spoke, a door opened in the gate and a servant stood there—a man maybe sixty, sarcastic of face, harried, round, and conspicuously armed. He said nothing. He simply stood there glaring at the two and their donkey.

Nicephorus felt a poke in his back. He said, in Latin, "Hail. I am Nicephorus. This is Tyun. We seek shelter from Turkmen riders."

The servant shook his head. He pointed at his own mouth. "Greek?" he said. He was a eunuch.

Tyun came forward, stooping and cringing, and said, "Yes, my master seeks shelter from the Turkmen horde." Apologetically: "Abbot Nicephorus is from Rome and cannot speak your tongue."

"Rome!"

"Papal Legate to Lycia."

"Papal Legate?" the eunuch asked the monk directly.

Dutifully, in Latin, Nicephorus told him, "I am the lowliest clerk of St. Benedict in Bari and my presence in your country is idiocy, sinful idiocy, and I wish I were back in my own cloister, praying at the altar."

"You're not really from the Pope," said the eunuch. He pointed. "A donkey."

"The Pope wishes his ambassadors to embrace a sublime humility," said Tyun.

"And you are—what?" The eunuch circled Tyun's steppe-nomad face with his finger.

"Relieved to serve so holy a master. You must have prayed hard today, since the Lord has directed St. Peter's own consecrated Legate right to your door."

"Have proof?" said the servant. "Of you?"

"A bull," said Tyun. "Signed by His Holiness. The Pope." He stumbled. Clearly he could not remember who was actually pope. "It is here."

Nicephorus turned incredulously to see where Tyun would pull a bull from.

The thief muttered, "A moment," and from the sleeve of his *qamis* drew forth a piece of parchment sealed in wax. Nicephorus recognized the written description of St. Nicholas's Basilica, bound shut by the dab of bottle wax Tyun had been thumbing by the fire. At some point in the evening, he'd pressed his nails into the wad to sketch a small but many-crowned papal tiara.

The thief brought the faux bull to his lips, kissed it, flashed the bogus papal seal, and stashed it again in his shirt before the servant's eyes could linger.

The servant looked perplexed. "The sisters know?"

"The sisters."

"The nuns."

"The nunnery!" said Tyun. "Then we've arrived. Letters were sent on before us. No? Ah. Perhaps marauders."

"They are everywhere."

"Including," said Tyun, pointing at the road, "behind us. Might the Legate step inside?"

"Welcome to the Nunnery of Saints Orestes and Episteme." The servant bowed to Nicephorus and let him pass. The donkey and the relic thief followed.

They were in a passage that led into a courtyard. As the servant led them to the stable, he said, now in hushed tones, "The sisters have been sequestered here in some disorder since—" he waved a hand at the outer world—"the barbarians."

Tyun said, "We apologize that you didn't receive the Legate's announcement of his tour."

"No worry," said the eunuch. "The sisters are prepared for guests." He pulled open the door to the stable.

They tied up the donkey and gave it hay.

The eunuch led them across the courtyard to a colonnade.

They came to two doors thrown wide open, and light within. They stood before a grand chamber, lit with many candles, walls painted with old pagan murals of gardens, nymphs, and herms. There sat six Byzantine nuns in an attitude of prayer. They all looked up. Their eyes were confused and unkind.

The servant bowed low. "Mother," he said, "new arrivals. The Papal Legate Nicephorus and his man."

The Abbess inspected the faces but did not move or speak. Small birds were flying around in the chamber, singing, upset by the candle flames.

"Abbot Nicephorus brings greetings from Rome."

The Abbess appeared unimpressed. She closed her eyes deeply and opened them again.

One of the lesser sisters said, "Mother is certain they are expected and a place shall be found for them on this night of nights."

Nicephorus felt a creeping in his scalp. He wondered, alarmed, *Expected?*

"I am glad she received word we were coming," said Tyun smoothly.

Nicephorus reached out subtly and pinched Tyun's arm hard in warning.

"To the guest chambers?" said the servant.

Like a serpent, the Mother Superior inclined her head once, dipping it low.

"This way," whispered the servant, and led them across the courtyard, up some steps, and into a bedchamber.

It was too large a room, mainly empty. There was a bed for the Legate and a mat for his man. One wall was built of faces:

the salvaged heads of old statues, *spolia*, one piled on another—marble, plaster, limestone, granite, all white, all glaring into the bedchamber. Fierce locks, sneers, aquiline profiles. They were emperors, kings, goddesses (both Roman and more ancient, more local, who'd hunted beneath the moon in the Taurus Mountains), senators, philanthropists, femmes fatales, Lycian patronesses, actors' masks in anguish. Their eyes were holes or blank marble, glaucous, staring.

The servant left them there. "The sisters will call for you when they're ready to speak, Legate." He closed the door behind himself, taking the candle with him.

They heard him lock the door before he shuffled off.

They were alone with the heads.

"Perfect," said Tyun, grinning. "Odd, but safe until tomorrow morning when they ask us questions we can't answer."

"Tyun, we cannot sleep."

"I can," said Tyun, climbing onto the bed, stretching out luxuriously, and starting to unwind his leggings. "The Legate of Saint Peter can take the mat."

The room was dark now except for a faint light coming in from a narrow window into the courtyard. It caught on marble cheeks and tousled hair.

"What?" said Tyun. "You want to sleep next to me? We can share the bed. I think that's Tiberius." He pointed at a massive face, bigger than the rest.

"Maybe it's better if I stay on the floor," said Nicephorus.

Tyun gazed at him in the half-light. "Do you think so?" he said. He reached out and took Nicephorus's wrist. Stiffly, the monk sat down on the mattress. He could feel the heat of the thief behind him.

The nuns began to chant. One called, the others responded. One droned.

Their voices were bright and light as crystal. The crickets added their own cantillation.

The monk and the thief remained like that: the monk, seated upright, the thief curled on the mattress, their bodies touching.

"This is not right," said the monk.

"What's wrong?" the thief whispered.

"Not you," said the monk. "It is no hour."

The thief rolled half-over. He made a noise of confusion.

"It is no liturgical hour. It is after Matins and not yet Lauds."

"I'm sorry . . . ?" said Tyun.

"There is no reason for them to be awake and chanting." Nicephorus listened. "There is no Office at this hour."

Tyun started to joke, but Nicephorus shushed him.

The monk said, "I know this chant. We do not sing it in Bari anymore." He asked the thief, "Do you know the story of Saint Kassiani? This is her best-beloved song."

"Is this the time for telling stories of saints? You could lie down instead."

"I cannot lie down," said Nicephorus. "There is something wrong here."

"They can sing whenever they want," said Tyun.

"Kassiani was a beautiful maiden. When she was a girl, her sharp wit embarrassed the Emperor of Byzantium. The story goes that once, in a lineup of possible brides, he saw her and said, 'Ah! Too bad that through women came all sin.' She snapped back, 'But from a woman came redemption, too.' Everyone was horrified that she'd spoken back. The Emperor fell in love with her on the spot. She confounded him by becoming a nun. Months went by, and he could not stop thinking of Kassiani and her clever tongue. I think she could not stop thinking of him, either. So she moved out of Constantinople to be farther away from him. She founded a nunnery to the West. They wrote letters to each other and argued about the sanctity of icons. She moved farther and farther off into the islands."

"Why, if they wanted each other?" asked Tyun, a dark shape on the bed. "I do not understand Christians."

"She had to move away, or the temptation would have been too great."

"This is a terrible love story."

"No. It's one of the most beautiful love stories I know. Years went by and they got older. The Emperor married someone else. Kassiani wrote hymns in her nunnery, some of the most famous of the Church in the East. She disagreed with him violently on matters of theology. He fined her nunnery. He still could not stop thinking of her. As he ruled, he could always feel her eyes on him across the mountains, across the Aegean.

"One day many years later, the Emperor was marching his army out on a campaign, and he realized that he would be passing within a few miles of Kassiani's convent. So he took his retinue and went to visit her.

"She was in her cell, writing music. Writing this hymn." Nicephorus pointed at the air, at the window, at the rapturous chanting of the nuns. "She was writing this hymn, and she heard the sound of many horses on the road. She heard the jingle of elaborate trappings and medallions, and she knew it must be the Emperor of Byzantium. He had finally come."

"Will this lead to fornication?"

"She got up from her desk and hid."

"Why?"

"You can tell the story however you want. Either because she despised the Emperor and wanted to avoid him—or because she desired him too much: too much and so she knew they should not meet. Perhaps both."

Tyun was now curled so close to Nicephorus that his breath stirred the sleeve of the monk's habit. "Why would you avoid someone you desired?" Tyun asked softly.

"The Emperor came into her cell. He could tell immediately that she was hiding behind the door. He saw her pen and ink on the desk and her half-written hymn. He went to the desk and read it. She watched him from behind the door. She saw him write one line in careful script. Then he straightened up, adjusted the imperial paludamentum on his shoulders, and walked away. He did not trouble her.

"When he had gone, she went to the desk and read what he had written: 'Eve hid herself when she heard His footsteps walking through the Garden in the cool of the morning.' Then Kassiani knew that he had seen her hiding in the room. But she did not erase his verse or scratch it out. She let it stand. It was a sign of his great love and respect for her that he had known she was concealed there, but did not acknowledge it. There could be no greater token of their bond than silence.

"Without speaking to her, the Emperor rode away with his retinue. She watched him go.

"They never saw each other again. Years passed and they died. There was just that one collaboration between them. Nuns still sing it to this day."

"That's your great love story. People who never touch each other."

"I can't tell it without my voice trembling."

"I think you should lie down."

Nicephorus looked at him. The thief lay in the dark, now straight upon the mattress, holding out his hand. Gently, Nicephorus said to Tyun, "After the story you just told me by the fire . . . ?"

Even in the shadows, Nicephorus could tell Tyun looked away from him. "I made it up," Tyun said. "Like everything else."

Each waited for the other. The hundred faces of marble and stone stared at them. The women sang the words of Kassiani: *"My night is an ecstasy of excess, gloomy and moonless, and full of sinful desire. You who gather the waters of the sea up into the clouds, bend down to me."*

The monk lifted his hand from his lap.

Tyun reached for him.

There was a ghastly wail.

The thief sat up. The monk ran to the narrow window.

They looked out into the courtyard: stone pithoi for storage, an olive press, hay, a dark portico. The moon. No motion.

"It's not coming from outside," said Nicephorus. He turned and saw eyes from the wall behind Tyun gleaming with faint light. The face was in agony. Nicephorus did not speak. With mouth agape, he pointed mutely.

Tyun turned, saw the glowing eyes in the wall. All the other faces were dark. The wail continued.

Tyun bared his teeth and drew his dagger.

It was the head of Medusa. The snakes were blunted with time.

"Tyun—" Nicephorus warned. "Statues can be invested with night wanderers. They can kill."

"Fuck that," said Tyun, and licked his thumb and made a sign of warding on his forehead. He crept closer and held the dagger blade to Medusa's stone throat. He squinted at her eyes. He stooped lower, put his eyes right up to hers. When he had peered into her head, he said to the monk, "Take an eye." He moved over.

Side by side, they squatted before the statue and looked in.

The eyes were holes drilled through the wall. It appeared the monk and the saint hunter had been placed in a room built for observation. Only, now they were peering back into the room beyond.

In that chamber was a candle, and by its light they saw something perplexing: a barbarian weeping. He was dressed roughly in furs and a loincloth. A Northman. He sagged against the plaster wall and sobbed, one shoulder covered with marten, raked. He was scrawny. He hid his face with his hand and his helmet slid around on his pate until he grabbed it.

It was not the crying of a normal sorrow, but something mortal, something that would never be healed.

"What's going on in this place?" Tyun whispered in a voice of awe. "What's wrong with him?"

"The standard," said Nicephorus.

Leaning against the wall in the barbarian's cell was a pennant colored white and blue.

"Those," said Nicephorus in confusion, "are the colors of the Varangian Guard. The *tagma* of Northerners who protect the imperial palaces in Constantinople."

"Why are they here?" whispered Tyun.

"Some mission?" Nicephorus wondered. "Sent especially by the Emperor?"

"To attack the Turks?"

"Or to negotiate with them?"

"Then why is he crying?"

The door in the Varangian's room opened, and the weeping standard-bearer backed away from it, fumbling his pennant.

The candle in the barbarian's chamber was blown out. The eyes of Medusa went dark. There were low voices. Whispers. Feet scraping along the floor.

Nicephorus and Tyun backed away from the peepholes.

"I do not like this," said Tyun.

"This is what I meant," said Nicephorus. "One other thing about the Hymn of Kassiani—"

Tyun looked at him in astonishment. "No! What? No! Shh!" The thief ran to the door. He rattled the latch. It was locked. They were locked in from the outside.

The chanting stopped. The crickets continued.

Out in the courtyard, a woman's voice called, *"It's time."*

The faces of a thousand years, emperors and gods, glared out from the wall, passive and fascinated.

· · ·

Rollo de Bailleul, Matteo Tradonico, and the two guards stood in the bushes near a road.

"I tell you," said Rollo. "It is this way."

"It is not." Matteo pointed to the left.

With relief, the Factor said, "Then here we part."

Matteo nodded, and they were about to continue on their separate ways when they heard slow, sad hooves, the creak of wheels.

They backed into the bushes to wait for a stranger to pass.

The Factor counted in lazy hoofbeats the moments until he could abandon the little Venetian shit to his fate.

He looked through the dry fronds.

It was one of the Guardians of Saint Nicholas leading a mule that pulled a two-wheeled cart. On the cart were six amphorae.

Matteo exclaimed, "Ha-*ha!*" He stepped out into the road. The Factor, still in the bushes, wished he had strangled the boy earlier.

Matteo Tradonico's guards, picking up on the cue, stepped out behind him.

The Guardian crossed himself and stumbled. The mule stopped.

"I am back, because I am sly as a serpent," said Matteo Tradonico. "A viper," he revised.

"There is nothing more that I can give you," said the Guardian.

Rollo de Bailleul stepped out onto the road. "Guardian," he said, "you can tell us where you are going in the dark of the night."

"I cannot," said the Guardian.

Matteo said to one of his soldiers, "Put your sword at his throat. When I say, cut."

The one soldier held the Guardian. The other applied the edge of his blade.

The Guardian clearly was struggling to smother fear in thoughts of the golden clouds of martyrdom, the winged faces greeting him, the divine hands applauding.

"You are going . . . ?" said Matteo.

"What are those amphorae?" said the Factor.

The Guardian said only, "Supplies."

Rollo de Bailleul walked back to the cart. He dug the cork out of a neck. Something pungent glugged out. He ran his hand under it and sniffed. "Olive oil and myrrh," he said. He stopped up the bottle.

"For cooking."

"No," said Rollo de Bailleul. He set his jaw. He made quick calculations. "You are going to run this oil through the actual sarcophagus of the Blessed Nicholas to sanctify it. Then you'll return with it to the basilica to replenish what we spilled. You have his body hidden in the hills somewhere."

"His body in death is more important than mine in life," said the Guardian defiantly, or meant to, except he became confused in the pronouns and said "than yours in mine in . . ." and did not finish at all.

Matteo Tradonico said, "Cut him."

The soldier looked to Rollo de Bailleul for approval. "Don't look at *him*," bitched Matteo. "Me. Here's my voice." He pointed at his own throat. "Cut him."

The soldier made a gentle slice, just enough to draw blood.

"So," said Matteo: "Where?"

The Guardian closed his eyes and began a prayer to Nicholas the Wonder Worker.

"Now!" said Matteo. "Does it look like I'm joking?"

But the deacon still prayed to his saint for intercession, lips mumbling supplications, as if the holy cope would be lowered from the sky and would draw him up; and the boy was angry, and so the boy said, "All right, kill him! Kill him!" And louder, to the soldier, *"Just kill him if he's going to do that."*

M. T. ANDERSON

"Don't kill him," said the Factor.

The monk's throat now bled quietly. He fell silent. His eyes were great with fear, and even under the moon, it was obvious his skin was green.

The soldier waited for clarification. The blade trembled stiffly against the man's taut neck.

Rollo de Bailleul stepped up beside the soldier, took his arm, and drew the sword away.

"Of *course* I did not really mean to *kill him yet!*" Matteo Tradonico screeched.

"Quiet yourself," said the Factor to the boy behind him.

"*You* will be quiet!" shouted Matteo Tradonico. "Face me!" he demanded. "*Face me!*" And in rage, he thrust his saber up and into the Factor's back, through his ribs, and the Barese Factor, Rollo de Bailleul, reached up to touch what passed through him, to find it real, and half spun. His head jolted and one leg kicked, and then he dropped to the ground. That quickly, it was over. His mouth was open in astonishment at his own death.

"Do you think I am *stupid?*" the Venetian shouted at the corpse of the Norman.

"Mary the Mother!" croaked a guard.

Matteo Tradonico was trying to get his sword out of the Norman. It was stuck between the ribs. He went to put his foot on the man's back for leverage, but he found he could only touch it with his toe. He pulled back, like a child from a cold bath.

"You *see?*" he bellowed at the monk. "You see I am . . . who I am? You see?" His whole body was trembling.

With effort, he planted his heel hard on the corpse of the Norman and yanked his saber free.

The Guardian was touching his forehead again and again in hectic prayer.

"Will you show us?" said Matteo Tradonico. "Will you show us where you've hidden Nicholas?"

The Guardian looked at the Venetian boy in fear. He whispered, "Yes."

Matteo goaded him angrily: "Now you will tell us? Why? Now that you know death is real? Wasn't there death a minute ago? What did you think? That there wasn't death? Wasn't there death an hour ago? Wasn't there death as soon as the world was born?"

In the janky cloister of Sts. Orestes and Episteme, Nicephorus and Tyun were trapped in the chamber of a thousand faces. Tyun kicked at the door, then knelt down, peering through the joints of the thumb latch. It was too dark to see.

Nicephorus was at the window.

There were shouts in a rough language he did not know. Something Nordic, harsh as the scrape of a blade across ice. Men calling to each other. There was a terrible banging with fists on doors.

The nuns of Orestes and Episteme had processed out of their ceremonial chamber and stood in two rows in their courtyard. "Get the sacred things," said the Mother. "Then we will close ourselves in the great room and put ourselves in God's hands."

The nuns filed swiftly off through a door on the far side of the courtyard. They returned shortly after with cups and crosses and an icon of Mary so large it had to be carried under an arm. They retreated into their great room, and the doors closed.

There was a loud shout, a bellowing of warriors, a hammering and slamming of doors, as if the gates to the nunnery were being battered down.

"What are we witnessing?" Tyun said. He realized, "They must be coming for us. The Turks. We've got to get out of here."

"It's not Turks," insisted Nicephorus, but Tyun had already smashed so hard into the plank door with his shoulder that the doorframe came away from the plaster. "Come on," he said, and together, they pulled the cracked frame away from the wall. They ditched the door. They were out in the corridor and running down the stairs.

Tyun said, "We can claim sanctuary, right? That's a thing Christians do?"

"It depends . . ."

"You talk a lot. I want to hear 'Yes.'"

But they stopped short. They were still in the darkness of a doorway that led out into the courtyard.

"They're in," said Tyun. "The man we saw through the Gorgon's eyes must have let them in. The standard-bearer."

Tyun wondered at the tears, the sobbing; but there was no time for thought. The Varangian Guard was in the courtyard. They stalked across the pavement, brutal and armed with axes and short swords. They were half-naked, smeared with pig grease. As they progressed, they made a terrible roaring and clamor, beating their weapons against walls and doors, hammering the butts of spears on the flagstones. Their leader— apparently—he had a sash bound across his chest and ribbons on his *Spangenhelm*—howled something in his sleet-drenched tongue. He walked to the double doors of the nunnery's great dining chamber and threw them open.

Inside was light and warmth. The nuns all were on their knees around the sacred furnishings: the silver cross, the icon, the cups and sacred trinkets. The little birds flew between the rafters, singing in sweet panic.

"Tyun!"

"What?"

"The barbarians did not break in," hissed Nicephorus, pointing to the closed doors to the compound, still locked fast with a crossbolt. *"They were already in the nunnery."*

The Varangians trod forward slowly, murderous intensity to their open mouths and swinging blades. Their faces were painted, like ghosts of the Gauls who once had ravished Rome.

Before Nicephorus could stop him, Tyun was darting forward, knife drawn.

"No! Tyun!" said Nicephorus. "You don't—"

Tyun padded swiftly and silently as a panther and then he was among the barbarians, swinging his dagger.

The barbarian nearest him screamed and backed away. They all did.

Tyun stood among them, legs spread wide, ready to strike.

Tyun lunged. Surprise—that was his element. He was under-armed.

The closest barbarian parried with a hide shield but instead of striking back shrieked and tried to stow his sword behind him.

Tyun bore down on the man ruthlessly, ready to feint and then gouge.

"A coward?" he said. "Will you fight?"

He sliced at the man, who bled and squealed, backed away.

Tyun looked at the others. They had formed a wide, wide ring around him. All of them looked terrified: gaping, white-eyed, in their woad.

"Not one of you?" he said, defiantly. "Throw me a sword and I will fight you all!"

The tallest and chubbiest of the invaders cried out, in perfect Greek, "Whose is he?"

The eunuch came from the corner of the courtyard and said, "He came with the Papal Legate." The man pointed at Nicephorus, still lurking in the shadows.

"Whose is the Papal Legate?" the Abbess of Sts. Orestes and Episteme demanded. "Charikles? Is he yours?"

"He is from Rome," said Tyun, dazed, still hoping to keep up a pretense. "From the Pope in Rome."

"Tyun," said Nicephorus, coming forward. "This is not an assault."

The chieftain of the Varangians pointed at the Abbess and said, "That is my wife."

She said, "I am Eirene."

Tyun looked around at the assailants. Well-fed men, late in their middle years, not one of them battle ready: some with bellies, others bellies but scrawny. Not warriors at all.

"We have been holed up here together since the Turks came," said one of the other men. "We hardly ever go out. We just send the servants."

"What? You—?"

Nicephorus offered, "They create their own diversions."

Tyun looked at the crowd in astonishment, maybe even disgust. He wobbled his knife around to indicate both invaders and nuns. "So this was going to end in a clench? On the cushions. Sweetmeats. The habits come off . . . ?"

"It should at least," said the gaunt Varangian standard-bearer with tear tracks through his battle paint, still snuffling and crying, "be our own dear nun who embraces us, instead of her lusting for Michael."

He cast his eyes at one of the huddled sisters and mouthed her name, but she would not look him in the face.

"She asked for me," said Michael, chief of the Varangians. "A man can't help it."

"Get the donkey," said Tyun in irritation. He went over to Michael, grabbed the man's wrist, and squeezed. Michael dropped his sword. Tyun plucked it up from the ground. He said, "Scabbard."

Nicephorus was untying the donkey. The donkey did not want to leave his fodder.

"We will wish you all a good and pleasant night of revelry," said Tyun, settling the sheathed sword on his hip.

The Abbess Eirene said, "You could stay. In a fur girdle you would look a very Avar."

Tyun gritted his teeth and turned away. Nicephorus yanked the donkey out into the yard.

There was a thunderous knock upon the gate. As the servant went to answer the knock, Eirene yelled at him, "Why did you let these two in?"

"They showed me a fake Papal Bull, ma'am. It was an ecclesiastical evening. Who but a guest of yours would trump up a—?" The banging on the gate persisted. The eunuch marched to answer it, grumbling, "Doubtless the Patriarch of fucking Constantinople."

The tear-stained barbarian lamented, "All sacred division of rank, degree, and station are in sick disorder since the Turks came. No one knows their master."

Myrans entered through the gate. At their head, the paterfamilias who had recognized the League of St. Nicholas earlier. He was now dressed for combat in corselet and helm. He announced to everyone in the courtyard, "Citizens! Excellent that you are armed! Join the hunt! Thieves have stolen the body of the Blessed Nicholas from the basilica!" Luckily, in the shadows of night, in the welter of strange costume, he did not at first notice the monk or the saint hunter.

The man called Michael—plush, even in his dangling dress-up furs—said, "They have not. The body of the Blessed Nicholas is not in the basilica. It's safe, hidden in the necropolis." He pointed vaguely in a direction. "The Guardians removed it when the Turks came, so the infidel could not practice an outrage upon it."

"The remains are in the necropolis? We have seen the thieves, though . . ." said the paterfamilias.

"John—the relics are just down the road. They're safe."

"The thieves broke open the Wonder Worker's tomb. There were thirty of them. They've scattered into the fields."

"There was nothing to steal in the basilica but oil," said

Michael, in some irritation. "I am telling you, the Guardians moved the body half a year ago, when the Turks were first sighted in the mountains."

Tyun, head down to hide his face, was quietly pulling something out of the donkey's saddlebags: the votive candle he'd made in the dark of the morning, marked with a cross and Chi-Ro. He whispered to Nicephorus. "We are going to light a candle in prayer for our safe passage. Fix the gate in your mind and run for it."

Boldly, he walked right for the eunuch with the torch.

"That!" cried the paterfamilias, pointing his blade at Tyun.

Tyun had reached the eunuch's torch and lit the candle in his hands.

The flame bobbed on top of the candle. It flared.

Tyun tossed the candle at the new arrivals, and when it hit the cobbles and rolled, he sprinted for the gate. Behind him, Nicephorus dragged at the reluctant donkey's bridle. Not reluctant long: as the candle began to bellow huge clouds of smoke, the donkey lunged forward, startled.

Yellow smoke. Gouts spewed out as the wick hissed. There was great confusion in the courtyard: men running, men coughing, men choking, women shouting orders, weekend barbarians slamming into the city militia. Nuns grabbing swords. Mourners with javelins. The eunuch valet laughing crying.

"Hah!" Tyun shouted to Nicephorus as they stumbled out of the gate. "To the ship!"

They pelted down the road, the donkey going faster than either of them.

"Is this the way to the harbor?" Nicephorus said doubtfully.

"No," Tyun said, sotto voce. "Of course not. It's where he pointed to the necropolis."

"Oh, Tyun. Nicholas does not want us to remove him. He belongs to Myra. It would be theft." He panted from exertion. "Kidnapping."

"You don't have to come with me."

Nicephorus looked behind him at the mansion in the burned orchard on the darkling plain. Yellow smoke rose out of the courtyard.

The two of them and their donkey ran together toward the necropolis.

Reprobus greeted each straggler with water and hard paximata to eat.

Pirates and Norman guards sat in various attitudes of defeat. The Venetians who had escaped returned to their own ship. Musarat and Tornik huddled under his old horse blanket together.

Reprobus had questioned each returning soldier and thief. The count was this: six of the rank and file had definitely been captured. All the leaders of the expedition were missing, out in the chaos of the night and the plain and the foothills of the grim Taurus Mountains: Tradonico and two of his personal guard; Barese Factor Rollo de Bailleul; Tyun himself, almost certainly caught, probably killed, last seen charging *into* the scrum of the basilica; and Nicephorus, the dreamer, weak and noncombatant, doubtless beaten to a pulp shrieking Latin prayers for mercy.

Gunnlaug in her bonds commented loudly, "It is not surprise, failure for you, dog-man. You thieves are weak and stupid. Your master is idiot."

"Muffle her," Reprobus told the Merv brothers.

He stood on the prow, looking up the river toward the black hills. It would be dawn soon.

To worry, for a dog, is to wrestle a thing clutched in the teeth, unable to let it go. When he was young and his mother and father returned to the village after a successful hunt or a skirmish against the demigods of the mountains, victory was embodied by worrying the tripe of the victim. The face, the tongue, the brain belonged to the great hunters; the flanks to those who'd coursed along with them through the snow. For the children: the numbles, the intestines, the tripe; and so this is what celebration became for Reprobus when he was young: tearing at the spongy stomach of the yak with the rest of the litter as his mother smiled from the high table and the pack was a unity. The disunion of the prey, torn apart (hooves, heart, haunches), was a sign of singleness of purpose, community luxuriating in their coordination. Small Reprobus ate the tripe in wonder at the impossible inversion: that you could eat a stomach, that a stomach could be in your stomach. As the litter fretted the tripe, the tissue pulled apart into a lacework, and that which was a bag became holed, swallowed, held. The kelpy texture, which he knew others disliked (Tyun, for example, could not stomach a stomach), still spoke to him of victory and his mother beaming and the whole pack of children tumbling over each other to feast together.

And now, looking out upon the hills and worrying, fretting, thinking of his beloved friend Tyun captured and all the others dispersed through the rocky hills, Reprobus recalled tripe pulled to ribbons, the tissue which should be whole now yanked into shreds and spread across the stones, muddied by paws; and the company of relic thieves appeared like this to him, scattered, tenuous; for the victory feast of one creature, he knew well, was always the corpse of another.

A Roman amphitheater stood, stark, alone, and white as bone, at the edge of the black foothills. It had risen out of the plain, step by step, for almost a thousand years.

Tyun and Nicephorus were exhausted. They wandered past its great arches, the vomitoria that had once spewed out fans. Once the site of noise and action, its abandonment now was total. It felt like the last human building still standing at the end of time.

Nicephorus could imagine the seats filled with a city's people, all watching some Senecan tragedy. Gestures with the wrist, platitudes of sorrow in metrical verse, messengers reciting spectacles too awful to witness. Then, two hundred years later, when the empire of old Rome was bloated and falling to pieces and a miasma of desperation invaded the provinces, gruesome combat games held there on the whited stage, the animals led forth to fight and bleed, the men with trident or gladius savaged before the eyes of betting citizens. Don't sit in the front row unless you want to get wet.

Now silent as if there had never been sound.

They lifted their eyes to the hills above, Tyun and Nicephorus, and saw the necropolis. The tombs surrounded the amphitheater, carved right into the limestone crags of the cliff a millennium and a half before. Doorways, pillared porticoes, huts of stone projecting out of the rock, piled haphazardly, one on top of the other.

"Which one?" said Tyun, taking in the full scope of the valley wall with all its beetling tombs.

They tied up the donkey, lit an oil lamp from the saddlebags, and began checking the mausoleums one by one.

Many had no doors. No one had been laid to rest in them for thirteen hundred years. A few had only the twelve faceless gods of ancient Lycia, hunter gods, carved on their walls. The interiors were just rough caves. Occasionally there was an empty, smashed sarcophagus. "Sarcophagus" means "eater of flesh": limestone devours the body quickly.

Other tombs had been used again more recently by Myra's rich and honored. They had doors of brass or of wood embossed with crosses. "Nicholas is in one of these," Tyun said, rattling a handle. "We'll come back to them. There are only six shapes to Byzantine keys."

In the dark of one tomb, Nicephorus reached out his hand and put it on Tyun's shoulder. The saint hunter turned, his eyebrows stark in lamplight.

"What is it?" said Tyun, alarmed.

Nicephorus quieted himself and shook his head. He did not know how to answer. He had touched Tyun simply because he'd discovered his hand reaching out. The shoulder was better than the cheek, less obtrusive. Comrades in adventure.

"Yes?" Tyun waited.

Nicephorus strained in the silence.

When there was no explanation, Tyun turned back to their task, examining the socket of the tomb. "Oh," he said, stepping over a fallen entablature. "How did you know the attack on the nuns was a party game? Smart boy."

Nicephorus dropped his hand. "A feeling. Also, the Hymn of Kassiani speaks in the voice of Mary Magdalene, who walked the streets. It has been taken up as an anthem by devout prostitutes. It declares them holy in the eyes of God. Prostitutes or, I suppose, wives who are set on sinning."

Tyun's faint smile shimmered in the flame. "You are also set on sinning."

"I did not say it in judgment. We all want to sin. It is the only way we have of knowing the full measure of creation."

"God wants you to sin," Tyun argued. "It will make his evenings livelier."

Tyun left the mausoleum. Over the door was carved a harpy carrying a squeamish soul to Rhadamanthus, judge of the dead.

"Back!" he suddenly hissed, and stepped away from the entrance, handing Nicephorus the lamp.

"What is it?"

"A cart with some . . . It's Matteo Tradonico. And three . . . no, two guards, one Guardian."

The four small figures led the donkey up a cart path between the tombs, the empty doors and desolate sockets and weathered porticoes that dotted the steep cliffside, the city of the dead.

"We've got the bastards," said Tyun. "Put out the lamp. Let's crawl."

The procession to the tomb of Saint Nicholas was glum and silent. The Guardian had a strong suspicion he would be discarded once he was no longer of use. He told himself he would alert Myra somehow. He would fight in the last moments. But he was keenly aware that so far, he had only sniveled and then complied. He had brought them here, the sanctum sanctorum. He prayed God would not condemn him for weakness. He asked for forgiveness in advance.

He was not sure that the vast, engulfing ocean of God's mercy would actually extend to someone who betrayed a saint and a city to protect his own life. The waves, he feared, were roiling.

Halfway up the sheer hillside, they reached an old tomb that had been given a new door. Above the tomb was a giant cross of wood casting a blue shadow across the cliff face. "We are here," said the Guardian. "Do I need to give you the key?"

"How else will we get in?" Matteo Tradonico asked.

"Break down the door."

"But you have the key."

"Must I yield to you, even to the last measure?"

"I guess yeah."

The Guardian took out his set of keys and chose one with teeth in the shape of the cross. He unlocked the door to the crypt of Saint Nicholas.

Shaking, Matteo Tradonico entered, his hands up and ready to seize.

The low, stone-cut chamber had been outfitted as a

temporary chapel. The capital of a broken column had been rolled to the back of the room, set up as an altar, arrayed with precious candlesticks and eucharistic furnishings. There were silken banners on the walls proclaiming the protection of armed archangels. A door into a side chamber was open, and inside were extra amphorae for the transportation of the saint's miraculous grease. A statue of Nicholas, balding, bearded, gaunt, and caustic, stood to the side of the altar.

Against the back wall there was an old, blank sarcophagus, without a lid but welling with oil. It smelled of perfume.

"We pour the oil and myrrh and holy water in," said the Guardian. "Let it touch the bones for a blessing. Then drain it out and cart it back to the basilica. That is a . . ." He did not feel it was worth it to continue speaking to the men who would soon kill him.

"I brought a bag of velvet," said Matteo Tradonico. He went hungrily to the sarcophagus to commit his gleeful sacrilege.

There was a voice from the entrance to the tomb. "We were wondering when the rest of the team would get here," said Tyun, sword drawn. The monk followed awkwardly behind him.

The two soldiers jolted and spun in surprise. Matteo Tradonico glared at the saint hunter. "We don't need you," he said. "Your services aren't necessary."

"My friend is necessary," said Tyun, nodding to the monk. "He had a dream of the saint's benediction."

"He's not your friend. He's your client," said Matteo. "And your whole mission is over." He boasted, "I killed the Barese Factor Rollo de Bailleul."

"From behind," commented one of the soldiers.

"With my own blade," Matteo Tradonico pointed out, irritably.

"Oh, Matteo Tradonico, you are shameful," said Nicephorus, wincing.

"I'm going—I'm going to kill this one too," said the Venetian, pointing at the Guardian. "We don't need him anymore either. Or you. Any of you."

"Hogtie the Guardian," said Tyun. "It doesn't make any strategic sense to kill him. We don't need a blood price on our heads."

The Guardian did not wait: he bolted.

Tyun was about to go after him, but the soldiers raised their swords against him.

It was a cramped room: both guardsmen could not attack side by side. Tyun thrust and parried in a corner, feeling naked without a shield. So much body exposed.

Nicephorus panicked, helpless, with no weapon but the idiot slingshot in that confined chamber.

Tradonico did not participate, but sat cross-legged on the edge of the sacred tomb, watching with pleasure.

"You could go around this way," Tradonico suggested to the second guard. "He's left-handed."

The second guard darted in from the side. Tyun was now confronting two blades, looking back and forth rapidly, creeping backwards along the wall, into the storeroom.

The two guards crowded the storeroom door. He swung at them wildly, and when they balked, he kicked a foot backward, hooked it around an empty amphora, and rolled the jug right at their feet. They tripped and the ceramic shattered, and one of them hopped sideways, slicing at the air.

Matteo Tradonico, enjoying the entertainment of henchmen sure to succeed, reached out, dunked his hand in the sacred liquor, and raised it to his lips. He poured it from his fingers into his mouth, his second dose in a day. He licked his palm with a broad tongue, like a child with a treat.

"I'm going to go kill the Guardian," he announced. "Right back." He got up, walked past his struggling soldiers, pushed Nicephorus out of the doorway, and left the mausoleum.

Tyun was on the defensive. The guards had forced their way

into the storeroom. Tyun was overwhelmed. He looked from one to the other.

One swung. The blade smashed through an amphora—Tyun had snatched it off the workbench, held it up as a shield, ducking back—sending fragments spinning across the floor. The saint hunter was left holding just the jagged neck in one hand, his stolen short sword in the other. The guards came at him.

He parried, grabbed the leg of the greasy workbench, and wrenched it into the middle of the little storeroom, sending pottery rolling and smashing. The bench was between him and the Venetians and their blades. He dove for the door, swiveling to fend off attack, and staggered backward on his heels out of the little room. He slid on shattered pottery and hit the ground; shards of ceramic cut into his shoulders. Looking up, he saw the merciless faces of the soldiers, both framed in the doorway, raising their swords to finish him.

Nicephorus slammed the storage-room door shut, kicking it with his foot. He threw himself against it as it thumped with angry blows from the other side.

Weary, bleeding, Tyun stood up. "Thanks," he said, and went to the statue of St. Nicholas. "Give me a hand."

"I can't," said Nicephorus, back against the thundering door.

"Move," said Tyun, and pushed the marble statue off its plinth.

Nicephorus leaped. The statue fell, struck the door, slid, scraping wood. It lay in front of the door, rattling as the soldiers tried to punch their way out.

"Now let's get that little fucker," said Tyun, and headed out to chase Matteo Tradonico.

The Guardian was climbing hand over hand up the sharp karst cliffside, desperate to escape. The Venetian boy was not far below. He was using only one hand to climb; the other held his saber, his paramerion. They crawled between the mouths of empty crypts carved into the cliff.

Tyun scampered up behind Matteo Tradonico, leaping from hummock to limestone spike. The cliffside was sharp. It bit into his hands. He planted his foot on the head of a long-dead Lycian god, reached up, and grabbed Matteo Tradonico's ankle. The patrician struggled. Tyun tugged.

The kid swung his saber down at the thief, but it was a weak swing. It missed Tyun's face.

The drag on his leg was too much for the Venetian. He lost his hold. He slid backwards. Rubble bounced around him.

He and Tyun now faced each other, almost vertical, wedged against karst spikes, both fiddling with their swords, wondering how much force they could exert before they'd topple off the cliffside entirely.

From fifteen feet below, standing near the old, rugged cross, Nicephorus watched anxiously as once the Marys, at the foot of another cross, had been aghast audience to the Harrowing of Hell.

Tyun held on to the wall with his right and sliced with his left; Matteo Tradonico, facing him, hung on with his left, parried with his right.

The Venetian lunged and his saber gouged deep into Tyun's right hand. Yelping, the saint hunter fell.

Nicephorus watched his friend topple down the cliffside and roll as if things were slowed.

The Venetian, thrown off balance by his own swing, lost his hold and spun away from the rock, his feet pedaling at nothing.

Bracing himself against the wooden cross, Nicephorus opened his arms to receive his friend.

He half caught Tyun—half was smacked by him. Tyun's skull snapped backward and Nicephorus felt his own nose explode with the impact. But Tyun was in his arms. They lurched backwards together. The cross held them both.

The Venetian rolled and bounced helplessly down the cliff

face and slammed heavily into saint hunter and monk, saber clanging.

At that, the cross behind them cracked.

As it toppled backwards, Nicephorus could see a great drop down to the ground below.

Impact. No breath in him. Three lay upon the cross—sledding down the hill—veering sideways—flung—

And again, impact. Nicephorus's body was thrown to the side.

Dazzling light.

When he came to his senses, he was lying on the dirt, the cross suspended a couple of feet above his face. It had landed flat, balanced precariously on a spur of limestone. Slowly, it spun, pivoting on its crux.

On one arm of the teetering cross, Tyun rose from a crouch, gathering himself again for battle. On the opposite arm, the Venetian youth, quivering with horror and excitement at his first evening of homicide, crawled to his feet.

They fenced, the weight of each balancing the other.

Jabs—parries—feints.

Wheeling like icons of night and day, some celestial battle, they passed over Nicephorus's head.

The cross shifted, rocked, almost fell. If one of them made the wrong move, one clumsy *appel*, they'd both be flung to their deaths thirty feet below. They slid their feet, shuffled up and down the arms where once the holy hands were nailed.

It was, at least, a Greek cross, so the four arms were of equal length. Nicephorus found himself wishing—*Ah, if only, provident God!*—it had been the Cross of the Patriarchs, which would've allowed Tyun a couple extra planks, more secure footing.

The cross spun lazily on its axis as the two men fought. They rotated out over the chasm; they returned and swung over the slope. Nicephorus squatted near their feet, afraid to tip the balance.

Tyun was haggard: right hand slashed to immobility, back scraped up and bleeding, knees quivering with vertigo. The Venetian was also shaking, but with a dreamlike, adolescent mania—alert, eager, insane. His hair and chin, despite everything, still looked great.

Tyun shifted his weight, his knees. He dipped and made the cross wobble and spin faster. The trick would be to fall toward the rocky slope, not into the chasm.

The swords lashed out and clacked above the central axis. The Venetian beat madly at Tyun, trying to force him backwards until he toppled off the end of the wooden arm into the void. Tyun retreated a step. The earth revolved giddily beneath him.

One penultimate slice by Tradonico's saber, and Tyun's sword went flying. It clattered down the slope.

Then Tyun faced the Venetian boy unarmed. *This little prick,* he thought irritably. *And now I die.*

He panted.

Then Matteo Tradonico hacked downward—a final coup.

Nicephorus leaped up from his squat—spun the cross—seized Tyun's ankles.

The cross dipped wildly—

Tyun skidded backwards—dropped onto the slope—

The cross bucked back upwards—

And Patrizio Matteo Tradonico flew off, flipped, and with the instrument of his sacred Lord's torture, plummeted to certain death on the rocks below.

Tyun and Nicephorus lay side by side on the slope, breathing heavily, both head-down.

"You have excellent balance," said Nicephorus to the sky.

"Once," Tyun recalled hoarsely, "once in Awdaghost, once when I was stealing an urn for a client . . . there was a weight trap in the pedestal . . . I knew it, part of the plan . . . I had to perch there on that fucking pedestal, motionless, for ten hours . . . till the changing of the guard . . . I couldn't shift my weight at all, right, or there'd be arrows, or a boulder . . . So there I was, balanced . . . ten hours. If I could just stay that way, I'd be a rich man . . . But it was incredibly hot. Edge of the desert. Baking hot . . . Shit, it was tough. Our plan was that Reprobus, through a window, lowered in a hollow piece of straw so I could sip some water . . . But here was the trick: To keep my weight constant, I had to piss at exactly the same rate as I drank . . ."

"That's a lie, right?"

They both started to laugh. Lying on the cliffside near the tombs of ancient Lycians, they laughed helplessly, heads down, bodies sore and bleeding.

"Now," said Tyun, "at last, the body of the Blessed Nicholas."

"Oh, no, Tyun. No."

Tyun did not respond. He crawled to his feet. He held out his hand, and the monk took it. He pulled the monk erect with a jerk.

They walked back up the cart track to the saint's mausoleum, moving like their bones were all unjointed.

They walked gingerly into the tomb. They no longer had a lamp or any light, so instead they felt their way around the makeshift altar with its furnishings. This was all they knew of the room: shadow, the sweet smell of myrrh, and the pounding of the two soldiers, still imprisoned, trying to escape the storeroom.

Tyun and Nicephorus came upon the cold stone of the sarcophagus. With their hands, they traced the lip of the bath of oil in which the bones reposed. Someone had to fish them out.

"Who?" said Tyun. "You?"

"Tyun?"

"You are here as a witness to authenticity."

"Tyun."

"You have to sign an affidavit."

Suddenly Tyun found himself grabbed. He was in the monk's arms.

At first, he was startled. He twitched. His hand stung. Then he gave himself up to it. He pulled the monk tighter to him. Blood from the monk's nose was on his lips, but its taste made him hungrier. He felt the tonsure beneath his fingers, the coarse robe.

They kissed by the bones of Saint Nicholas, yearning even as they were satisfied.

The pounding continued.

Then it was time to remove the sacred bones. The two kneeled down, side by side, before the sarcophagus, like children saying prayers before bed. Tyun started laughing.

"What are you laughing at?" asked Nicephorus.

Tyun said, "The wonder of the world."

Stiff from his injuries, he took off his battered silken coat. He laid it out upon the floor to receive the bones and smoothed its skirts.

"Now," said Tyun. "It's time."

Nicephorus whispered: "As Alexander the Great said, when you are in the Land of Darkness, you must reach down and grasp whatever objects you find."

They reached into the oil with all four hands.

O blessed bone. The skull, the seat and throne, the citadel, the watchtower. Then the cage. Let scholars and mystics argue whether the body is integument and tomb or vehicle, vahana, the stilted assemblage that allows us to walk freely in the world, our only perch.

Once bathed in flesh, this brittle manikin stood in the bath two hours when first removed from another, gravid skeleton, another tomb of flesh. And these jointed pieces were augmented, growing many times their own height, before they were laid again in a brimming bath, this time to stand no more.

Seven hundred years have gone—the tomb's sockets stare out across a different city—what were the sensations concocted in the skull of this simian in brocade, this Primate? What now remains of Nicholas? Yes, the chilly globe, the ass's jawbone that once made music, but also disjointed, also incubating: the shards of his story that remain. No longer bound by sinew. We try to organize fragments into the outline of a living creature.

Not just for saints, but for those we loved and ancestors we've heard of from our parents as we sat around the drying carcass—I mean the casket or the family bird. Recall their stories. Otherwise, they are once again disarticulated and their remains scattered.

Now warm hands grasp again at the fragments in the greasy murk. Once again, the bone is pressed with flesh.

A figure is laid out and assembled. This scaffolding, upon which we climb up out of the earth just long enough to see the pear trees catch on fire.

The dawn was silent.

Rank by rank, sun climbed down the steps of the amphitheater.

Tyun the saint hunter and Nicephorus, lowliest clerk of St. Benedict, walked almost lazily away from the necropolis. The donkey walked behind them. They still had three miles to go to get back to their ship. They didn't know how they were going to get through a hostile town. They didn't really care.

Stone masks of antique actors looked down on them from arches and piers. Silenus and the satyrs, Medusan grimaces. Medea wild with grief and her vendetta. Thundering Jupiter. This was the world: the comedy always turns eventually to tragedy. Just wait long enough, and the wedding of Helen and Menelaus becomes the stabbing of Agamemnon in the bath.

They were crossing the ancient stage with their donkey when Matteo Tradonico limped out from some gaping archway to confront them. He had his saber in hand.

"I don't think we need to have this happen," said Tyun, holding up his hands and the donkey's bridle. His scabbard was empty. His sword was somewhere back on the hillside.

"I am versed in the ways of honor!" the kid cried out. His voice echoed in the empty cavea.

"Heaven bite me," complained Tyun, and wearily drew the dagger out of his boot. He handed the bridle to Nicephorus and went to face the Venetian one last time.

It would be almost impossible for Tyun to close on his opponent, with only a dagger to defend himself.

Nicephorus watched, almost delirious with the confusion of the long night. He felt there were shadows moving behind him, spilling out onto the steps and seats of the theater, and at first he assumed it was the motion of light at dawn. Then, as he watched the Venetian and the saint hunter circle each other, he began to feel eyes upon him: the undead audiences who once gathered here to watch gladiators die. He looked back quickly. He was startled to find that, spread throughout the arena, there were in fact mortal bodies: ten Turkmen shepherds, their companions of the previous night. The nomads, weathered and grim, stared down silently at the combat on the stage, as the gods once surveyed the contest between Achilles and Hector at Troy.

Matteo Tradonico no longer looked good. There was at least

that blessing. His face was scraped and bleeding. He limped, possibly with a broken leg or ankle. Every time he stepped on his right foot, he winced. But he had his saber.

Tyun circled him warily, ready to spring. He could not approach.

The boy hollered and swung—a feint. Tyun had to back away.

The boy whipped the saber back and forth crazily, gaining ground, forcing Tyun into a crouching retreat.

Then an arrow slammed into the kid's hand. Matteo Tradonico screamed and dropped his saber.

"Now fair," said a voice in broken Greek. The Turkmen archer pointed at Tyun's bleeding hand.

In the sudden break in action, the large, sarcastic shepherd—Taptuk, the skeptic—called out to Tyun, "As we told you, we will be handing you all over to the Byzantine dogs. You and the bones. Do you still want to fight the boy? We can take him alive or dead."

Tyun looked at Matteo Tradonico. The boy was on his knees, gasping, grappling with the arrow that projected out the back of his wrist.

"No," said Tyun. "I'm tired. I don't want to fight."

And so the shepherds all descended and surrounded the three thieves and their donkey, and the long, strange night of flight and deception was over.

IV

JUST AFTER DAWN, THE CICADAS STARTED THEIR RHYTHMIC CALL AGAIN. THE HILLS SIZZLED WITH THEM. THE LIGHT of day was uncompromising. The searing eye of justice.

The parade passed through the streets of Myra, and everyone who saw them followed. The word was spreading quickly that the thieves had been caught. Everything beneath the sun was sharp and defined: the walls glaring with whitewash, bisected in shadow.

Matteo Tradonico rode, humiliated, on the back of the donkey. His foot and leg were at an awful angle.

"We were trying to stop him from stealing the bones—the real bones—from the tomb," Tyun protested. "You saw us. We were fighting!"

"When two thieves fight," said Taptuk, "that does not make one of them a chief justice."

"That is our donkey," said Tyun.

Taptuk said, "Now it is a donkey that belongs to the righteous."

The crowds were shouting at the prisoners, throwing slops and rinds.

Tyun put his arm around Nicephorus so he could say quietly, "I don't know exactly how we are going to land on our feet this time."

Nicephorus answered, "I think I do."

Tyun looked at him curiously. Nicephorus frowned and

faced forward. Blood from his nose had dried all the way down the front of his habit.

The crowds grew, and now they shouted: *"Thieves! Thieves! Give us back our saint!"*

The mob was held back only by the presence of the Turkmen escort. Otherwise, it would have moved in and pulled Tyun and the monk and the Venetian golden boy apart, limb from limb.

The menace grew as they approached the harbor. *"Let us have them! Let us have them!"* Hands in fists, feet stamping rhythmically on the cobbles of the plateia. Hurling a terracotta roofing tile which smacked the donkey. The animal started, yelped. The injured nobleman on his back swayed dangerously. He had a fever by now and seemed both too red and too white.

The shepherds did not flinch or look at the seething of the crowds. They marched forward with the prisoners between them.

"Where are you taking us, Uncle?" Tyun demanded.

Taptuk said, "Our brothers in the Turk garrison, then the city elders. Someone will pay us."

They now could see the harbor down the rocky slope. They could not pick out the *Epiphany*. The whole was blue and dazzling. The crowd had swelled to hundreds, Tyun guessed, and execution was definitely in the air.

They were shoved and grabbed. The way became treacherous. Feet tripped them. The shepherds had a hard time pushing the crowd back. Nicephorus looked ready to vomit. Tyun reached out and squeezed his arm. Nicephorus reached up and pressed his hand.

They were brought to a halt in the port's wide agora, beside the great Roman granarium. Behind them stretched shoals and dunes of crushed murex shells discarded in the making of purple.

Heaven stank of fish, and seabirds circled in great flocks, crying like the crowds.

The elders of Byzantine Myra processed out, dressed in their robes of office. They stood in a phalanx like the scowling bishops in judgment painted upon the arches of Nicholas's basilica. Next to them, sergeants of the Turkish garrison, sour and armed. And in the middle of all of them, the Guardian who had fled the necropolis. He pointed at Tyun, at Nicephorus, at Matteo Tradonico, and told stories that could not be heard over the cries for vengeance.

"Tattler," muttered Tyun. "I let the bastard go."

The ten shepherds could no longer hold the line. Angry men and women tore their way past and stumbled toward Tyun, clawing at him, hollering, "Thief!" He noticed Nicephorus did not back away, but stood shoulder to shoulder with him, determined, though terrified. The shepherds drew their swords and cried *"Get back!"* in their own language as the city elders shouted for order, but the crowd was louder, more desperate, as if by assaulting thief and monk and golden boy they could pry apart all Myra's calamities: the loss of their ancient prestige, the Turkish invasion, the nomad sorties, the burned houses, the citizens slaughtered, the abandoned farms—and now this final outrage, the theft of the corpse that defined them all, that made their city a wonder of the world.

Tyun held up his hands in front of his face. He did not want his eyes gouged out, and that was where they were aiming.

As the wave crashed down upon him, he fell backward and caught himself with his hand, and with the other, shoved at a butcher, and felt someone knee him, and surrounded by legs—nothing but kicking—he heard a sound: a blast, a trumpet, a signal.

And there, by the broad steps that led down to the harbor, stood a dog-man in a brocade *qaba,* blowing upon a horn. Behind him were ranked soldiers, Venetian and Norman and his own piratical crew. On one side of Reprobus stood the shaved Rus, Shchek, with his tasseled spear. On the other, the Northwoman, Gunnlaug, dressed almost anonymously in her mail, face hidden coyly by her aventail, armed with a sword few could lift.

The sight of cutting blades and corselets quieted the riot.

Reprobus called out, "Myra! Release these prisoners or we will burn this port to the ground." He raised his sword. "If I lower this blade, the destruction starts!"

Tyun said softly to Nicephorus, on the ground beside him, "Sometimes a bad boy is a very good boy."

"This is an affront!" an elder called. "The saint will curse you all. The sea will swallow you," but another was already smothering the curse by calling out, "Who are your leaders? Who has led this criminal invasion?"

Everyone looked to Matteo Tradonico. He, puling child, did not raise his hand.

So Nicephorus got up. Much to Tyun's astonishment, the monk stood up tall, masked and painted in his own dried blood, and declared loudly, "I am." Tyun shook his head desperately at his friend, but Nicephorus continued, "The Barese Factor Rollo de Bailleul is dead. I was sent by the Archbishop of Bari as a legal witness. I will answer for the expedition. Let me speak to the city's elders alone."

Tyun muttered through clenched teeth, "You don't know how to lie."

Nicephorus said to him, "Then I will tell the truth." Again, in a louder voice, he called out, "This man on the donkey is Matteo Tradonico, scion of one of the Twelve Apostolic Families of Venice. Bring us into the granarium and we will make all clear."

"Don't do this, dream boy," said Tyun.

But Nicephorus had already moved forward, taking the donkey's bridle. Though he wore a monk's rough habit, dirty and torn with a night of running, hiding, rolling, leaping, kicking, fighting, and falling, he advanced through the crowd like a prince.

Saint Nicholas himself once foiled thieves.

As the bandits sat around in their cavern, counting their loot, the saint appeared before them, bellowing, threatening, blazing with holy fire, calling them demons and demented, impudentissimi, *pointing at the entrance to the cave: "Take back what you have stolen and you won't be hoisted on the gibbet!"*

Now Nicholas himself is stolen. He is the treasure. Nicephorus, watching Tyun wrap the bones in a coat of brocade, asked himself: What would be the saint's retribution?

Relics are treated as stand-ins for saints, though once they were the saints themselves. We each own a skull that identifies us, an attribute we carry. We are all our own icon, our own avatar; an idol made in our shape, haunted by a spirit longing to intervene in the calamities we witness.

The people of Myra waited for an hour while negotiations went on inside the granarium. Tyun and Reprobus and their band of marines waited by the entrance. The crowd did not disperse.

"Thank you for coming," said Tyun.

Reprobus said, "I hear a riot, and I know you're nearby."

With the deep echo of a crossbar dragged aside, the doors to the granarium swung open. The Turkish soldiers and the Turkmen shepherds issued out first, even before the elders of the city. They showed nothing on their faces.

The elders next, in their ranks. Their looks were severe.

And then, alone, the monk, his hands folded before him. A saddlebag was suspended from his shoulder. He squinted in the sunlight.

Tyun and Reprobus went to his side. The monk said, "Let's go—let's go," with an urgency they had never heard before from him.

"What did you do?" said Tyun.

"Quickly," Nicephorus urged, and began stalking down toward the quay.

The crowd, seeing him go, seeing the saint hunters follow, began to roil again. They followed down the broad steps, getting louder. Crying, *"Justice! Justice!"*

"Quickly," said Nicephorus again, and he pointed to the *Epiphany*. Then started to say to each soldier and sailor who boarded, "Go! Go! Go!"

It was not like him. Energy, command. Tyun watched in amazement.

Gunnlaug was suspicious. "Where do we go? The Venetian party?"

"To your ship," said Nicephorus. "All of you. Quickly."

"What is this?" the woman asked Tyun.

"I do not know the ways of monks," said Tyun. "So listen to him."

Through the veil of her chain mail, she looked back and forth at the two of them, reading their faces, their comity. "I go to wash myself," she said in disgust. She turned around and walked away.

The Barese soldiers and Tyun's men were aboard the *Epiphany* and readying their oars. Tyun and Nicephorus were the last to climb on deck. From there, they could see the swelling crowd spilling down the wide steps between the columns and the countinghouses and the harbor's pillared tombs, standing on the roofs of storehouses, all of them pushing forward.

Their elders called out to them, but were not heeded.

"What are we doing?" Tyun asked the monk.

Wordlessly, Nicephorus lowered the donkey's saddlebags to the deck and opened one. He pulled out the brocade coat and unrolled it on the deck. There were the bones, glistening with their holy grease, grinning at the blue heavens.

"How?"

"Let's go, Tyun," said Nicephorus. "We're done."

Tyun gave the order to cast off, and the crowd heard the command and a great cry went up, unintelligible, as their saint deserted them—as he pulled away from the shore. Men and women ran along the dock as the ship pulled away, as the oars touched the water and glided backwards. The *Epiphany* left the dock, and still the crowd surged forward, toppling into the sea, running along the sand of the beach, tripping on the waves, and people in the water grabbed at the two great steering oars, pleading, praying, demanding the sky give back their beloved Nicholas, Navigator, Wonder Worker.

And Tyun asked: "Nicephorus, what have you done?"

We have records that show the ports they stopped at as they fled: Kekova, Meis, Patara. Three days, three nights, and that is hardly any distance at all.

Kekova is an island barely out of sight of Myra, surrounded by pinnacles of stone that rise out of the blue waters. At its peak is a fortress that looks down upon the bays and archipelagos in all directions. We might imagine they were uneasy that night, the fortress above them manned while they slept in the harbor.

And the next day: almost no progress. The air must have been too still for sails. Clearly, they were rowing. The heat was overwhelming. The clacking of the cicadas on the slopes was like a fever.

A stop that night was necessary: They were out of water. Rowing is thirsty work. They stopped at an island; the mainland was too dangerous. Even someone walking steadily, spreading news, could have beat their pace.

"Are you going to tell me, Brother N?" said Tyun.

Nicephorus had imagined that once back on the safety of the ship, he and Tyun would at least sleep side by side as a promise of future intimacies. He wanted to touch Tyun's chest, his arms, his thighs. Instead, Tyun hardly slept, crouched up in the prow of the ship, arms around his knees, staring out at the islands. Nicephorus lay curled in the stern, thinking about saints and God and duty.

The crew that night was sullen and unhappy. They wanted more distance between themselves and the crime. One sailor complained that he had dreamed of swallows swarming. They bit at his tongue in a frenzy.

On the third day, near Patara, the storm hit.

It began with wind rather than rain. The chop was obvious. The blue water turned steely. The ship began to shudder from small impacts. At least, with steady wind, they made good progress for an hour or so, but the weather was getting blustery. Finally, a gust hit them, the ship heeled, and everyone hollered and slid. Tyun and Reprobus called for the sail to be lowered.

Then the storm was full upon them: swells and hot rain. Dimly, they could see mountains to starboard. They were being pushed toward the coast, an impossible complication of stony shoals and half-submerged islets.

"We're coming to Patara," Tyun called out over the storm, pointing at the gray hills. "Where I normally would say we should anchor. Excellent harbor. But they might have heard the news."

Reprobus, his wet snout close to the monk's face, translated for Nicephorus: "What our friend means, but does not say, is that the crew is convinced that the myroblyte Nicholas is impeding us, that the fury of the storm is the fury of the Navigator—that Nicholas is bellowing in the heavens that he does not want to go to Bari. And so to anchor at Patara, his birthplace, right now will lead all of them, Christian, Muslim, and—" he waved a bewildered paw at Shchek—"devotees of Stribog, god of the winds, to conspire and cast you and the bones ashore."

Tyun turned and, rain-streaked, yelled out to his crew, "We are going forward! Row! It is Nicholas's will!"

The rowing was hell. The oars slammed down into the waves—then suddenly were lifted up and skated across the surface—touching nothing—yanking the arms of the men—or were caught and dragged by the surf. The sea spilled across the deck. Water poured in through the oar ports as the thwarts dashed down under the waves. Rowers half rose from their benches, drenched.

Half an hour passed. An hour. They could no longer see where they were.

"Tell me, monk," said Tyun darkly. "Is this the saint?" He jabbed his finger at the sky. *"Is it the saint?"*

Nicephorus felt abruptly alone. He locked his mouth closed. He shook his head.

The mast dipped down almost to the swells, heeling hard, the ship close to capsizing. Water gushed aboard. Sailors screamed. Nicephorus was holding on to a stanchion, almost vertical where he lay. Water shot up around him. It was in his nose, and he coughed and gagged.

The ship righted itself. Bodies toppled past.

Tornik was crawling across the deck toward the box of sacred bones, coughing, "Look—save us! Wonder Worker, save us!"

And we are told that they reached the eye of the storm; and suddenly, for a space of time at least, all was still and creepy and green; and they found themselves at a place called Perdicca.

We do not know where this was. It appears on no map.

Nicephorus was not pleased when he heard the name, because it sounded like the Latin *perdita,* which means "lost."

We will imagine Perdicca was a harbor with cedars on its slopes. We will give the crew a sandy beach. The rain still falls, and the trees on the heights thrash, but the League of St. Nicholas are safe. Shivering at the edge of the forest.

Tyun, Nicephorus, Reprobus, and Shchek hunched under a sweet bay bush. They had the bones with them in a box used usually for millet. Tyun was staring at the box as if it would speak to him. Nicephorus wrung water out of his sleeves. It was no good trying to light a fire. The rain was softer now, but the winds above them were loud again, and the waves were fierce.

Abruptly, Tyun rose. He clapped his hands. The crew looked up at him. He said: "I know you are worried about the saint." He paced between them, catching their eyes. "You are worried we are kidnapping him. But that isn't it, is it? That's not the problem here. We know what has happened—the secret some of you are keeping. So step forward, those of you who are guilty."

Nicephorus had no idea what was going on. He shifted in the dirt.

Tyun crouched down and stared in the eyes of the Merv brothers, one at a time. He did not find what he was searching for. He stood and walked to where the Factor's bodyguards were all propped against cedars around a fire that would not light.

"It's you," he said. "It's you." They did not look at him. He reached down and put a finger on one man's forehead. Pressing, he forced the head to crane back. "Your name?" he prompted.

"Romoald," said the man, blinking. "Romoald Bulpanna."

Tyun held his hand flat in front of Romoald Bulpanna's face. "Give it," he said, tightly. The rain fell. The forest pattered with it. The waves crashed against the shore. "Give it now," said Tyun.

Romoald Bulpanna reached inside his bag. He drew out a little roll of cloth and put it in Tyun's hand.

Tyun stared down at the miserable cloth.

"Finger?" he said.

Romoald Bulpanna adjusted: "Thumb." Thinking better of it, he whined, "Stephen has the pointer finger. It's used for blessing." He held up his hand, feebly demonstrating some Christian mudra of grace.

Tyun kicked him right in the chest. The man went sprawling, and reached for his blade, but it wasn't on him.

"You fucking idiots," said Tyun. "How many?" He looked around the little group. "Five? Five fingers?"

Members of the crew were getting to their feet, scowling darkly.

Grudgingly, four Norman guards drew forth their amulets, their stolen relics.

"*Integrity!*" Tyun shouted so loud it echoed in the lost bay. "Integrity is what I demand! Integrity of the body!" He pointed over at the box of saint. "Now!" he said. "Now! And pray! Pray we all are forgiven!"

The clouds were red and heroic, full as the sails of a departing argosy. The storm had lit out for the wide Mediterranean. Once the body was whole, the wind died down.

It was evening, and Tyun and Nicephorus sat upon the crest of the hill, looking out across the Aegean. Below them, the men lit campfires and told shitty jokes, calling to each other between the cedars. They all were alive, and the evening was warm. Tornik and Musarat were overseeing a small task force of impromptu fishermen.

"Did you like that?" Tyun said. "Absolutely intuition."

"The saint was not angry about the theft of fingers," said Nicephorus.

"Back together again," said Tyun. "Reunited." He raised his hand, five fingers spread, to put it against Nicephorus's.

Nicephorus did not meet it. "It wasn't the theft of fingers that endangered us," he insisted, "because the Blessed Nicholas is still whole, and back in Myra."

Tyun dropped his hand. He shifted on the duff. "What do you mean?"

"That's how we got away. You must have worked it out."

Tyun pointed, raggedly, down the hill, one, two, three times. "That is . . . ?"

"The decoy skeleton you brought. Slicked up with some olive oil."

It had been a tense conference, there in the echoing granary down by the docks. The city elders wanted execution for the leaders of the League, imprisonment for the rest. The warrior-shepherds wanted payment, and the Turkish militia, the *ahdath*, wanted peace restored at whatever cost.

And so Nicephorus had told them everything. He drew out the brocade coat with the saint's bones, still fragrant with myrrh and *hagiasma*. He also showed them the fakes. He explained that there were two expeditions, and that the Factor, the leader of the Baresi, was dead, murdered from behind by the Venetian boy. He offered to stand trial in the Factor's stead. He pointed out, however, that the city now had their sacred bones again. And moreover, the Basilica of St. Nicholas had already retained a hundred golden Byzantine solidi the Factor had donated to the church during the theft. The Guardian spoke up and complained that Matteo Tradonico had planned to kill him. It was only due to squabbling between the thieves that he was alive at all.

At that point, Matteo Tradonico, half-loopy with fever, chose to boast meticulously about how he was indeed in charge of the expedition. He expounded upon his honors and his deep importance to the Most Serene Republic of Venice.

And the more he enumerated his excellences to the council (". . . when I am in my regalia, people bow to me on the steps . . ."), the more Nicephorus indicated to the gathered men with looks, gestures, and a few whispered words that while execution for a murder was always gratifying, the kid would rack up a spectacular price for a ransom. What if they held the young Venetian prisoner and demanded a fortune from the Doge? Who needs another severed head?

When Matteo Tradonico realized his freedom was being bartered off, Nicephorus assumed he would back out of his titles. Instead, he brayed about the riches he'd fetch. "Ask my grandfather," he said with condescension. "I'm worth worlds, I guess. I guess I'm worth worlds."

"Gentlemen," said Nicephorus. "Humbly: There is an armed force waiting outside this building to tear the port apart and burn Myra to the ground. I have offered myself as a victim for execution, and I do so wholly and gladly, if that is your wish. But I suggest, instead, you let me take the fake relics and leave this harbor with that whole bloodthirsty crew. I will convince them: they will leave your city without violence and return to Bari. You will keep the corpse of St. Nicholas the Navigator, sacred to your city. Send the Venetian ship back to their lagoon to take word that Matteo Tradonico, scion of one of the Apostolic Families of Venice, is a murderer. He has killed a Norman knight. Wait for his fortune to arrive. The wealthy are never allowed to suffer long for their crimes. He will be fine. You will release him. He will go on to kill again and steal. And you, members of the council and those who caught us, you will be rich, and your city will be rich, and the Church of the Blessed Nicholas will be rich, with the only harm done to that church being cracked plasterwork. That, in the end, was our crime. We accomplished nothing more than broken masonry. That is the conclusion of all we strived for. That is the full measure of what we achieved. May St. Nicholas, who spared three prisoners from execution by seizing the blade of the sword with his naked hand, guide you in your deliberations."

The elders of Myra were not quite unanimous. But they were close.

"You gave them back?" Tyun hissed. "You gave the whole thing—*the whole fucking thing*—you gave it back?" His face was savage with anger.

"What, then, Tyun?" said Nicephorus. "Sack the city? Kill people on the wharves? Destroy Myra for the body of God's saint? The soldiers and sailors who died at sea, the Factor—they were combatants. They made their choice. But were we going to slaughter citizens for this farrago?" He said, "The Blessed Nicholas did not wish to accompany us."

"'The Blessed Nicholas'!" Tyun scoffed. "The fucker died seven hundred years ago! What do you think they pay me for? What was this—?" He waved his hand in the air, indicating everything, the whole cycle of violence and action: the Greek fire battle, the plot, the plans, the subterfuge, the strange night of flight and danger. "What was all this for?"

"The bones of a stranger, wrapped up like a saint," said Nicephorus. He reached out and grabbed Tyun's hair. The saint hunter froze. The monk said, "Don't pretend you're not already thinking about how you're going to produce a miracle with these bones back in Bari."

Tyun thought about this.

"I had to do the right thing," said Nicephorus, and dropped his hand. "The sick and the dying back in Bari . . . the relics of St. Nicholas, even complete, all ten fingers, would have been worthless if we'd stolen them from that town, if we'd betrayed the saint and his city and left such sorrow behind us."

"So you betrayed *me*," said Tyun. Yet it was not wholly an accusation. There was a dawning wonder in the saint hunter's eyes. "You betrayed me." The tone was oddly delighted. "You *beat* me! You clever bastard. You actually lied!"

"I didn't lie. I only told the truth." Nicephorus smiled. "But you will lie. To the crew. To everyone else."

"You son of a bitch," said Tyun in admiration.

Nicephorus said nothing.

Tyun looked out toward the sunset in the west. It spread over the isles where so many famed adventurers and rogues had met wonders: sea monsters, sorceresses, one-eyed giants and their flocks. "We could do something again with niter," he said. "Smoke. I really enjoyed that smoke." He turned to Nicephorus. "The Archbishop of Bari and the Abbot have to swallow it. Will you lie with me?"

"Oh, I'll lie with you," said Nicephorus, holding out his arms, putting his hand on Tyun's chest. "But first," he whispered as they kissed, "you lie to me. Tell me the lie I want to hear."

And Tyun did, fondly, again and again.

Finally.

Now lovers see each other as in a glass, darkly—and assume when the other moves a hand, it is because we have reached out too, both of us desiring reflection—*but then we shall see each other face to face.*

Face to face: how close may eye read eye without knowing truth—(blinks)—if in that moment, the truth of both is a longing, hard and pure, extended well into the world of things, a truth that, when tested, proves solid enough to hold, and calls the senses to flock like seabirds . . . ?

No thought left, but only seeking the animal face that declares itself in crisis. And the man is shed away, the history, the father falling off the cliff, the Normans on the sand, the routine of hours, and there is only action and observation and coruscating soul remaining—radiant, for you are encircled by a body that is not your own.

But (thought Nicephorus somewhere) *so invested with the body—held.*

Ah, Lord, was the True Cross not found buried beneath a temple to the divine Venus?

"Inside," he gasped, "the sanctum sanctorum," and the saint hunter took it not as a floor plan, but as a demand.

The arms about him—and his hands on hands—and they both were in the world together, wound tightly, as tight as a trick knot that would never come unraveled.

The birds settled quietly on the islands in the evening, and the breeze blew from the south.

In hagiography, we have the record of the company's voyage home: across the Aegean, stopping at Milos, then bumping along the shore of the Peloponnese, then across the Adriatic to San Giorgio, and finally to Bari. But the itinerary does not tell of the pleasure of those days, now that they were out of danger. The whole crew swam in the blue, blue sea. They bathed in streams that trickled into coves. They played drinking games. They wondered at a gull who landed right on the bones, as if honoring the Navigator. The crew, unaware of the deception, felt certain that the whole of Bari was about to be cured of its pox. Nicephorus and Tyun told each other stories. Tyun's were of cons, Nicephorus's of the bizarrerie found in old lambskin manuscripts. The crew's one Sufi mystic taught everyone how to breathe. One evening, in a small, brief ceremony, Reprobus performed a marriage between Musarat and Tornik. The two of them huddled under a single old horse blanket. They were both extremely shy.

And then, the arrival at Bari. Imagine the crowds swarming down to the bay. Abbot Helias came aboard and prostrated himself before the bones. The relics were so profoundly holy that there was argument over where to stash them at first. But Abbot Helias prevailed and announced he would build a new church just for the Blessed Nicholas's remains. There was a solemn procession with the relics through the streets. People threw themselves down before the box. We have records of the healings, which immediately began:

Now I should like to tell you, beloved, how the folk, running from the four corners of the city, gathered in the church, suffering from various sicknesses. And there were cured that night and the following morning forty-seven men, women, and children.

On the next day, the people came in droves from all the environs to honor the sacred remains. Among them, seven men were cured up to the fourth watch of the day. And from the fourth watch until sunset, fourteen others were cured.

And on the next day, twenty-nine others who were suffering dreadfully were cured.

Nicephorus and Tyun wondered, in deep seclusion, at the healing power of the bones, though they were not Nicholas's, but random substitutions. Tyun shrugged. "The Sufis say that all the world is a precious artifact, and every place is holy. Every single object in the world is a reliquary."

"You would not have said that to me two months ago."

"Two months ago, I would have avoided talking to you entirely."

The relics of St. Nicholas attracted pilgrims to Bari from

all over Europe and beyond its distant boundaries. The city pulled down the old palace of the Byzantine governor, where Nicephorus had spoken to Tyun for the first time one morning at dawn. In its place, by the city's eastern wall, Abbot Helias built a church dedicated to the stolen saint. There were steps down to the burial crypt so wide that fifteen pilgrims could progress downwards on their knees at once. Everyone who had been on the expedition, even those who straggled home from where they'd been stranded on Crete, got a special dispensation to be buried in the new Church of Saint Nicholas; and many of their names are still scratched on its walls. By the time the Abbot Helias died, he had become archbishop and the church he had founded in Bari was one of the most famous pilgrimage sites in Christendom. Helias did not even notice when, in 1100, on the way back from the First Crusade, the Venetians stopped over in Myra and claimed to steal the bones again.

In Myra, the Basilica of St. Nicholas was finally abandoned. By that time, the Byzantine Empire had died entirely. Over the centuries, silt filled the church and it sank beneath the earth.

Eventually the Russian tsar, himself a Nicholas, paid for its restoration. Now it is a site of urgent pilgrimage once again. Russian bus tourists gather by a broken sarcophagus and launch into sonorous chants for the Wonder Worker, the Gift Giver, the Navigator. The sarcophagus where they pray is clearly not the sarcophagus of Nicholas: on its shattered lid lie two reclining Romans, man and wife. The tourists press their children's heads up hard against the plexiglass. The child faces smear; the parents pray ecstatically. They toss in money for good luck. They worm their fingers under the plastic shield to touch the coffin's base.

The Church of St. Nicholas in Bari still sells the blessed

ichor. A strange, miraculous change, though: In Myra, the bones had to be doused in oil, which they then blessed. In Bari, they simply drip water of their own accord.

"If you don't have faith in miracles," said Tyun, "you must make your own."

They were standing in the monastery garden. It was time for Tyun to leave. It was a hot night. All the flowers and the lemon trees exhaled their scent.

"What will you do, now that you have seen how wide the world is?" Tyun asked.

"The Abbot Helias has asked me to write an account of the expedition," said Nicephorus. "He suggested I simplify it somewhat."

"I can imagine," said Tyun. "So now you're going to be shut up again in your jewel box here." Tyun gestured at the cloisters, the high walls overgrown with bougainvillea. "It's going to clap closed, and at the concussion, you'll fall back down on your knees. I hope I'll see you again, someday."

Neither wanted to speak. They waited while the bells throughout the city rang.

Nicephorus started, "It is said that the star which rose above Bethlehem at Christ's birth was first seen from an observatory on a mountain in India called the Hill of Vaus."

"Please," said Tyun. "This is not a time for stories." He put his arms around his friend.

"The three kings, the three mages who traveled to Christ's crib, went back to that observatory in India after they had seen the miracle, and for the rest of their lives they lived together in brotherhood. Years later, the star they had followed flared up again, and they knew it was time to die. That league of three adventurers was buried there together upon the Hill of Vaus, in the sight of that star."

"That is a sweet sentiment."

But Nicephorus persisted: "So there may be an abandoned observatory on a mountain in India, full of forgotten Chaldean wisdom and the treasure of three kings."

"It's a good story," Tyun admitted.

"Herodotus says that in India, powdered gold is so thick beneath the ground that the people there trick huge ants the size of dogs into fetching it to the surface. Imagine the wealth the three kings might possess in their graves, and the good it might do in the world."

"This is all immaterial."

"If you had someone who had read the right apocrypha, you could follow the route of the kings back to their home. Pace backwards out of Herod's palace. Pursue the star in retrograde. Find the observatory and the tomb of the magi."

Tyun looked at his friend. "You have taken vows. You're cloistered."

Nicephorus pointed. "That wall is low. I wouldn't be missed for some hours."

"Three kings," Tyun calculated.

"The thought of it is making your saliva thicken."

The bells rang on all the slopes.

Nicephorus ran his hand down Tyun's taut body. They stood in the sweet-scented shadows.

"What are you doing?" Tyun asked, and gasped, and Nicephorus replied softly, "As Alexander the Great said: When you are lost in the Land of Darkness, you must reach down and grab whatever objects you find."

And so I leave them there in the shadowed garden, with the city celebrating its newfound saint, and the sick healed, and the campanili all ringing. Here where I sit, ten centuries later, a bitter snow is falling, which is right, because this is a story of St. Nicholas, Navigator and Thaumaturge, gift giver and magician, who flies through the snow to remind us of wonder, and of how we deceive the ones we love most into believing in miracles; and how that deception might be a betrayal or, perhaps, a gift in itself. There is no line between vision and delusion. The bones, dry seventeen centuries, still produce a holy manna. The afternoon falls from the sky. The face looks up into yours. The door opens. A raised hand can be a slap, a greeting, or a blessing.

Yet you stand, and you too raise your hand.

AFTERWORD

Despite all appearances to the contrary, this book is closely based on real events. In the year 1087, an expedition from the Italian city of Bari actually did sail to Lycia and steal the corpse of St. Nicholas. The heist happened much as described here. The saint's bones still repose in the crypt of the beautifully severe church that the Abbot Helias built for them in Bari. Once a year, priests still open the tomb and draw out about a half liter of fluid which has built up around the remains. It is dispersed in holy water and sold to pilgrims.

My primary sources for the novel were the two stunningly detailed contemporary accounts of the theft left by John the Archdeacon and by Nicephorus, "the lowliest clerk of Bari." Some details of the Venetian expedition were taken from a later narrative by the anonymous Monk of Lido. I have followed their accounts quite closely in writing this historical novel. Given how scrupulous I have been in some regards, historians of the event may wonder why I have deviated from the record in other matters. To this objection, I would point to the nature of medieval nonfiction: We have only a few bare sentences in Greek and Persian that cover, for example, the spread of the Seljuks into Lycia; whereas a nation of dog-headed people is attested at length in Herodotus, in the Chinese *Classic of Mountains and Seas*, and in most Eurasian travel narratives written for the next millennium and a half after them. I wanted to write a historical novel with the love of a good story, incidental detail, and willful inaccuracy demanded by the European Middle Ages themselves.

The business of saint hunting is described at great length in contemporary sources, most notably Einhard's *Translation of the Relics of Saints Marcellinus and Peter,* Guibert of Nogent's *On Saints and Their Relics,* and Christopher of Mytilene's tirade "To the Monk Andrew." Those looking for a modern discussion of the trade should read Patrick J. Geary's *Furta Sacra: Thefts of Relics in the Central Middle Ages* (1990). Other details of the heist were inspired by passages in the *Itinerary* of Benjamin of Tudela, the satires of al-Jahiz, the *Maqamat* of al-Hariri, the *Seljuqnamah* of Zahir al-Din Nishapuri, and the superb *Book of Charlatans* by Jamal al-Din 'Abd Rahim al-Jawbari, who is your man if you want to burgle a house using a ladder, a bag of sand, an iron hand with iron fingers, a candle, and a small turtle.

I wish to thank in particular Thomas Moody and Nicky Bangs for their assistance in the translation of the Nicholas *Translationes;* and Lauren Mancia, Adam Gidwitz, Alasdair Grant, Lev Arie Kapitaikin, A. C. S. Peacock, and Bilge Usta for their generosity in responding to my historical queries. I apologize that this is the book that came out of it.

All errors and exaggerations are of course my own.

Thanks to Zach Phillips and the team at Pantheon for their hard work on this novel, and to my agent, David McCormick, for sealing the deal.

And thanks, finally, to Dr. Erin Thompson, who has taught me so much about the theft of art and human remains.

December 6, 2022

A NOTE ABOUT THE AUTHOR

M. T. Anderson has written stories for adults, picture books for children, adventure novels for young readers, graphic-novel adaptations of ancient French tales, and several books for older readers (both teens and adults). His satirical science fiction novel *Feed* was a finalist for the National Book Award and was the winner of the Los Angeles Times Book Prize. Both *Time* magazine and National Public Radio have included it on their lists of the one hundred best young-adult novels of all time. The first volume of Anderson's *Octavian Nothing* saga, *The Pox Party,* won the National Book Award and the Boston Globe–Horn Book Prize. The second volume, *The Kingdom on the Waves,* was a *New York Times* best seller. *The Assassination of Brangwain Spurge*, a tragicomic spy story written with Newbery Honor winner Eugene Yelchin, was a finalist for the National Book Award in 2018. Anderson's nonfiction book *Symphony for the City of the Dead: Dmitri Shostakovich and the Siege of Leningrad* was long-listed for the National Book Award. *Landscape with Invisible Hand,* another satirical science fiction novel, was made into a movie starring Tiffany Haddish and Asante Blackk, directed by Cory Finley. Anderson has published stories for adults in literary journals such as *McSweeney's, Northwest Review, Colorado Review,* and *Conjunctions*. Several of his stories have appeared in *The Year's Best Fantasy and Horror* collections. His nonfiction articles and reviews have been published in *The New York Times*, *The Washington Post, The Boston Globe, The Improper Bostonian, BBC Music, Slate,* and *Salon.* Anderson is a lifelong New Englander and lives in a small, haunted eighteenth-century house in the hills of Vermont.

A NOTE ON THE TYPE

This book was set in Hoefler Text, a family of fonts designed by Jonathan Hoefler, who was born in 1970. First designed in 1991, Hoefler Text was intended as an advancement on existing desktop computer typography, including as it does an exponentially larger number of glyphs than previous fonts. In form, Hoefler Text looks to the old-style fonts of the seventeenth century, but it is wholly of its time, employing a precision and sophistication only available to the late twentieth century.

Composed by Westchester Publishing Service, Danbury, Connecticut
Printed and bound by Berryville Graphics, Berryville, Virginia
Designed by Maggie Hinders